PRICE ONE SHILLING

SHEET ANCHOR JACK

LONDON:—HOGARTH HOUSE, BOUVERIE STREET, FLEET STREET E.C.

THE HOGARTH HOUSE STANDARD LIBRARY

The following Original Editions are now in Print in Volumes and Penny Numbers. Be sure in ordering that you get the "HOGARTH HOUSE" ORIGINAL EDITIONS, as other INCOMPLETE Works are in the Market:—

GENTLEMAN GEORGE, THE KING OF THE ROAD.

Complete, price 1s.—A Startling and Romantic Story of the Road in the Days of the Regency. "Pardon me, your Highness, I would not rob a parent"—The gold room and Italian cabinet at Carlton House, and what happened there—The warning of the black horseman—The hall of the council of twelve—Gentleman George encounters the black horseman of Hampstead Heath—The judgment of the council of twelve—Wellington speaks his mind, as does the Regent—Gentleman George breaks the bank—The eve of the Battle of Waterloo—Gentleman George in the charge; "Up Guards, and at 'em"—The return to England—The Queen's messenger upset—Attempt to rob the Bank of England—The rescue of Annette from Newgate—A midnight visit to Carlton House, and an interview with the Regent—Escape—The marriage in Epping Forest—Attacked by soldiers—Capture—Condemned to death—On the road to execution—The rescue by the four kings and the pack—The escape to France—Freedom.

KING OF DIAMONDS.

A SEQUEL TO "GENTLEMAN GEORGE."

Complete, price 1s.—Being the adventures of the Pack in France—How they become noblemen and soldiers, and form themselves into Napoleon's body-guard—The attempted escape from the Island of St. Helena—The plot frustrated—Seizure of a man-of-war—Fighting the King's ship—Defeat—Alone on the ocean—Cast on a desolate island, &c., &c., forming one of the most exciting romances ever written.

THE TROUBLESOME TWINS.

Complete, price 1s.—The Twins are rescued from the wreck of a vessel by Von Bunk, who takes them to his frow—The compact—The Twins go to school—Their adventures there—The Dutchman's boat—Von Bunk and Jack and Joe, together with their sportsman friend, go to sea and visit many foreign lands; have many very narrow escapes and funny adventures—The Dutchman and his sporting friend's mishaps—full of mirth, fun, and drollery, intermixed with many startling episodes of savage life.

BOYHOOD'S BATTLES.

Complete 1s.—The History of an Orphan Boy who was left to the care of a brutal uncle, who tried many ways to kill him for his money—His wonderful escapes and adventures—How he, in the end, triumphed over all his enemies and became a great man. Boys, read this tale; it shows what honesty and pluck will do. Beautifully illustrated by a well-known artist.

FOLLOW MY LEADER;
Or, Lionel Wilful's Schooldays.

In Three Vols., 1s. each, or complete in One Vol., bound in cloth and gold as a Prize Edition, price 3s. 6d.—The funniest and most laughable story ever written. Illustrated by the celebrated Phiz.

CARACTACUS, THE CHAMPION OF THE ARENA.

Complete, price 1s.—The cheapest shillingsworth ever published.—A Romance of Rome and Britain. The period which the talented author has chosen for his story is one which abounds with the most exciting and romantic interest for all our boys. Who among them has not felt his young blood thrill with fiery ardour at the mere mention of the British hero's name? And it is the most interesting period of the warrior's history which our author has selected for the romance. Read of the captivity of Caractacus—of his adventures amongst the gladiators—and how, even in that band of skilled and daring men, whose trade was Death, not one could be found to match him. Read how the youthful hero conquered the wild beasts, the wrestlers, the boxers, and the swordsmen.

ON THE QUEEN'S SERVICE.

Complete, price 1s.—Being the exciting adventures of a Queen's messenger.—All who would like to read about the war between England and Russia, deeds of daring of the British troops in the Crimea, the Balaklava Charge, the fall of Sebastopol, the heroic defence of Kars, and the hairbreadth escapes of a Queen's messenger, should send for this Volume at once, and see how an Englishman behaves in the time of deadly peril.

DICK DAUNTLESS, THE BOY PRIVATEER.

Complete, price 1s.—Acknowledged by all who have read it to be the most exciting story of privateer and pirate life ever published.

BLUECAP THE BUSHRANGER;
Or, the Australian Dick Turpin.

Complete, price 1s.—This thrilling story of deeds of daring and adventure is written by a retired Victorian trooper, who has been engaged in countless conflicts with bushrangers, and it gives its readers a graphic realisation of life in the Australian Bush.

HANDSOME HARRY OF THE FIGHTING BELVEDERE.

In Four Vols., price 1s. each, or complete in cloth gilt, 4s. 6d.—In this splendid Story of the Sea will be found vivid descriptions of the mysterious captain and his wrongs—The fight in the storm—The pirate captain of the Black Jaguar—Alone among the cavemen—Encounter with the Russian three-decker—Gallantry of Handsome Harry and Tom True—Samson the nigger, and Ching-Ching the Chinaman—with a thousand-and-one eccentricities of the "Heathen Chinee" to divert and charm the reader.

THE DEVIL'S DIAMOND; or, the Fortunes of Richard of the Raven's Crest.

Complete, price 6d.—This is a magnificent romantic story of an English Adventurer in Mexico in the days of Pizarro.

OTHER VOLUMES IN PREPARATION.

THE HOGARTH HOUSE PENNY LIBRARY.

The following New Crown Octavo Volumes, each complete in itself, containing 32 Pages of well-written and closely Printed Matter, in a Beautifully Illustrated Wrapper, Printed in Colours, are now ready:—

1 HURON'S DAUGHTER.
2 WILD HUNTRESS.
3 YOUNG RANGER.
4 SILVER SEEKERS.
5 SLEEP WALKER.
6 WATCHMAN PRINCE.
7 PIRATE'S PRIZE.
8 THE PHANTOM CUTTER.
9 GAMBLER'S VICTIM.
10 BRIGANDS OF PRAIRIE.
11 OLD CAPTAIN.
12 PALE-FACE BRAVE.
13 SWAMP BANDITTI.
14 CAPTAIN TOM.
15 KITTY, THE FACTORY GIRL.
16 THE FEUD. THE PROPHECY.
17 LOVE AND REVENGE.
18 BACKWOOD BETSY.
19 WHITE SERPENT.
20 A NIGHT BY THE CAMP FIRE.
21 FALSELY ACCUSED.
22 EAGLE PLUME.
23 BATTLE OF THE CLIFF.
24 RED HAND.
25 STRIKING EAGLE.
26 BLACKFOOT RAIDERS.
27 THE FOREST KING.
28 RATTLEPATE THE WANDERING NABOB.
29 NORMINSTER DIAMONDS.
30 PAUL ST. LEGER.
31 CORSAIR'S NEST.
32 WITNESSED BY MOONLIGHT.
33 DEMON ALLIGATOR.
34 THE GOLDFISHER.
35 A BROKEN BARONET.
36 BERTIE'S ADVENTURES.
37 THE WRECKER CHIEF.
38 RUTH MOSELEY'S SECRET.
39 MILES HILL MYSTERY.
40 WINNING NUMBER.
41 WIFE FOR WIFE.
42 HOW HE WAS POISONED.
43 LOST IN THE LONDON SEWERS.
44 BEHIND THE FOOTLIGHTS.
45 BOUND TO THE WHEEL.
46 THAT BROTH OF A BOY.
47 THE HALSHAW MOOR MYSTERY.
48 THE BLIND SOLDIER OF FRANCE.
49 THE MAID'S REVENGE.
50 A CLOSE SHAVE FOR LIFE.
51 SELF DOOMED TO DEATH.
52 ENTOMBED ALIVE.

This Library is continued by a New Novel every other week.

HOGARTH HOUSE, BOUVERIE ST., FLEET ST., LONDON, E.C.

SHEET ANCHOR JACK.

BY GEORGE EMMETT.

AUTHOR OF

"*Midshipman Tom,*" "*Alf's Well,*" "*Pirates Isle,*" "*Yarns from the Locker,*"
etc., etc., etc.

PROFUSELY ILLUSTRATED

BY

HARRY MAGUIRE.

Publishing Office:

HOGARTH HOUSE, 32, BOUVERIE STREET, LONDON, E.C.

CONTENTS.

SAVED FROM THE DEEP.

SHEET ANCHOR JACK.

BY GEORGE EMMETT.

PROLOGUE.

THE vivid beams of a vertical sun played upon the glassy waters of the Southern Atlantic. The vast and trackless expanse was undimmed. save by the motionless hull of what had once been a noble ship. The masts, rudder, figure-head boats, and sails had been torn away, as was evident by the few remnants of the cordage which hung over the sides.

The bulwarks, in more than one place, were stove in ; but whether this shattered remnant of a large vessel had been mutilated by the power of the elements or the merciless hand of man, there were no eyes, save those of the Great Omnipotent, to behold.

Low, very low, in the water was the vessel's stern, and the forefoot, with its broken fragment of the bowsprit pointing upward, showed the waters were slowly, but surely, claiming another victim.

From the unfathomable depths came the sea monsters, and, as they swam around the wreck, their course was marked by a line of fleecy foam.

They seemed the only things of life about the ill-fated craft, until the stern sank yet lower, and the waters began to lave the poop; then from the fore hatchway crept a human being, who staggered towards the bows, and looked, piteously, first at the sunny heavens, then at the tranquil surface of the treacherous waters.

A few minutes after, another figure crawled from the same place, and, supporting himself by the bulwarks, he came stealthily behind the seaman who was taking his last farewell of the glorious light.

The second figure clutched a pistol firmly in his wasted hand, and, by the maniac-like glare in his sunken eyes, and the weary cat-like manner in which he glided forward it was evident his purpose was to cheat the dark monsters who mustered around the ship of a living victim.

Twice he raised his hand to fire, but either owing to weakness or the dazzling rays of the sun he was not able to take a steady aim at the unconscious form which stood out in such bold relief against the azure canopy of heaven.

While creeping forward to get close to his victim, another form slowly emerged from the hatchway—this time a woman's, a mere girl—who, as soon as she beheld the attitude of the two men, dropped upon her knees, and raised her transparent wasted hands supplicatingly upwards.

She would have cried out, but famine and thirst had deprived her of the power of speech.

It was a strange and awful tableau—a shattered hull fast sinking to the ocean's mystic depths, a youth taking a long and yearning look at the sky and water, another armed with a deadly weapon about to destroy a companion whose span of life was fast drawing to a close.

A strange and awful tableau! indeed What could it mean?

The glistening sea convulsed the after part of the ruined fabric, and, entering the hatchway in large volumes, caused the whole structure to lurch forward.

At this moment there came a flash from the pistol, and the figure at the bows threw up his hands and fell forward; then the girl's hands dropped to her side, and he who had pulled the trigger uttered a shrill cry.

The vessel gave another lurch, then careened over, and disappeared beneath the surface of the ocean, carrying with it the murderer, the senseless girl, and the figure which lay prone across the shattered bows, and the sunlight as the mutilated fabric sank to rise no more played for a second upon a line of golden letters which told that the name of the lost ship was the GLORIANA.

CHAPTER I.

MIDSHIPMAN HORATIO NELSON.

HIS Britannic Majesty's ship, the Seahorse, twenty guns, and commanded by the renowned Captain Farmer,* and bound from Plymouth to Bengal, in crossing the line encountered a stiff gale of wind.

Perched in the foretop of the gallant barque was a young midshipman, about fifteen years of age. He was a pale, slight lad, feeble in body, and seemed possessed of scarcely sufficient strength to retain his perilous position, as the vessel lurched from side to side, under the combined effects of the heavy seas and the howling winds.

Although the young middy had been three years at sea, he was not yet admitted to watch over the quarter-deck; his post was the foretop, and there, undismayed by the terrible grandeur of the elements, he kept his dangerous post until relieved.

Drenched to the skin, the boy descended to his berth, and, not noting the raillery of his more robust companions, he shifted his wet garments, and, rolling a blanket around him, lay shivering in his hammock, his mind and body both enfeebled; and wishing himself overboard and his misery ended, he soon fell into an unquiet slumber.

Little thought the devil-may-care middies, when they taunted the poor boy, that their feeble companion was destined to become the greatest hero ever England possessed on land or sea.

His career hitherto had been but a source of misery to one who seemed so utterly unfitted for the hardships and privations of a sea-boy's life; added to this his mind had acquired, apparently without any cause, an utter aversion to the king's navy, and it was long before these prejudices could be overcome, or that he could reconcile himself to the service on board a man-of-war.

This was brought about by appealing to the boy's ambition, and the future idol of England was promised, if he behaved himself, he should not only be promoted from the foretop to the quarter-deck, but moreover, he

* Captain Farmer commanded the Quebec in 1779, and gallantly engaged a French frigate of superior force; the fight lasted nearly four hours, then the Quebec took fire, and the heroic officer, although desperately wounded, refused to leave his vessel, and when she blew up, he was shattered into fragments.

would have command of the cutter; and the fulfilment of these promises created that confidence within the boy's mind, which soon formed and established his undaunted character.

Years after this, when the name of Nelson was extended to the utmost limit of Europe, he spoke of the feelings which he at that time endured.

"I felt impressed," said the hero, "with an idea that I should never rise in my profession. My mind was staggered with a view of the difficulties I had to surmount; and with the little interest I possessed I could discover no means of reaching the object of my ambition. After a long and gloomy reverie, a sudden glow of patriotism was kindled within me, and hope presented my king and country as my patrons, 'I WILL BE A HERO!' I exclaimed, 'and confiding in Providence, I will brave every danger.'"

Should these words be read by any youth, whose mind is agitated by the fluctuations of hope and despair concerning his future, let him, like the brave Nelson, confide in Providence, and resolve to surmount every difficulty in his path to fame and riches.

Here was a lad, the son of a rector, and when only twelve years of age, taken from school and sent on board the Raisonable—sent on board, for he was sent in a stage coach to join his ship, which lay in the Medway—sent without a friend near him, and at the end of his journey he was put down with the other pasengers, and had to find the ship the best way he could.

After wandering about in the cold for some time, an officer, who knew the captain of the vessel, spoke to the poor forlorn boy, and took him home and gave him some refreshment; and when he at last got aboard, he walked to and fro the deck during the remainder of the day, not a soul on board taking the least notice of him.

Who can picture the feelings of the little sea-boy when he found himself thus cast upon the world? for there is nothing the young feel so poignantly as the want of a friendly voice when they first leave the haven of home.

Nelson, although feeble in body, had a loving heart, and he remembered through life the first days of wretchedness he passed in the service

From this time until the hour he is introduced to the reader perched on the Seahorse's foretop, he had seen considerable service for one of such tender years.

From the Raisonable he passed into the merchant service, and his voyage to the West Indies gave the young mariner a practical knowledge of seamanship.

After this we find him in command of a cutter, which was attached to the commanding officer's ship at Chatham.

In 1773 a voyage was undertaken to the North Pole, and although orders had been issued that no boys were to be received on board, the enterprising Horatio Nelson, rather than submit to be left behind, begged to be appointed coxswain to Captain Loftwyche.

This officer was so struck with the undauted spirit which the lad displayed, yielded, and at length received England's future hero in the humble capacity he had solicited.

As a proof of the cool intrepidity which animated the bay even amidst the dreary scenes of the frozen ocean, the following anecdote is related by an eyewitness:

Young Nelson was one day missing; and, though every search was made for him, it was in vain, and at length he was given up for lost, when lo! to the astonishment of his shipmates, he was seen at a considerable distance on the ice, armed with a musket, and in pursuit of an immense bear.

The lock of the piece being injured, he could not fire, and he had, therefore, followed the animal, in hopes of tiring him, and being able to effect his purpose with the butt-end.

Upon his return, the captain severely reprimanded him, and demanded what motive could have induced him to undertake so rash an action.

To this the little fellow, with great simplicity, answered:

"I wished, sir, to get the skin for my father."

Upon his return to England he longed to explore the torrid as well as the frigid zone, and for this purpose he used every endeavour to be appointed to the Seahorse, then fitting out for the East Indies.

The gale had somewhat abated, when young Nelson again ascended to the foretop; but the sea, as though unwilling to return to that placid state from which it had been aroused by the angry winds, still ran high.

The ship danced upon the white-topped waves, now with her bowsprit under water, the next moment careening over, and dipping her yard-arms in the sullen waves.

It was at such a moment as this, and when the bright copper sheeting was visible above the water, that the young look-out gave warning that there was something floating directly in the vessel's course.

The word was passed to the first lieutenant, who immediately passed forward, and said:

"What is it you say, Mr. Nelson?"

"There is something ahead, sir."

"What does it look like?"

"I cannot exactly say, sir; one minute it

seems like a boat keel upwards, the next it looks like a portion of a wreck."

"Is there anything alive upon it?"

"I cannot see anything, sir.'

"Keep a good look-out, my lad, and when we come near enough to make it out clearer, send for me."

"Aye, aye, sir."

Owing to the ship making so much leeway, it was some time before the midshipman could make out the strange object which the heavy head sea drove towards the Seahorse.

That it was a portion of a wreck soon became known even to the crowd of seamen who were clustered upon the forecastle.

"Tells you what," said a saucy captain of the afterguard, "it's a dead whale, or I ain't a true blue."

"Bill Jinks," said a seaman, "is always to the fore in making out things that float upon the sea. Stand clear, you lubbers, the Seahorse wants a drink."

The mariners retreated as the vessel dipped her bows in the frothy waves, and when she again righted they ran forward to watch the dark looming object which by this time had excited the attention of all on board.

"Well, Dick," said Bill Jinks, shaking a shower of salt spray from his pigtail, "p'raps you'll finish your yarn about a chap they calls Bill Jinks, captain of the afterguard in this here ship."

"Right, my hearty." "Well, as I was a sayin', you are always pretty ready to shove your oar in when anything is going on."

"Avast, there, Tom Cox!"

"Hold on, Bill Jinks, until I've payed out, and——"

"A fragment of a ship's bows, sir," sang out the little mid from the foretop, "and either a piece of sail-cloth or a human being clinging round an anchor which lies athwart the wreck."

"Blest if I didn't say so," said Bill Jinks, "a bit of a wreck, and the t'other what Mr, Nelson says."

"May I turn as many colours as a dolphin a-dying," said Tom Cox, "if you ain't one of the biggest liars aboard the Seahorse."

The boatswain's shrill whistle caused the watch to run to their stations, and prevented an angry retort from Bill Jinks.

A slight alteration in the position of the yards caused the vessel to edge towards the strange object, and Tom Cox ran nimbly out upon the bowsprit and flung a grapnel at the moment the Seahorse buried her nose into the water.

The barbed claws of the hand grapnel caught one of the flukes of the anchor, and as the ship rose the sudden tightening of the line Tom Cox held tumbled that worthy head foremost into the sea.

"A man overboard!" rang out fore and aft, and a rush was made by the boats' crews to lower the boats; but ere the tackle could be loosed, the light form of the young midshipman was seen upon the bowsprit, throwing a rope to the seaman, who, puffing and blowing like a porpoise, had by this time scrambled aboard the piece of wreck.

"Thankee, Mr. Nelson," he sang out; "make fast the end, sir, or when the barkey rises you'll find a berth alongside of Tom Cox."

The midshipman followed this advice, and the lieutenant, calling the men from the boats, ordered two or three to go forward and assist in getting Tom Cox aboard.

Bill Jinks, Sandy M'Culloch, and Joe Davis obeyed, the latter prudently taking a coil of rope in case of an accident accruing to the thin line the young middy had thrown to the seaman.

"Make this fast, Tom," said Joe Davis, "then come up, hand over hand, and we will hoist that bit of a craft aboard and take the anchor off; Davy Jones don't want anchors, and that's a good sheet-anchor, or I'm a Frenchman."

The strange waif held by the line rose and fell with the sea, and as Tom Cox pulled aside the cloth which partially covered the anchor, he gave an exclamation of surprise.

"What's up?" demanded Bill Jinks; "found a mermaid there, Tom? Bring her aboard if you have."

The broken timber having by this time got close under the Seahorse's bows, the doings of Tom Cox were not visible to those who stood on the forecastle, where Bill Jinks had retired when Davis threw out the rope.

Those who remained on the bowsprit were, like Tom Cox, too much surprised to speak when they saw the object which had caused the seaman's exclamation.

"Mermaid!" answered Tom, after a pause, "come down, one of you, here's a fellow-creature on this bit o' junk, and there ain't much breath left in him."

Joe Davis descended with the rapidity of lightning, and soon after those on deck heard him say:

"Cheer up, my hearty! That's it, open your mouth; you've had enough salt water for one trip. Cheer up, you've cheated Davy Jones, anyhow. Where are you? You're aboard the Seahorse—gently, Tom Cox, those mawleys of your'n ain't used to handling anything except ropes and rammers—leastways, my lad, you'll soon be aboard the Seahorse, when I've made a whip to hoist you with. Now then, you lubbers, hoist away."

A dozen eager hands drew the thickest of the ropes gently upwards, and fastened securely to the end was the drenched form of a young sailor.

He was soon released and led forward by the men, and the rope again being thrown overboard, was made fast to the broken timber, which had borne him beneath the Seahorse's prow.

Tom Cox and his companions ascended the strange craft, and went down aboard.

The piece of the wrecked vessel was considerably larger than it had seemed when in the water; this was in a great measure owing to the weight of the heavy anchor, which not only kept the floating timber steady, but sank it within a few inches of the surface of the ocean.

Bill Jinks brought his pigtail over his shoulder, and while effectively striking the well-greased appendage, gave his opinion of the matter.

"This here barkey," he said; "has struck on a rock and gone clean in four pieces; now I wonders how long that young chap has been afloat, and I wonders, too, how he weathered the gale we've had."

"Who told you it struck on a rock?" said Tom Cox, from pure mischief; "it looks to me werry like as though old Davy Jones had come up from his caboose, under the water, and, being in a rage, had broken the craft in four bits with his thumb and finger, and most likely he's taken the other pieces to light his galley-fire, for——"

Tom Cox paused, as Bill Jinks, too indignant to reply, walked from the forecastle savagely tugging at his pigtail.

"You have settled him, Tom," said a topman, "and it ain't everybody as can do that aboard the Seahorse."

"You are right there, my hearty," said Tom Cox; "but what's become of the young chap as came aboard just now?"

"I saw him being taken down to old Bloodstick, the doctor."

"He was qneer then."

"He was, for as they led him aft he fell down all of a heap, and although Mr. Nelson tried to put some brandy atwixt his teeth, he wouldn't swallow it, so the mid sends him down to old Bloodstick."

Sandy M'Culloch drew the back of his hand across his mouth, and said:

"What became of the grog, man? But it was a pity he couldn't take it."

"Here comes the youngster," said Tom Cox, as the waif was being taken before Captain Farmer and his officers; "come on, and maybe we shall hear what he says."

The seaman drew as near the quarter-deck as they dared, and listened to the following dialogue:

"Well, young fellow," said the captain of the Seahorse, "what ship did you belong to?"

The young mariner hesitated before he answered.

"The Gloriana, sir."

"Man-o'-war?"

"No, sir, a merchantman, bound from London to the East Indies."

"Where were you wrecked?"

"We were not wrecked, sir, a privateer or pirate overhauled us, and because we would not give in, shot away our masts by the board, smashed up the hull with shots, then boarded us and took out the cargo, and all that were left alive on board were made to walk the plank."

"How did you escape?"

"By hiding in the orlop deck along with another seaman and a young lady."

"They died, of course?"

"They went down with the hull, sir, when she foundered."

"How long is it since this fellow overhauled you?"

"Three weeks, sir, as near as I can reckon."

"Three weeks," said the officer, in astonishment; "then the hull floated after the pirates left?"

"She floated until yesterday morning, sir, for the fellows had not time to scuttle her, in consequence of an English brig-of-war heaving in sight."

"Did nat the brig offer you any assistance?"

"A boat's crew came aboard, sir, but we thought they were from the pirate sloop, and didn't find out until the brig had taken in boat, and was in chase of the sloop."

"That was unfortunate. So you have afloat on this piece of wreck since yest morning."

"I have, sir."

"I understood you to say the foundered."

"Such was the case, sir, but the bow broke away and floated as the other part went down."

"I understand. Possibly your companions also clung to a portion of the wreck?"

"No, sir; I am sure they are both dead."

"Well, we can do no good by driving about for them."

"It would be useless, sir."

"Very well, you can go forward with the men. But stay; would you like to serve on board this ship?"

"I should, sir."

"What is your name?"

"Jack, sir."

"Jack—your surname?"

"I have never been called anything but Jack."

"You ought to be called SHEET-ANCHOR JACK," said Tom Cox to a shipmate, "I'm blessed if you oughtn't."

"The purser will find a name for you," said the captain, "when he enters you upon the ship's books."

The young seaman left the quarter-deck, and the purser, when he inserted his name in the books, having been prompted by one of the petty officers, wrote John Anchor; but the crew, loudly taking up Tom Cox's idea christened the castaway

SHEET-ANCHOR JACK.

CHAPTER II.

SAUL MASON.

IN a mean-looking, dingy, red-brick house, which stood in Blackwall, resided Saul Mason, whose profession, if the brass plate upon the door of his dwelling could be relied on, was that of a "Ship Chandler."

Those who disliked Saul Mason, said he dealt in other matters besides ship chandlery; and report added to the evil repute of his name by asserting that he purchased leaky vessels and sent them to sea freighted with barrels filled with hides, and bales made up with old sails and disused tarpaulins.

Report further added, these vessels and cargoes were invariably heavily insured, and not one ever returned from their voyage.

The more charitable of Saul's acquaintance attributed these reports to the envy of those who disliked the ship chandler because he was rich, and shut himself up in the dingy brick house with his wealth.

Whether true or false, Saul Mason never troubled himself about them. True, upon more than one occasion his house had been broken into by burglars, but whether they tried the front door or back windows they were equally unsuccessful in capturing any booty, and those who went upon this errand had good cause to remember Saul Mason.

The interior of his dwelling was so well furnished with spring traps, that every robber who crossed the threshold found himself seized by the saw-like teeth of those trusty guardians so that escape was impossible.

Saul allowed the disturbers of his repose to remain in the most excruciating agony all night, and when morning came they wer politely handed over to the Bow-street officers.

Thus, although many coveted the yellow gold popularly supposed to be stowed in huge iron-bound boxes in the ship chandler's cellars, none after a time were bold enough to pay a midnight visit to the house of Snaky Saul Mason.

A stranger passing the dingy house at Blackwall would have imagined the premises were unoccupied and in Chancery, for the windows had not been cleaned for years, and, to add to their gloomy appearance, the interior of the glazed panes were covered with a network of iron wire, the work was so close that had any one been standing inside their faces or forms could not be distinguished from the street.

Yet, in spite of the gloom which hung over the place, and the evil repute of the owner, a day seldom passed without several visitors coming to consult Saul upon matters of business.

Unfortunately, these visitors were generally needy tradesmen, who ran to Saul for assistance when pressed by their creditors.

If he approved of the securities they brought he would tender them seventeen guineas for a three months' bill for twenty, and glad enough were the poor wretches to stave off the inevitable day of collapse even upon those terms.

So much for Saul Mason's house and his visitors, so much for the ship-chandler who managed this portion of his business without the smallest pretence of keeping a store for his goods; so much for the ship-owner whose name never appeared in any document relating to the vessels he owned. Now we will pass the threshold, and see the inside of this strange house.

The back room on the ground floor was Saul's office, and the door and walls were cased in sheet iron, covered with a dark-coloured paper.

Under the window stood a square writing table and a chair, and on the opposite side of the room was a large cumbersome piece of furniture, half chest of drawers, half cupboard, the upper part of which was raised when Saul had any business to transact, and the portion of the interior exposed to view formed a writing desk, behind which were several small drawers and two rows of pigeon holes.

The strangest sight revealed when the top

THE COMPACT ON THE RIVER.

was raised was four pistol barrels set horizontally upon small carriages, the muzzles of which were facing the opening; from the triggers of the barrels were four wires, connected with a corresponding number of locks.

The opening of this repository of Saul's secrets was a very delicate matter, and no hand but the owner's knew the number of turns to the right and left made with the key, but all who knew Saul were well aware that one false turn would send them into eternity, with the contents of the four barrels in their heart.

Nearly four months after the Seahorse had picked up the strange waif upon the ocean, Saul Mason sat at the piece of furniture we have attempted to describe.

At the table under the window busily writing, was a man whose hair was as white as the falling snow, yet by his muscular frame and features, although the latter bore more than ordinary marks of the hand of sorrow—it was evident he had not yet passed the prime of life.

This broken-spirited looking being was Saul's only confidant, his clerk, his amanuensis, servant; and besides Saul, the only dweller in that strange house, the outside of which he had not seen for *six* long years.

He was prisoner—Saul's slave, body and soul, and although his heart loathed the work he was compelled to do, he dared not attempt to break his thraldom.

Six years before this hapless wretch had been a wealthy merchant, but misfortune coming upon him, he had to apply to Saul for pecuniary aid, and in an evil moment he forged an acceptance for five thousand pounds. Saul lost the money, but he gained an abject slave, for with the document in his cabinet he could at any moment have placed the hangman's noose around Edward Blendell's neck, for in those days forgery was punished by the gallows.

Saul Mason was a man of about forty years of age; in figure he was a little above the middle height; thin, but wiry; his face strongly reminded one of a snake, for his month was half circular in shape; his eyes wide apart; a forehead very low, and flat eyes, small and piercing; thin straggling light hair adorned his head, and to complete the picture, four large rusty-looking teeth standing prominently out, which, with his sallow complexion, gave him a harsh and forbidding aspect.

For nearly an hour the only sounds audible in the room were the scratching of Blendell's pen, and the rustling of paper, as Saul keenly examined a pile of documents before him.

Suddenly the pen dropped as the writer, in extending his hand to the inkstand, caught sight of a paragraph in the *Shipping Gazette*, which lay open upon the table before him.

As he read his nostrils dilated, his breast rose and fell, and a deep groan escaped from his lips.

Saul turned partly round, and looking angrily at his companion, asked—

"What now, fool?"

"The Gloriana," gasped Blendell;. "she has foundered, and not a soul has been saved."

A peculiar smile flitted over Saul's lips as he asked—

"How do you know this?"

"Read for yourself."

"There was, we learn, nothing found except a portion of her bows, with the name printed upon it."

"Well, it's no affair of mine, or yours either."

"None of mine, certainly," said Blendell, except that I loved that poor boy you sent on board that ill-fated ship. Saul, Saul! when is this to end?"

"When is what to end, fool?"

"This foundering of ships at sea—ships in which you have had a hand in——"

"Fill in those papers; I have nothing to do with this."

"I cannot write; that poor boy——"

"Silence; do as I tell you, fill in those papers, then look down the *Gazette* and see if there are any old vessels to be sold.'

"What, again? Are you human, Saul, to send so many beings to the bottom of the sea for the sake of the insurance upon the vessel? You are rich——"

"And you are an ass; do as you are bid."

"My God! when is this to end?"

Saul's small eyes blazed angrily, as he said:

"Sooner than you expect, if I have much more of this."

"Do your worst," said Blendell, throwing the pen he had been writing with upon the table; "better ten thousand deaths than the life I have been leading here."

"The life you have led here!" said Saul, sneeringly; "a forger with the gallows waiting for him is housed and fed by me; well, certainly, you have much to complain about."

"I have to bear that," Blendell fiercely answered, "which would have driven many men to suicide long before this; for nearly six years have I been kept a prisoner in this accursed house, and been compelled to assist in your villanies by making out false——"

"Hold your tongue; think you I am fool enough to let you leave this house with the knowledge you posses? When you cross the threshold of my door, Blendell, it will be to go aboard one of the *stout ships* I intend buying; but mark me, you will not be able to talk of matters which do not concern you."

Blendell shuddered; he knew the man was capable of any villany, and, as he took up his pen, he thought:

"I am a fool, indeed, to lose my temper; the secret of the spring-lock will soon be mine; then the accursed papers in my possession, and the gallows shall be your due, Saul Mason."

He had waited and watched for an opportunity to open the cabinet, but the complications of the lock had as yet baffled his vengeful watchfulness.

He knew the lock was opened in safety by turning the key first *three times to the right*, then *twice to the left*, there was only one more turn to learn; but hitherto Saul had succeeded in keeping this to himself.

As these scenes were of frequent occurrence, Saul took no further notice of Blendell, but went on with the heap of papers before him, until a sharp ring at the bell announced a visitor.

The ship-chandler closed the cabinet, and as he passed out of the room shut the door after him. The lock, like all that were in his house, was of peculiar construction, and when the door was closed could only be opened by a key which he alone possessed.

But for this, Blendell would long ago have made his escape during Saul's absence; but when the doors were closed he was as much a prisoner as though shut up in one of the dungeons of the Inquisition.

The windows, too, were guarded not only by heavy sashes which were not made to open, but the iron gratings we have before alluded to.

"I can read his thoughts," chuckled Saul as he went towards the street door, "and if he were not so useful I would leave the key of the cabinet where he could find it. He, he, he! there is many a worse way of getting rid of a troublesome fellow than this, but none so sure."

He opened the door, and beheld a lad garbed in a seaman's dress.

"Well," Saul asked, "what do you want?"

"I want Saul Mason."

"I am Mr. Mason."

"Here's a letter for you, and I am to wait for an answer.

Saul adjusted a pair of tortoise-shell spectacles before he opened the letter.

"The Saucy Jane," he read, "is at anchor in the Pool, and close under the batteries of a line-of-battle ship. What think you of that, friend Saul? Will it be safe for you to come to-night and see me? There will be two blue lights hanging over the sloop's stern. Send answer per bearer, and rest your mind easy about the Gloriana. She is at the bottom of the sea. All on board have gone the same way to——"

"Tell the Captain," said Saul, "I shall be there at eight. That is all. Go."

The last word was spoken savagely, for the boy, much to Saul's anger, peered in at the doorway, as though more than ordinary curiosity prompted him to behold the interior of Saul Mason's house.

The ship-chandler watched the lad walk down the street, and, as usual with him when he felt very pleased, he begun rubbing his hands, and from his lips came sounds, the nearest resemblance to which we can give in words is this:

"Hum, hum, hum—all gone to the bottom; hum, hum—that boy is well out of the way—hum, hum; he knew too much—hum, hum; besides the gain—hum; let me see, about £20,000—hum; that is a good day's work—hum, hum; the half idiot I set to kill the boy. Should Anstey Phillips not come up with the Gloriana, he's gone too. Well, hum, hum, so much the better—hum. All that remains to share my secret is Anstey, the captain of the Saucy Jane—hum—and he is at anchor under the guns of a line-of-battle ship—hum; there is a reward of £1,000 for him who shall place the Saucy Jane and her captain in the power of the law—hum; let me see, a thousand pounds, and a riddance of a man who knows too much."

He stood at the door for some time, the soft humming noise from time to time accompanying the polish he was giving his hands.

"It's worth the trial," he muttered at last; "but first I must see him and hear the account of the Gloriana—hum, hum—then to the commander of the line-of-battle ship. Anstey will never suspect me—hum, hum—of betraying him; if he does, and tries to peach upon me? Hum, hum—no one will believe him. The story will sound too improbable. Hum, hum—it's worth trying; a short and a safe means of getting rid of a man who knows too much! Hum hum—hum, hum—it's worth trying!"

He closed the door and re-entered the office, and Blendell handed him a list of the worn-out vessels, which were to be sold on the morrow, to be broken up.

"Hum, hum," he buzzed; "here's one, Blendell—a full-rigged ship?—hum, hum—a little paint and pitch and a few guineas slipped in the Government Inspector's hands will make her sea-worthy—hum, hum--we will see about it to-morrow; hum, hum—I have an engagement this evening."

Blendell sighed, and placed the list he had copied from the *Shipping Gazette* upon the table, and Saul Mason went to his cabinet.

Blendell's eyes shone with a peculiar light as he watched the key turn to the right and left, and each click the lock gave he made a mark upon the blotter before him.

CHAPTER III.

BILL WEBB THE WATERMAN.

When Saul Mason left his dingy house to visit the captain of the Saucy Jane, there was no swift railway to take him in a few minutes to within a stone's throw of the spot where the vessel was at anchor.

The best means of conveyance was a boat, and to the water side went Saul and hailed a passing wherry.

The ship-chandler was well known to the boatmen, in consequence of the daily visits he paid to the ship-yards.

Better known than liked; for Saul believed "that a fool and his money are soon parted." Mr. Mason could not by any possible stretch of the imagination be called a fool in this respect.

Thus Saul's summons was disregarded by the

boatman, who continued to pull deliberately a-head, as though he had not heard the sweet voice from the riverside luring him to turn his prow that way.

"Confound the rascal, said Saul; "he pretends not to hear me; this is not the first time I have been served so by these men; no, no, I must get my thumb upon them—hum, hum, hum—why, this is the very fellow I wished to speak with."

Mr. Saul Mason rubbed his hands and gave a peculiar humming noise which characterised him before he called out:

"Waterman! ho, ho, hi! Bill Webb, I want you."

There was no means of evading this; so the waterman turned the prow of his boat towards the shore, and ran it aground.

"Did you call afore, sir?" he said, touching his cap; I beg pardon if you did. I'm getting plaguy deaf."

"Hum, hum! it don't matter; I did call," replied Saul, as he took his seat in the stern. "Now my man use your oars, and pull me down the river to where the Mameluke man-of-war lies at anchor."

"It's a long pull, sir," said Bill Webb; "but as I've been that way twice to-day, I s'pose as this time won't make much difference."

"Been to the Mameluke, Bill Webb?"

"No, sir; not 'zactly; but very close to."

Hum—oh indeed. Not to the Mameluke, Bill, eh?"

"No, sir, a little vessel close 'lonside the brig—a saucy-looking craft, sir, and one with as clean a run fore and aft, if I may say so, as I've ever seed. That 'ere craft it's my opinion is—"

But Bill Webb stopped short when he felt Saul Mason's snake-like eyes were fixed upon his face.

"Is what, William Webb, boat No. 20?" said Saul, "is what? Bill Webb, is what?"

"A regular right down fast goer, and no mistake, sir, I should say."

"Very likely she is, Bill Webb—very likely; she was built for quick sailing, William Webb."

"You know her then, sir. La! you seems to know every craft as floats on the Thames, if I may say so, sir.

"You may say whatever you think proper, Bill Webb, except abuse me before my face; you do that, William Webb, behind my back, eh? Hum, hum, hum."

Snaky Saul chuckled when he saw that waterman's look of surprise and terror.

"Keep steady in your seat, Bill Webb," Saul Mason continued, "and don't trouble yourself to make any reply; it was at the 'Blue Anchor' tap, William Webb, and not content with calling me an old miser, you said I bought rotten ships and sent 'em to sea; you said this, William Webb, so do not deny it."

"He's the werry devil out and out," thought the waterman.

"I'm a respectable man, William Webb," old Saul went on; "I'm a man of feeling, Bill Webb, or I should have you punished for a libel against me; but I thought of your wife, and—how many children, Bill Webb?"

"Five, sir," answered the waterman, keeping his eyes fixed upon the bolts of the boat; "none on 'em, sir, able to do much yet for me."

"I thought of that, Bill Webb, and didn't have you punished; so be careful for the future, William Webb, and don't talk about Saul Mason until he gives you a cause."

There was a long silence after this. Saul was evidently silent because he wished his words to have their full weight with the boatman, and the latter, feeling a peculiar dread of his strange companion, remained with his eyes cast down.

"You're a young man," old Saul said, breaking the silence, and speaking in a slow voice, "a very young man to have such a large family, Bill Webb."

"Not thirty yet, your honour."

"A strong man, too," continued Saul, not heeding this interruption; "quite young and strong enough to serve the King, eh?"

The waterman turned pale, and actually trembled at these words, for he remembered men who had offended Saul Mason being torn away from their homes by the press-gang.

"It's almost a wonder," Saul continued, "the press-gang have never caught you, Bill Webb."

Bill Webb plied his sculls quicker, and evidently wished his fare at the bottom of the river.

"I may say it's a great wonder, Bill Webb—but perhaps they don't know where you live, eh?"

The waterman looked his fare straight in the face as he ceased rowing, and said earnestly:

"No, sir, they don't; surely you wouldn't betray a man because he's said a few words when the drink was in him."

"Betray you to the press-gang, Bill Webb! Ho, ho! he, he! Well, come, you have but a poor opinion of me. Pull away, my man, pull away."

Webb resumed his labour.

"So," old Saul said, "you have taken people to that sweet little craft across the river, eh, Bill Webb?"

o parties have gone across with me to- Webb answered, anxious to ingratiate into Saul's favour, "and they comed that's more."

ey came back, did they; and pray did they start from, William Webb?"

ne party as looked like an old sea officer, ed from London Bridge."

"Oh, oh—hum—a stout man with a red—very red—face."

"That's him, sir, to the werry life."

"He used wicked words—swore, you know, Bill Webb, which is very bad."

"Yes, sir, he did as you says."

"The other party, William Webb, what was he like?"

"It wasn't a he, sir, leastways not one wasn't."

"A lady, then, one of them—eh—hum—hum."

"Yes, sir, a lady and a gentleman was the second fare."

"Ah, ah—hum, hum! What sort of people, eh, William Webb?"

"Good sorts, sir, for they gave me a guinea."

"Ah, indeed, very generous, but very imprudent—a whole guinea—too much, too much—but what were they like in appearance, William Webb?"

"Werry handsome, sir, and great people, I should think, for they wore wonderfully fine clothes, and when they had left the boat—I—I——"

"You found something belonging to them, Bill Webb," said Saul, "and it's in your right-hand pocket."

The waterman opened his eyes and stared at the speaker in silent bewilderment.

"He's the very devil," he thought; "how did he know that?"

Saul found it out very easily, for while Webb was speaking he glanced at the pocket referred to.

"What is it, William Webb," said old Saul, "a diamond shoe buckle, or a pocket handkerchief?—the latter I should think by the look of your pocket."

Bill Webb held the handles of his sculls with left hand, as with the right he slowly drew embroidered handkerchief from his pocket."

Saul Mason bent forward and took it sharply way; then examining an embroidered crest and monogram in one of the corners, he gave an exclamation of rage, and his face became perfectly livid.

Saul was taken off his guard or he would not have allowed his astonishment and anger to have been seen.

"A pretty device," he said, quickly recovering himself—"a very pretty device, Bill Webb, and as it is no use to you I shall keep it—eh?"

"Your honour's welcome to it, if you like."

"Thank you, William. I shall not forget you when one of my ships returns from India. You shall have a real silk one, William. He, he, he! Yellow and red. Ho, ho, ho! When one of my ships returns from India."

"Your honour's very kind. Here we are, sir. There's the big man-o'-war and the little saucy wessel. She has two b'ue lights astern, I think."

"Quite right, William Webb. Pull under the ladder, and await my return."

"Boat ahoy!" said a man looking over the vessel's side, as the wherry ran under the ladder. "What do you want?"

"The Saucy Jane," said Saul. "This is the vessel, I believe?"

"You believe right; this is the craft. Who are you?"

"A friend of your captain's."

"Hold on a bit afore you come up. What's your name?"

"Confound your impudence! Is it not sufficient for me to tell you I am a most particular friend of your captain's?"

"It aint half sufficient," said the sailor, "So out with your name, or sheer off before I drop a cold pill into your boat."

It was evidently of no use to argue with the man. He was but doing his duty.

"My name's Mason—Saul Mason. Will that do?"

"Stop where you are till I pass the word aft. Pass the word," the man added, turning to a shipmate, "that Salt Mason wants to see the skipper."

Saul had his name transmitted from mouth to mouth as Salt Mason; then, after a few moments' pause, the words "Let him come aboard," were heard.

"Come aboard," said the sentry. "Hold on by the main ropes, for the ladder is slippery."

Saul did not neglect the caution as he ascended the side of the Saucy Jane.

The vessel which Saul Mason had left his home to visit deserves an introduction to the reader, for a more beautiful vessel the ocean had never borne than the swift, graceful Saucy Jane.

Her hull was low in comparison to the height of her spars—which, by the way, partook of both the appearance of brig and sloop, the foremost being rigged like a brig, the aftermost like a sloop; yet so faultless was the adjustment of her spars and rigging, that, owing to the great height of her masts, they assumed an unusual, fantastic, yet graceful appearance, more befitting a model of a ship than one which had the repute which clung to the Saucy Jane.

The low hull was exquisitely proportioned and so well balanced, that it rode the water like an aquatic bird.

Above the water-line this beautiful hull was inted a delicate blue, relieved by two lines of rilliant vermillion; and, if she had any ports, they were so well fitted and concealed that the keenest eye could not detect the slightest break in the close timbers.

Under the bowsprit was a brazen figure-head, representing a gigantic wasp; but in the present instance, this strange figure-head was skilfully concealed by the wooden figure of a woman.

The interior of the vessel was of somewhat peculiar construction, and fitted with the most refined taste, and a total disregard to expenditure.

There was one large cabin beneath the main deck, and nearer the stern were two chambers fitted with truly Oriental splendour.

Saul Mason, as he passed through the large cabin on his way to the state-room, cast a quick and somewhat anxious glance at the silken hangings which shrouded the entrance, and was let into the bulk-heads.

The state-room of the Saucy Jane exceeded in splendour the cabin through which Saul had been led.

The glass in the stern windows was coloured in such a manner that a misty stream of subdued golden light, not unlike the tints of the setting sun, filled the air.

The floor was covered with a thick carpet, which, by its elastic softness, told that the looms of Persia had weaved the crimson and gold threads of which it was composed.

The beams and ceiling were painted of an azure tint and studded with tiny silver stars, which at night, when the lamp which hung in the centre was burning, gleamed and twinkled as though they formed a portion of the firmament.

There was not a vestige of the wood-work to be seen, for oval mirrors festooned with yellow silk met the eye upon every side save the windows, which were draped with heavy hangings of rich brocade.

There was but little furniture in this luxurious state-room.

A table, a few chairs, and a cabinet of ebony inlaid with gold, a couch in each corner of the cabin, and one in the centre, heaped up with cushions and shaped like an Eastern divan, comprised the whole of the furniture.

Along the transom * glittered an array of defensive arms of all nations, from the common ship cutlass to the jewelled Eastern yatagan.

Such was the Saucy Jane externally and internally, and although with the exception of the stud of arms mentioned above, and which seemed to be collected more to gratify the taste of the captain of the vessel than for use, there was not a weapon visible in the ship.

The white polished decks had not as much as a small piece of ordnance to use for a signal, yet Saul Mason knew the beautiful craft possessed or did possess as goodly a train of guns as ever were cast.

A young sailor who had conducted the ship-chandler to the state room now turned towards the door and said,

"The captain will be on board directly; he has gone to dine with the officers of the man-o'-war that lies within a half cable's length of us."

Saul's Mason's visage expressed the perfect astonishment he felt at this intelligence, and when the mariner closed the door he walked to and fro the cabin biting his nails.

This act proved that Saul Mason was in a state of rage and perplexity, more than any words he could have used to proclaim the unpleasant sensations which filled his crafty brain.

CHAPTER IV.

SHEET ANCHOR JACK MAKES A FRIEND.

FROM the coarse, vulgar ship-boy to the brave commander of the Seahorse, all had a good word and a thorough liking for the lad who had so strangely come aboard the King's ship.

He was a smart broad-chested fellow; his limbs were as faultlessly symmetrical as those of the Belvidere Apollo, and all those parts of his body which were not exposed to the sun were as delicately fair as a lady's rounded arm.

His face was more expressive than handsome, and of a type which proclaimed him a cast above the common herd.

His feet and hands, too, were small even to effeminacy, and even the rough work on board did not destroy the whiteness of the well-formed hands, save on the palms, which from handling ropes soon became of a horny substance.

There was much of sadness in his deep blue eyes when he thought himself alone and unnoticed; in these moments he would gaze earnestly at the rippling wavelets, and, as though unconscious of where he stood muttered strange and incoherent words.

* The cross-beam over the stern-post of a vessel.

At other times he was as jovial as any blue jacket aboard; would sing a good stirring sea-song if asked, or dance a hornpipe until it was almost impossible to watch the movements of his tiny feet.

By nature Jack seemed unsuspecting and simple, affectionate and grateful for the slightest favour; of wonderful good temper, except when taunted by the ignorant side-boys; then he was as fierce in his resentment as at other times he was genial and good-humoured.

He was not deficient in education; but few exceptions there was not an officer or man but would have done anything to have served him.

There was one subject upon which Jack would never converse; that was, the loss of the vessel to which he had formerly belonged.

His messmates attributed this reticence to the sorrow the young sailor felt at the loss of his former shipmates.

Among the friends he made on board the Seahorse, the most attached was the quiet young midshipman, Horatio Nelson.

SHEET ANCHOR JACK TRIES A SHOT

whether it was the result of education or merely what he had gleaned by his quick intellect, his shipmates were not sufficiently versed in the matter to form an opinion.

He was a good sailor, too, as active as a squirrel among the rigging; first aloft in a storm, last on deck; clean in his person and clothing, and never had to be called twice by the bo'sun when it came to his turn to relieve the watch.

These natural and physical advantages made him a universal favourite on board; and with a

The man-of-war, like most of her class, carried a great many lads to train for England's future navy.

These midshipmen, although in many cases of good family, were upon the whole a set of graceless, fun-loving scamps, and they looked upon the unassuming studious Nelson, as a parcel of mischievous lads would look upon one who was endowed with more intellect than they themselves possessed, and not thinking that so brave a heart existed in so small a body, they were more apt to play off their practical jokes upon the embryo hero of Trafalgar than was at all pleasant.

When the Seahorse arrived off the Sunderbunds,* a dead calm kept the men inactive, and the middies on the alert devising all sorts of mischief to pass the irksome time away.

A group of the lads were hanging over the side whistling away with might and main for a breeze to fill the sails and waft them to the uproarious delights of a cruise ashore; but although every sail from stunsail to royal was shook out in anticipation of the breeze, not the least movement was visible aloft.

"I shall give it up," said one who was known as Chubby-faced Joe; "made my teeth and jaws ache for nothing."

"I tells you what young gemmen," said an old sailor who was basking at full length alongside a gun, "I once knowed a barkey as was becalmed, and all hands set to a whistling, and a big black cloud come in the 'sky, and it got biggerer and biggerer until all of a sudden it opens, and down comes a wind that upsets the barkey as clean as you'd upset a can of grog, and although they wasn't one o' the other vessels, and there was a whole fleet of 'em waiting for the wind, touched or a inch of canvas moved, this ere barkey I am telling you about turns keels up'ards and down she goes—live stock, blue jackets, marines, and the whole blessed lot, and was never seen again."

The middies grinned at this lesson, then looked mischievously at the old tar.

"You saw this?" asked Chubby Joe; "eh, old yellow chop?"

"Seed it with my own eyes, young gemmen."

"What shall we do with him?" Joe asked. "Of all the old liars, this is the king of them all."

"Let's kick him up from there," suggested one.

"No; let's dowse him with bilge water," said another.

"Kicking is the best," Joe said. "It's too far to go for water. Now, then, lads, charge!"

They scrambled down from the side, but the old tar gathered himself up and ran forward, and did not feel himself safe from the enemy until he had gained his berth in the forecastle.

"These young gemmen," he said, "is as full o' tricks as a Gibraltar monkey after a feed o' nuts."

The captain being on the quarter-deck at the time, prevented a chase, or the middies would certainly have run the old sailor pretty close.

* The name given to the numerous creeks and channels forming the delta of the Ganges, which extend for nearly two hundred miles along the sea-coast of Bengal.

The escape of the old tar caused the lads to look around for another prize, and to their joy they saw young Nelson sitting on the bulwarks, his legs outside.

A book was open in his hand, and he was so occupied with its contents, that it would have been an easy matter to approach him unnoticed.

The middies saw this at a glance, and, being ripe for any mischief, they at once determined to give their messmate a ducking.

"Nothing like a bath," said Joe, when a fellow has been reading too much, and young Nel is always at it."

"Can he swim, Chubby?" a big youth asked, "because there'll be a row if he can't."

"Swim," said Joe, "like a fish, Hollyhock"

Hollyhock was the sobriquet of the long youth and a fitting name it was.

"Well, we must wait until the skipper goes below before we begin skylarking, then one of us must run against him."

The captain went below, and the young scamps began chasing each other among the guns, and in a scuffle which ensued the studious middy was pushed overboard.

Anchor Jack was upon the main yard, creeping along at full length to catch a bright-plumaged bird which had alighted on the end of the spar; and when he heard the splash, he at once sprang into the sea, and as the middy rose to the surface, caught him by the collar.

A dozen hands were ready with as many ropes, and the pair scrambled to the deck, the young officer shaking the spray from his clothes, and clearing the moisture off the book which he yet held open at the place he had been reading.

"Thank you, Jack," he said, "I must have forgotten where I was seated or I should not have bent forward as I did."

"You fell overboard then, sir."

"Decidedly; I was sitting there reading and became so interested that I lost my balance—go below Jack and change your clothes."

"I feel convinced," Jack thought as he went to the forecastle, "these young imps pushed him in."

The middies, to do them justice, were sorry when the saw their messmate in the water, and Chubby Joe, when young Nelson went below, followed him, and in a penitent voice said:

"Look here, Nel, you didn't fall overboard, we pushed you—it was only for a lark—are you angry?"

"No; but it was not right for you to do so; suppose there had been any sharks about the vessel."

"I'm very sorry for it," the lad said, "and so are all the other fellows—you are a good

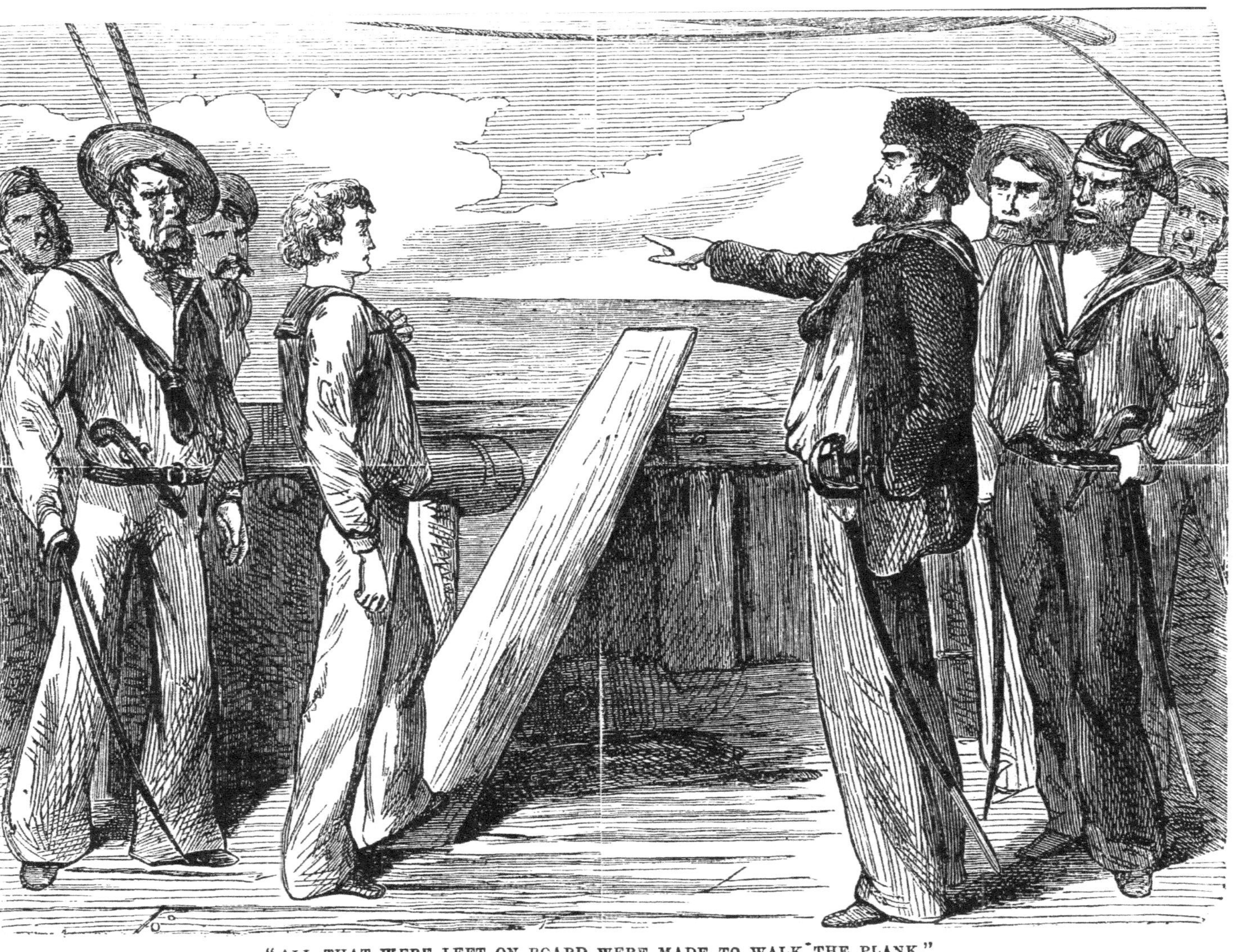

"ALL THAT WERE LEFT ON BOARD WERE MADE TO WALK THE PLANK."

sort, Nel, you never get angry with us whatever we may do."

"Why should I?" said young Nelson, as he changed his clothes; "is it because I am not of the same temperament as yourselves nor fond of practical jokes, that I should interfere with your amusements? I must say I wish you would not let down my hammock so often when I come off watch."

"Give me your hand, Nel," said Joe; "now look here, no fellow shall touch your hammock, if they do I'll cram my fist in their eyes."

Joe was as good as his word, for more than once he had to fight to protect Nelson's hammock from being lowered when the tired middy was asleep.

CHAPTER V.

BOARDING A PRIZE.

THE Lowestoffe, a frigate carrying thirty-two guns, was driven in sight of the Keys—a cluster of islands on the northern side of Hispaniola.

The day was rough, and the wind blew a fierce hurricane, but the frigate dashed onward in chase of a suspicious-looking sail, which had tried the sailing powers of the King's ship to keep within sight of the chase.

Upon the frigate's quarter-deck stood the captain, and by him a mere youth, in the uniform of a lieutenant.

The latter had not long joined the vessel, and being the youngest officer who held the rank of lieutenant in the British navy, for he was barely nineteen years of age, it was a matter of envy to the older officers in the ship that the captain should so often take the young officer's counsel when there were so many on board who thought themselves well qualified to give an opinion upon all matters relative to their profession.

"What does that man of yours think of her, Mr. Nelson," Captain Lockyer said, addressing the young officer—"he's a smart fellow; by the way, I wish you had brought a few more like him on board the Lowestoffe."

"He's a good seaman, sir," answered the young luff; "and none better than himself in watching a chase; he tells me there has been a gradual rising of at least a foot of the stranger's topsail since we set our royals."

"I am glad to hear it. Here, Mr. Yarnley, take the trumpet and signal to the foretop."

The master, a grey-headed old mariner, did as he was desired, and, in answer to his hail, came the words:

"Deck ahoy!"

"Ahoy!" said the master.

"Tell the captain we are losing the advantage we had a few minutes since; and unless the frigate makes more way, we shall lose the light-heeled craft."

The captain heard the young sailor's words, and after surveying the sails, which threatened every moment to fly into ribbons, turned to the lieutenant.

"The main-top bends like a piece of whalebone," he said; "think you, Mr. Nelson, it would be advisable to trust the fore-royal up in a hurricane like this?"

"The case, as it stands at present," said the young officer, "is the certain loss of a prize, against the probable loss of a spar and an unimportant sail."

"You are right—up with the fore-royal, Mr. Yarnley; it would be a disgrace to a King's ship to lose a prize, after keeping in her wake for two days—up with it, sir!"

The master shook his head, as though doubtful of the stick bearing the extra strain; but in deference to his superiors he had the sail set, and the frigate, like a goaded steed, dashed swifter through the boiling sea.

They were gaining fast upon the chase, for, bit by bit, the whole of her masts became visible, then the hull rose above the water.

For some time a state of silent excitement reigned on board the frigate, the men were clustered thickly forward, and in spite of the waves, which at times threatened to wash them from the forecastle, they clung to their posts, a gruff laugh every now and then bursting from their lips as the sea washed completely over them.

The strange sail, now plainly visible to every eye, could be seen at one moment rising upon the summit of a huge wave, the next her hull was hidden in the trough of the sea.

The excitement was nearly as great among the officers, and young Lieutenant Nelson, whose keen eye and clear judgment told him the heavy press of canvas the stranger carried could not much longer resist the fury of the gale, stood with folded arms awaiting the inevitable fall of her top hamper.

A sudden change in the wind gave the frigate a slight advantage in sailing, and Captain Lockyer, tired and somewhat annoyed at the long chase, ordered a shot to be fired across the stranger as a warning to show her colours.

Anchor Jack, who had descended from his perch on the foremast, ran forward, followed by Lieutenant Nelson.

"This is scarcely a time for courtesies, Jack," said the young officer," "so send the shot through her bows if you can; one hole made, the gale will do the rest."

"I'll try, sir," Jack answered, shading the portfire with his open hand. "Steady there messmates; make the lashings fast and keep the gun steady."

Jack ran his eye along the dark barrel of the gun, and as the stranger rose to the crest of a wave he sprung to his feet and fired.

Mingled with the bellow of the gun came the voices of several seamen, as they shouted—

"Hurrah! Well done, Sheet Anchor Jack!"

The mischief of that shot soon became apparent, for the chase began to roll about unmanageable upon the billows.

"You have smashed the wheel," said young Nelson quietly, "therefore the fellow will have to give in or be swept from the face of the water by our battery."

"There goes her flag," said a dozen voices; "she's struck."

The American colours floated for a few moments in the gale, then were slowly lowered in token of surrender.

"She's our's," said the captain, "thanks to your gunner, Mr. Nelson. Tell him I shall not forget his conduct."

Jack who was within hearing blushed to the temples.

"Now, Mr. Walton," said the captain to the first lieutenant, "board the prize, and remain there until the sea goes down."

The first officer left the ship in the cutter, but to the mortification of all on board the frigate, the boat when it reached the stranger's side, after a fruitless attempt to put her crew aboard, turned back and gave up the attempt.

The captain paced the deck chafing like an angry lion, and when the crest-fallen officer returned, he exclaimed—

"Have I, then, no officer who will board the prize?"

"Ay, that you have," said the old master, running to the gangway; "old Bob Yarnley will board her, or go to Davy Jones in the attempt."

Young Nelson's pale cheek glowed when he heard the captain's words and the old sailor's reply, and running forward, he stopped the master.

"It is my turn now," he said; "if I come back it will be yours."

Before a word could be spoken, he jumped into the boat, followed by Sheet Anchor Jack, and the tars gave a hurrah as the boat cleft her way through the seething water.

They watched the boat until it reached the stranger; then, as the young luff, followed by Jack and a dozen men scrambled aboard. they gave a shout which was heard far above the howling of the wind, and the roar of the water.

Here may be seen the early indications of that intrepid spirit in Nelson which no danger could dismay or appal, and that propensity for daring deeds which the subsequent events of his glorious life so brightly exemplified.

When the English Jack was run up on board the prize, the frigate's men gave three cheers for the young luff, and three more for his hardy follower, Sheet Anchor Jack.

CHAPTER VI.

THE CAPTAIN OF THE SAUCY JANE.

A SOUND of a person descending the ladder that led to the state-room caused Saul Mason to pause in his excited walk, and as a red glow suffused his sallow cheeks, he turned and faced the door, which was slowly opening to give ingress to the captain of the Saucy Jane.

The latter was in the bloom of youthful manhood, for his age could not have exceeded five or six and twenty. He would, possibly, have been judged older, in consequence of the dark bronzed hue which concealed a fair, almost an effeminate, complexion.

He was handsome to a fault, and of slight but sinewy frame, and there was that appearance about him which can only be explained by using that vague term, "Devil may care."

There was something peculiar in the expression of his large dark eyes when he saw Saul Mason, that told he bore his visitor but little love; but this transient gleam passed quickly away, and he came forward and extended his hand in token of friendship.

"Punctuality itself," he said. "I trust I have not kept you waiting, friend Saul?"

Friend Saul presented his parchment-like fingers to touch the other's extended hand as he answered:

"I have been here but a few minutes, Anstey, although each moment has seemed an hour under the feverish desire I have to learn the full particulars of the—the—wreck of the Gloriana."

Anstey Phillips's keen glance detected the restless, savage look in Saul's eyes, and a smile of contempt played upon his lips.

"Quite natural," he said; "but have you not seen the account in the papers?"

"Curse the papers! How could you have bungled so in——"

"Softly," said the privateer captain; "wait until you hear my version of the affair before you accuse me of bungling. Did you ever know Anstey Phillips to bungle, friend Saul?"

"Not before. But come, do not delay. I am burning with——"

"A bad sign," said Anstey; "be seated. Slightly feverish—febrile symptoms decidedly. Bad plan, friend Saul."

Saul Mason flung himself savagely upon a seat, and the privateersman opening a locker, which was covered with silk to represent an ottoman, took from thence a long, narrow-necked bottle, and placed it, with a couple of glasses upon the table.

"Good wine," he said, "need no bush, so I feel sure you will say when you——"

"I do not require your wine," said Saul sharply. "Pray give me the account of—of——"

"The destruction of the Gloriana," said the privateer captain, laughing. "Out with it, Saul. I am not ashamed to hear the truth. Ha, ha, ha! We have destroyed a few vessels in our time, eh, Saul? But you are a cunning dog: you do it without any risk—eh, Saul?"

"Go to the——"

"Hush, my friend; we shall both go there quite soon enough, if there is any truth in the mouthings of those sanctified fellows who——"

"You will drive me mad."

"I hope not, Saul. You look dangerous now. If you were to reach the rabid state and bite, the result would be a case of hydrophobia. Here, take this, it will steady your nerves.

Saul knocked the proffered glass from Phillips's fingers, and starting from his seat, exclaimed,

"Had I known you would have——"

"Be seated—there, I have done. Now, what is it you wish to know?"

"The full particulars of the—the destruction of the Gloriana."

"And all on board. You shall hear."

The speaker opened a cigar case, and after a short delay in obtaining a light from a flint and steel, he said,

"I don't think I should have sent her to the bottom had not the rascals had the impudence to salute me with a discharge of small arms and the contents of the only gun they carried, when I ranged alongside."

"Did you lose any men?"

"Aye, twelve of my fire-eaters went to Davy before we could board; then our work was soon over, for her hull and spars were pretty well damaged, so she lay like a log on the water——"

"Spare these details."

"Do not be so impatient, friend Saul," said the privateersman, provokingly. "Well, since you will not have the full account of this affair, I will condense it."

"For heaven's sake do."

"Well, I helped myself to the cargo as per agreement, friend Saul; then I made all who had survived our shot and steel walk the plank."

"All?" repeated Saul Mason, nervously "Are you quite sure? all—everyone?"

"Every living thing—aye, even to a dog, we sent to Davy."

Saul Mason wiped his brow, and his forbidding face looked paler than its wont, and the rusty discoloured teeth stood out more prominently as the thin twitching lips were drawn back, either under the impulse of fear or gratified revenge.

Anstey Phillips watched his visitor closely, a wicked look in his dark eyes, and the faintest curl of contempt upon his lips.

At last Saul spoke, and his words were uttered more in a frightened whisper than his usual suavity and tone of manner.

"So they all perished; the youth, the idiot, and the—the girl?"

"What——!" exclaimed Anstey Phillips, but checking himself, he added, "do you doubt my words, friend Saul?"

The ship-chandler did not reply. He was struck by the tone of astonishment in which the privateersman's exclamation was uttered, and his subtle brain was busy with the doubts he felt respecting the other's statement.

"Girl!" thought Anstey Phillips. "I saw no girl; yet there might have been one on board; yet, no, it is impossible that confounded brig could have found any one living on the wreck after my bull-dogs had been aboard; if there was any of the gender feminine she or they must have left the vessel before I overhauled it, or what is more likely, been dressed as a sea-boy."

"You seemed surprised," said Saul, breaking in upon the other's reflections, "when I asked about the girl."

"Indeed!" laughed Anstey; "you are the first man who has been able to surprise Anstey Phillips. Now let's have an end to this and settle the little business relative to the destruction of the Gloriana."

"Business," said Saul; "surely you do not expect more for the job than the cargo."

"Considering I could have helped myself to that without your assistance, I have much to be thankful for. Now, friend Saul, I require the £1,000 you owe me, then we can arrange about other matters."

Saul smiled maliciously, and threw a packet of notes upon the table.

"I'll trust to your honour," said the mariner as he flung the roll into the open locker, "respecting the correctness of the amount; now have you any commands for me?"

"None."

"What! no ship upon which you have effected a heavy insurance that requires a shot below the water line to send——"

"Peace. I have no commands for you yet."

"The Saucy Jane will not be in these waters another twelve hours," said the privateersman, "therefore, friend Saul, unless you can oblige me with the particulars of any little affair you may feel disposed to honour me with before that time, they will be useless."

"You are in haste to leave; I should have thought the attractions of London sufficient to have caused you to stay a few weeks."

"There are other and gayer capitals than London, and much safer for me to visit—much safer, friend Saul."

'But your friends, Anstey, of course you nave many in England.

"Many," replied the corsair, with a sneer, "but none to be so well trusted as my most attached friend, Saul Mason, ship-broker, money-lender, and——"

"Never mind the remainder," said Saul, "the information is not new——"

"And not agreeable," laughed the privateersman; "well, well, perhaps not."

Saul rose from his seat, and taking his hat, seemed about to leave the state-room when, as though struck by a sudden thought, he turned and faced the mariner, and looking him steadily in the face, said—

"You are sure all on board of the Gloriana perished?"

"Quite sure," was the reply. "Why do you ask again?',

"I have a reason."

"Saul Mason," the privateersman said, "seldom moves or speaks without a motive, but his motive for the Gloriana affair is quite beyond my comprehension."

"Let it remain so," said Saul savagely, "it will be better for us both."

"Ah, friend Saul, this sounds like a menace."

"It is not. But I do not like men to pry into my affairs. You understand."

"I do; yet were I disposed to fathom the mystery, I should eadeavour to do so in defiance of all you, my friend, could do to prevent it."

"It would not repay the trouble," Saul said, "besides the risk you would incur."

"Risk!"

"Yes. Anstey Phillips: I am a man of very quick passions, and possibly under a fancied sense of wrong I should forget our friendship and betray you to the very men you have had the assurance to visit within the last few hours."

"You refer to the officers of the Mameluke line-of-battle ship."

"I do."

"Listen, friend Saul," said the privateersman, "were a King's officer to place his foot upon the deck of that vessel for a hostile purpose, one pull upon that tassel would send him and the ship into eternity."

"Hum, hum, hum!" purred Saul; "you should have kept that secret, my friend."

"Why?"

"Because the world is wicked—very wicked, and anyone wishing to get rid of you would find it a very easy plan to set the King's officers upon you. They would not care, of course, who died with you, as long as they attained their wish."

"Those," Anstey Phillips said pointedly, "who betrayed me would share my fate."

"But you would not know—hum, hum, hum—you would not know, my friend."

"There you are mistaken, Saul; I trust no man; and all who visit my ship are closely watched when they leave."

Saul gave a start of surprise.

"Does this rule hold good in all cases?" he asked.

"In all cases whore I have reason to doubt my visitors.

The old man darted a keen glance at the privateersman to note the effect of his words, as he said—

'Your visitors of to-day were not watched Anstey Phillips."

The other did not betray the least surprise at these words, but, in his usual careless manner, replied—

"I have no occasion to fear their loyalty."

"Possibly not; yet perhaps their visit was of ——"

"Whatever it was," said the seaman, it "cannot matter to you."

Saul sprang from his seat, and exclaimed passionately:

"But it does—it does! and I will know or—or——"

"What! have you suddenly gone mad?"

"I have not; but know the result—the purport of their visit—I must and will; so do not attempt to hide anything from me—pirate, thief, and murderer!"

He seemed as though he would have sprung

SHEET ANCHOR JACK THREATENED BY THE AMERICAN CAPTAIN.

at the young mariner's throat while giving vent to this incoherent string of words.

"I'll tell you what it is, my friend," the seaman said coolly; "a ducking would do you good; and a ducking you will have, if you are not more careful in your speech."

"Do you refuse to tell?"

"I do; what is the matter with you——"

Before he could finish, Saul Mason sprang up the ladder which led to the deck.

The captain of the privateer touched a small gong which hung by a small chain from the roof.

In answer to his summons a sailor entered the state-room.

"Follow that man who has just left the ship in a shore boat; should he make any attempt to board a King's ship he must be prevented at any cost."

"At the cost of his life, cap'en?"

"Aye, twenty lives. You understand?"

"I do, cap'en, and will see to it."

When the sailor left the state-room, the officer stood for some moments in deep thought.

"What," he muttered, "can be the reason of old Saul's peculiar behaviour? Can there be any connection between the Gloriana and the mission I have undertaken for these people?"

He paced to and fro for a few seconds, then resumed:

"No matter to me, I must be upon the blue waters—England is at war with France and America, and I must not lose the chance of doing a little legitimate business."

CHAPTER VII.

ON BOARD THE SANDY HOOK.

THE crew of the Sandy Hook stood in sullen silence watching the approach of the lieutenant and his boat's crew, and when young Nelson scrambled up the side he was seized by the American captain and a pistol held close to his head.

The American captain uttered a deep threat, and tried all he knew to intimidate the daring youth, but finding that young Nelson was immovable, and fully bent upon taking charge of the prize, he replaced his pistols in his belt.

Perhaps it was as well he did so, for at that moment the prize crew, who had been vainly endeavouring to prevent their boat being crushed against the ship's side leapt on to the deck flourishing their cutlasses and threatening to cut down all who dared oppose them.

The captain retreated sullenly to the quarter-deck muttering curses on the hated English, and casting ominous glances towards the frigate, from whose side another boat was about to be pushed off to the young officer's assistance.

The Sandy Hook, an American letter of marque, was a stout-built vessel, a good sailer, and moreover carried one hundred men, from which it might be inferred she was not an enemy likely to be played with.

Nelson saw at a glance that Jack's shot had done a signal service, for had the Sandy Hook been manageable, there is no doubt the captain would have made an attempt to get out of range of the frigate's guns.

Had this been possible, there would have been a wholesale massacre of the Lowestoffe's men, or an unconditional surrender on their part.

The young lieutenant advanced to the quarter-deck, and raising his hat to the American captain, said:

"You will please to give up your sword, and order your men to lay aside their weapons."

The captain unbuckled his belt and flung the weapon to the deck. his men following the example and threw their weapons at the feet of the English sailors.

"Run up St. George's Cross," said Nelson to Sheet-Anchor Jack, "in order that those on board the frigate may know we have taken possession of the prize."

To the annoyance of the conquerors, it was found that in the hurry of the moment, the party had left the Lowestoffe without a flag.

"You needn't want for that article," said the American, with grim satisfaction; "for there's seven of them in my cabin, one for each of the ships I have taken belonging to your miserable patch of land which you call England."

The colour came to Nelson's cheek when he heard this, and turning sharply upon the speaker, he said:

"It ill becomes a man in the moment of defeat to boast of his former deeds. Go below, Jack, and bring up one of those flags."

"Defeat!" said the skipper. "Skyrockets and figure-heads! you call this defeat, do you? Listen, young fellow. Had your ship been a little nearer my own size, it would have gone hard with me, if I had not added another of your thievish colours to my stock."

Nelson turned upon his heel, and left the American to chafe at his leisure.

"Now, my lads," he said, rig a fresh wheel, if there is such an article aboard, and keep your eyes upon the prisoners, for we shall not be able to send them to the frigate with such a sea as this running."

A spare wheel was dragged from the hold and soon replaced the broken one. When this was done, the Sandy's Hook's sails were spread, and she bore towards the frigate.

With the exception of the captain and two officers, the prisoners was sent below, and over the hatchway a sentry was placed with strict orders to fire upon any man who attempted to force his way upon deck.

It was a delicate position for the young officer and his handful of men to be placed in.

The night was coming on, and there was no means of keeping close to the frigate; thus it became necessary to use the greatest caution to keep the prize they had so easily won.

Therefore, in addition to the sentry, a carronade was slewed round so as to command the hatchway, and in doing this, the young officer took especial care that the prisoners should see the charge of grapeshot placed in the gun.

With the darkness the sea rose higher, and the wind howled yet more dismally among the rigging, and the heavens became a dark as pitch.

For some time they were able to keep the frigate's lights on their weather bow, but suddenly they disappeared as though the stately ship had been swallowed in the dark void beyond.

A portion of the prize crew stood on the forecastle vainly endeavouring to pierce the inky darkness.

"What's become of the old barkey, I wonder?" said one of the men. "Why doesn't the skipper fire a gun to let us know where he is!"

"You know as well as the rest of us," replied a messmate, "that Cap'n Lockyer hates to signal at night. Doesn't he, Bill Morris, you ought to know, for you were his cox'un long enough?"

"In course I knows," said Bill Morris, with the air of a man who felt his importance, "and often's the time I've heard him say to the young luffs when they have gone on board a prize, 'No guns or rockets,' says he, 'young gemmen; for that ere way of signalling only shows the enemy, should there be any of 'em about, the exact place we are in, and many a good prize has escaped in the darkness when she seed the rockets, and heard the guns; and if it hadn't a-been for all this 'ere signalling they might have been took in the morning, which,' he says, 'ain't right, 'cos the men wants their prize money, when they goes ashore;' which is quite right, ain't it, shipmates?"

"Quite right, Bill Morris," chimed in his messmates, "and no one knows that better than we do ourselves."

"What's that?" exclaimed Jack suddenly, "the frigate's lights, or I'm much mistaken."

"Well, it are lights," said Bill Morris; "but to my mind they don't seem to be so high as the old barkey's."

"Maybe not, seem so," said a sailor, "and perhaps they ain't as high; but that may be because they've been lowered a bit."

"Right, Dick Sheave," said Bill Morris approvingly; "you can allers tell the exact way things happens; so now as we are all right unders the frigate's barkers, I shall turn in and have a sleep."

There was another watcher on the quarter-deck who felt quite as much relieved when he saw the lights, Will-o'-the-wisp like, dancing about in the darkness.

This was the young lieutenant, who, feeling the terrible responsibility which was apon his head, had refused to leave the deck until he was satisfied that the frigate was near enough to keep the turbulent crew of the Sandy Hook in subjection.

He had not left the deck about five minutes when two cloaked figures came up, and leaning over the bulwarks, one took from beneath his boat-cloak a battle lanthorn.

The ample folds of his garment shielded the light from the sentries' watchful eyes until he had lowered it over the side.

"Dip it twice," said the American shipper to his companion the lieutenant, and if it is the Boston she'll answer."

The light was dipped as ordered, and almost instantly answered from the other vessel, which was not more than a pistol-shot from the prize.

"The Boston, by all the snakes in Vermont!" chuckled the captain; "free States and eternal British slaves! but these infernal Britishers are in a tolerable fix if this frigate keeps away."

"I don't suppose the Britishers know these waters swarm with our light craft," said the lieutenant, "or they would not have sent such a weak prize-crew aboard."

"Not they, the dunder-headed fools; they don't see an inch beyond their noses, or they would go closer to land, and find out the reason of their merchant ships being snapped up as they are."

"So much the better for us," whispered the lieutenant. "Now, captain, is there no way to tell the Bostons of the fix we are in?"

"No way?—Creeks and alligators! of course there is. Let me see. Captured! eternal smoke!—yes, pass the light twice to the right, then let the line run out until the lanthorn nearly touches the water."

When this signal was made a green light shone for a moment in the distant vessel's rigging.

"He understands," chuckled the captain. "Now, then, for the warning. Let's see. Look out—dip three times—so—so—it's answered by the Jumping Joker! Frigate—put your cap over the light twice—hurrah! Now, Britisher, wave the light to and fro, then drop it into the water. That's a signal and a motto too; for as sure as there's a tree in the free country, we shall wipe these eternal skunks out. Eh! what's up?"

"The line's broken, and the light has gone to show old Davey the way home, for he has, I daresay, been out to liquor up—eh?"

"The Boston's signalling," said the captain. "Yes, yes, yes—bravo! Good, old nails and dollars, you don't say so?"

"Say what?" asked the lieutenant as the light disappeared from the distant vessel's side, for the private signals were only understood by the captains of the light armed craft which proved so destructive to the English shipping after the young country threw off the British yoke, "what does he say?"

"About the best bit of news I've heard for many a long day."

"What is it?"

"Well, just this · a large ship passed him about two bells since in chase of the Virginia," he thinks.

"I'll tell you what," the lieutenant said, "the frigate has gone after the Virginia, thinking it was this little beauty of a prize."

"I believe you are right, O'Brien. Ha, ha! it was a cute dodge for you to douse all the lights except that one over the binnacle. Wriggling serpents and dancing bears! but we have drawn the feather over those Britishers' eyes."

"And over those on board the frigate, too," said the lieutenant, "for, depend upon it, when she missed the light here, she saw the Virginia's and went after her."

"That's it, by gosh! Well, we can't do any more until the daylight comes and the sea goes down a little. Pumpkins and tallow! but the Britishers will stare when the morning comes."

"They will unless we can get to the men and rouse them up. Those fellows are tired; all asleep, except the sentries and a few men to look after the sails."

"We can wait," said the captain, "for the contents of that gun would knock half of our fellows to eternal smash if fired down the hatchway; and fired it would be, for that young fellow, though he ain't much to look at, has a devil of an eye, and it means mischief."

"Can't we surprise the sentry?"

"Better not try it, O'Brien, my boy."

"Be it so. But as sure as fate we shall make a mistake if we do not get a few lights up."

"That's easily done—— Hallo! Stoop, sit upon the gun. Here comes the little officer."

The Americans dropped into a sitting position upon a carronade, and placing their heads against the side, drew their cloaks over their faces, and pretended to be asleep.

"Most singular," said Nelson to a sailor who was by his side. "What could it mean? I feel sure if Captain Lockyer wished to speak to us, he would do it in the usual manner."

"Very likely, sir," said Sheet-Anchor Jack, respectfully, "but I am confident I saw the light move about as though signalling."

The American captain nudged his companion and whispered:

"I should like to have that cute lad tied up in a hammock, and a cold shot fastened to his feet."

"The varmint," said the lieutenant; "he'll spoil our game."

"I'll choke him if he does."

"You are generally very correct," said the young officer to Sheet-Anchor, "very correct indeed in your reports, yet I think—nay, I am certain—you have mistaken the rolling of the frigate in this heavy sea, and the consequent alteration in the position of her lights, for "——

An exclamation of surprise came from Sheet-Anchor's lips, which caused his superior to pause in his speech.

"It's explained, sir," said the young mariner; "our lanthorns, except the binnacle, have gone out."

"So I perceive. Well, how does this explain your theory about the signals?"

"Why, sir, the man on watch knows how particular the captain is about these matters, and they have been showing a lanthorn over the side to attract our attention before the report should be taken to him."

"Very likely; in fact, this is the only explanation of the affair," said the young officer, speaking in a tone of vexation. "See to the lights at once, and find out whose negligence has caused this want of attention to be noticed by the watch on board the frigate."

"I am to blame, sir," said Sheet-Anchor, "if there is any one to blame in the matter, for I lit the lamps, which looked as though they were trimmed ready to be hoisted, and I did so without ascertaining whether they were full of oil."

"Well, well, it can't be helped now. I shall not notice the matter unless Captain Lockyer hears about it."

"Thank you, sir," said Sheet-Anchor; "I will take care the lanthorns are in proper order for the remainder of the night."

The young officer left the deck; but before retiring to his cot he visited the sentry on the hatchway.

"All quiet below, Saunders?"

"All quiet now, sir," the man answered, "but they have been rather noisy, and using anything but nice words about King George and England."

"Poor fellows, it is but natural; be on the alert, Saunders. Good night."

"Good night, your honour; I'll keep on the 'lert—never fear."

After Sheet-Anchor had run a lanthorn up to the foremast and another at the bows, he returned to his station in the forecastle.

"What did the luff say?" asked Bill Morris "blowed up because you didn't call him at fust, I s'pose?"

"No," said Sheet-Anchor; "they were not signalling after all."

"What then, messmate?"

The young sailor narrated the interview between the lieutenant and himself.

"No light aloft," said a tall sailor, known as Lanky Dick; "well, I'm blessed if I wasn't right, after all, Bill Morris."

"Right, was you?" said Morris; "how was you right?"

"Why, did'nt I say I seed the light at the mast-head lowered all of a sudden?"

There was a general laugh at this, for Lanky Dick was an inveterate liar; and although in this instance he had spoken the truth, no one believed him then or at the time of the occurrence.

"Never mind," said the long one savagely, "if I has told a few of 'em in my time, this was as true as I am here."

"Aye," said Bill Morris, "as true as the island you saw grow out of the sea."

"It's only fools like you," retorted Lanky Dick, "as don't believe; ask Sheet-Anchor—now he's a scholar, and knows more than all of ye—if it ain't right."

"Such a thing has occurred more than once," replied the young seaman; "the cause, I may as well tell you, has been a volcanic eruption taking place under the sea."

"Good night, mates," said Bill Morris: "arter that I'll have a sleep. A 'ruption under the sea! oh, Lord! what next?"

"Where ignorance is bliss," Jack thought, "it is more than folly to undeceive the unbeliever."

He stretched himself upon the wet planks, and, like his companions, soon gave audible evidence of the most perfect repose.

"I never heard," said the American captain to his companion, as they leant over the side watching the Boston's lights, "of a lot of fools being in a bigger fix than are these here thick-headed Britishers."

"Pretty tolerable," remarked the lieutenant; "it will be worth sitting up all night to see their faces in the morning."

"A month of nights," said his companion, "to see this animal they call the British Lion as nicely muzzled as ever any animal has been since the whole tribe came out of Noah's Ark."

So passed the night; the two Americans exulting over the prospect of a speedy release: the handful of English tars sleeping in the fancied security of the stately frigate's protection.

CHAPTER VIII.

HANS KLEB IN A FIX.

WATERMAN Bill Webb sat in his boat, reflecting over the scene which had taken place between Saul and himself.

"If I thought," he reflected, "that old Saul would betray me to the press gang I'——I'd ——"

Waterman Bill Webb's thoughts were interrupted by the arrival of the gig belonging to the Saucy Jane.

The waterman saw the men pulled man-o'-war fashion, and he also noticed that the sailors, when a gaily-dressed individual mounted the Saucy Jane's side, tossed their oar-blades aloft likewise in man-o'-war style.

"Very smart chaps'" thougnt Bill Webb, "but to my mind there's a something about them and the craft they belong to a——"

"Get out of the way with that tub."

The waterman nimbly backed water, and, swallowing the insult, he watched the bow-oarsman make the light gig fast to a guess warp.

When the men went on deck, Bill Webb pulled his boat under the ladder, and, leaning upon his sculls, resumed his reflections.

"The night 'll be pretty dark afore he gets back to Blackwall, and, if I thought he'd do me any harm, I'd upset the blessed boat in the middle of the stream, and send him to the bottom if I had to hit him over the head with one of the sculls."

The longer Bill Webb reflected over this means of disposing of Saul, the better he liked it; and while thus occupied, the meagre figure of old Saul descended the accommodation ladder, at a pace considerably quicker than he was in the habit of moving.

"Push off, push off," he said as he plumped down on the seat and nearly capsized the boat. "Push off, William Webb, and get out of sight of——"

Saul did not complete the sentence; he seemed to remember there was a witness to his unusual excitement.

The waterman, as he pulled the boat up the stream, was certainly a little astonished at the evident signs of an excited mind which the usually cool and collected Saul Mason displayed.

The ship-chandler turned several times towards the ship he had just left, and shook his clenched fist at the graceful fabric, then he faced Bill Webb, and kept opening and closing his fingers and thumb, which looked not unlike a vulture's claw, they were so thin and so discoloured, and topped with long, sharp nails.

This occupation seemed to relieve the mind Saul Mason, for, when he desisted, he looked sharply at Bill Webb.

The boatman shuddered, for he fully expected e ship-chandler to accuse him of the act of violence which had occupied his thoughts ; but now he was face to face with Snaky Saul, he felt his resolution, like Bob Acre's courage, ooze out at his fingers' ends.

"William Webb," said old Saul in a persuasive tone, "you are a poor man, and you have a large family to support."

"That's true, your honour," answered Bill Webb, very much surprised at this address, "and hard lines I find it some times to keep the young 'uns' teeth from getting rusty."

"No doubt, William Webb, no doubt, and as your bad time is coming on, a present of five guineas, five golden guineas, Bill Webb, and full weight——"

Here Saul tapped his pocket, and the ring of the precious metal fell very musically upon the waterman's ears. Then, as Saul remained quiet, Bill Webb ventured to say:

"Yes, your honour, five guineas, and full weight."

"Ah—hum, hum, yes ; not a light one among them, Bill Webb."

"No, your honour."

"These guineas changed into shillings make quite a heap of money, Bill Webb, and properly used, when your bad time comes on, would oil the hinges of your youngsters' teeth—he, he he!—don't you think so, Bill Webb?"

"That I do, your honour; but I am afraid I shall not have the little heap, unless you gives it me, and—and——"

"And that's not very likely, eh, Bill Webb? Old Saul does not part with his money like that; oh, no—hum, hum!"

The waterman did not make any answer. He began to wonder whether it would be possible for him to knock Saul Mason down as he left the boat and help himself to the money.

"No, Bill Webb," Saul resumed ; "money is much too hard to obtain to throw away, eh, William Webb?"

"Yes, your honour ; but I may make so bold as to speak, I—I——"

"Of course you may, William Webb; of course you may make yourself as bold as you think proper."

"Well, sir, as you give me liberty to say what I think, I would say that your honour was about to ask me to do something for you to earn the five guineas.'

"Quite so, Bill Webb; quite so, William Webb. I shall require a trifling service for that money, and shall not pay until you have done the service."

"In course not, sir; I'm quite willing to attend to a agreement like that with a gentleman as I have known so long as I've known you—— Now then, stupid, where are you a coming to? Are you blind?"

The shadows of twilight had deepened into night by this time, and the waterman and his fare had been so interested in the matter in debate that one had ceased from rowing, and the other had not noticed this neglect.

The consequence was, that a light gig which had followed Bill Webb's wherry for some distance up the river, grazed the stern of the waterman's craft, before either party became aware of the other's proximity.

"What do you leave off rowing for in the middle of the stream?" retorted the occupant of the gig; "if you are going to cast anchor, why don't you hang out a light?"

This answer was given as the solitary rower backed his light boat clear of the wherry ; then with an adjective not necessary here to repeat, he shot swiftly, and—save for the ripple of the water under the gig's bows—silently ahead.

"William Webb," said old Saul, after the boat had gone ahead, "don't you think it's very lucky you ceased rowing for a few minutes?"

"Can't say as I do, sir, seeing as how at the very least there is some of the paint taken off the starn of my boat."

"You are a dull animal, William Webb."

"May be, I am, your honour."

"Very dull. Did you not recognise that gig, eh?"

"Now you speak, sir, I do. In course it belongs to that smart craft you went on board?"

"Exactly so, William Webb. Exactly so; does your remarkable intelligence suggest any cause for that man rowing with muffled oars?"

"Can't say as it does, sir."

"You are an ass, Bill Webb. That man has been following us, and had he not fouled us in the dark, we should have remained in ignorance of the interesting fact."

"Your honour is right; but I don't understand like what he wants a following of us for, unless he's looking after your honour."

"No, Bill Webb, he's looking after you. They are short of hands, one hand, and ——"

The waterman did not wait to hear any more, but bending his back, he drove the boat at an astonishing pace through the water.

Saul Mason chuckled to himself, and peering over the side of the boat, first on one side then on the other, he saw, or fancied he saw, a sm boat, spectre-like, overtaking the wherry.

Saul pressed and rubbed his hands, as though in high glee, and even when Bill Webb in his haste splashed the ship-chandler, the latter did not rebuke him.

Blackwall was reached at last, and as Saul stepped from the boat, he said:

"Follow me, William Webb, and we will talk over the little business I wish you to execute for me."

Bill Webb did follow the ship-chandler, and, as they left the muddy beach, the light gig and its occupant came swiftly towards the shore.

Slightly as the sand was grazed by the keel of the gig stranding upon the beach, it did not escape the quick ears of Saul Mason, and he chuckled.

"Did you hear that, Bill Webb?"

"I did, your honour."

"He's after you, Bill Webb. Ho! ho! ho!"

The waterman's teeth chattered audibly.

"But never mind, William Webb, we'll trap him yet. Ho! ho! ho!"

"Oh Lord!" gasped Bill Webb. Oh Lord!"

"Don't be a fool, William Webb. I tell you, we will trap him yet. Do you hear that, Bill Webb?"

"I do, your honour. I hope we shall."

THE STARS AND STRIPES FLUTTERED IN THE BREEZE.

"Ho! ho! ho! We shall, Bill Webb, if you follow my directions?"

"I'll do everything, your honour tells me."

"Very well, William, keep cool, and he won't have you—hum, hum, hum! Do as I tell you—ho, ho, ho!"

"Yes, your honour."

"When we reach my house you go straight forward, Bill Webb, straight up the narrow street that runs close to my house, and when you have reached the first oil lamp, wait until I join you."

"I will, your honour; but he——"

"No, Bill Webb, he will follow me, and I shall, ho! ho! ho! leave the door of my house open; then, ha! ha! ha hum! hum! but that's not your affair, Bill Webb."

"No, your honour, it ain't. Now here we are close to your honour's house."

"Quite correct, Bill Webb. Now go you on to the place I have named."

The waterman ran eagerly forward, glad of the opportunity to place Saul Mason between himself and the pursuer.

Saul jingled his bunch of keys as he unlocked the door, and, as though by accident, when he passed inside his house, he left the door partly open.

The sickly light from an oil lamp, which stood by the footpath, enabled him to see the form of a man walk stealthily across the road.

"Ho, ho!" Saul chuckled; "I shall have him—ho, ho!"

Still keeping his eyes upon the seaman from the Saucy Jane, the ship-chandler quietly placed a spring-trap upon the mat, then softly withdrew to the extreme end of the passage.

Here he waited for several minutes, rubbing his hands and purring to himself at the prospect of catching Anstey Phillips's spy.

"He's sure to come," thought Saul; "curiosity will cause him to step inside. Hum, hum, hum!"

Hans Kleb, captain of the afterguard, a devoted follower of Anstey Phillips, crept stealthily to the partly-opened door.

His orders were not to lose sight of Saul Mason, and for all Hans Kleb knew, the house he was so near might be a Government office; therefore, his best plan would be to see the interior, if possible, or at the least find out the occupation of the person he had been told to follow.

With his hand upon the hilt of his cutlass, he slipped inside the door, then he paused and listened, but could hear no sound.

As the place was in darkness, Hans Kleb, as a measure of precaution, drew his cutlass, then advanced further inside.

There was a sudden click, followed by a yell from Hans Kleb, when he felt his right leg seized just above the ankle, by the saw-like teeth of the man-trap old Saul had placed upon the mat.

The astounded Hans fully imagined his limb was in the jaws of a shark or an alligator, so he gave another yell and began to cut and slash wildly about him, but his weapon only encountered the wall.

In the midst of this cutting and yelling old Saul appeared at the end of the passage with a lighted candle in his hand:

"Ho, ho! my fine fellow!" he said, grinning horribly, and his rusty teeth standing out more than ever; what are you doing here?"

Hans glanced at the mummy-like figure, and gave a lusty oath of rage and despair.

"Swear not, my good man," said Saul; "you are caught this time; and there you will remain until the morning, unless you tell me the reason of your visit."

"Come closer," said the seaman, tears of pain running from his eyes; "come closer and I'll tell you."

"He, he, he! ho, ho!" laughed Saul; "what, come within reach of that cutlass? no, no; my name is Saul Mason—a name that is known not to belong to a fool; oh, no; speak out, my man—but at a distance—a safe distance—from that carnal weapon."

Hans made a savage but ineffectual cut at his grinning tormentor, and favoured him with a volley of the choicest forecastle blessings.

"Well my man," said Saul suavely; "you know best. Stay here if you like till the morning, then I will have you taken away by a Bow-street officer; so good night, and—ho, ho, ho!—pleasant dreams!"

"Here," said the seaman, as Saul was about to move away, "what is it you want to know?"

"The object of your visit here, my man."

"If I tell you, what pledge have I that you will release me?"

"The bond of Saul Mason, my man—an honourable pledge I——"

"The world is turned upside down then," said a voice outside, "when old Saul's word is—ah! hallo!—what's this, Saul, you old villain? What! have you caught a poacher?"

These words were spoken by a young man as he threw open the door and gazed upon the strange scene.

"Ah, Mr. Henry," said the old man, "you are always so full of your jokes—well, I daresay I was young myself once—but come in—come in."

The new comer, who wore the uniform of an officer of the King's guards, came forward at old Saul's words, and as he was in the act of passing the trapped seaman, the latter placed the point of his cutlass against the guardsman's breast, and forced him against the wall.

"Keep quiet," said Hans Kleb, savagely, "and do not attempt to draw your sword, or I will pin you to the wall"

This sudden change in affairs was as embarrassing to the Guardsman as it was astonishing to the ship-chandler, Snaky Saul Mason.

CHAPTER IX.

AN UNEQUAL MATCH.

When the grey mist of the new-born day rolled upward from the face of the mighty ocean, and the rosy tints of the red sun began to tip the wavelets, Sheet-Anchor Jack shook himself, and arose from his sleeping-place between the guns.

The young seaman's first look was aloft, and, as he gazed at the ship's swelling sails, he could not repress a slight exclamation of admiration at the graceful and fairy-like rig of the American Letter of Marque.

His next glance was directed around him, and as the light became yet clearer, he gave a start of surprise and anger at the scene which met his eye.

The watch, with the exception of the sentry over the hatchway, were fast asleep.

Owing to the absence of the proper officers, the command of the morning watch devolved upon the coxswain of the boat which brought the prize crew aboard.

The old sailor stood on the forecastle, one elbow resting upon the bulwark, and supporting his head; he had but just dozed off. Perhaps the feeling of security, consequent upon the close vicinity of the frigate, had caused him to yield to that drowsy feeling, which, but for the opportune awakening of Sheet-Anchor Jack, would have lost the prize, without a chance of striking a blow to keep her from the Boston.

Stepping among the sleeping men, the young mariner aroused them by a no means gentle application of his foot.

The American captain and his companion had fortunately fallen asleep just before daybreak, or they would have seized the opportunity to overpower the only watchful man on deck.

When Jack had aroused the watch, he began to bestow his attention upon the vessel which lay about a mile to windward of the Sandy Hook.

"Surely," he thought, "this cannot be the frigate—no, it is a light vessel of the same class as this, and by the rig an American—but where's the frigate?"

He took the glass and swept the horizon, but beyond a white speck which appeared to be a sea-bird's wings, nothing was visible except the vessel which Jack saw by the position of her yards was edging towards the Sandy Hook.

Discreetly refraining from making any communication to the men, he went below and tapped at the door of the cabin where the young lieutenant slept.

The sound awoke the officer, and when Jack entered he said:

"Well, my man, how is the weather?"

"The sea has gone down, sir, but the wind still keeps pretty fresh."

"And the frigate—how far is she away?"

"She is not in sight, sir?"

"What? Impossible! Have the watch not been able to keep the Lowestoffe's lights in view?"

"They have kept in view the lights you saw before turning in, but I am sorry to tell you, sir, the vessel which carried them is not the Lowestoffe,"

The young officer jumped from his cot as he asked—

"What vessel, then? One of the West Indian squadron?"

"I am afraid not, sir; she looks like ——"

The officer ran rapidly on deck, followed by the young seaman.

There was no glass required to learn the purpose and the nationality of the stranger, for from the mast-head there floated the stars and stripes of the young country, and the vessel was rapidly and skilfully edging in with the Sandy Hook.

Lieutenant Nelson's quick perception was not long in understanding the whole affair, and prompt in action while there yet remained a chance of saving the prize—

"Gentlemen," he said to the American officers who stood near the mainmast joyfully watching their country's flag floating defiantly in the breeze, "I must request you will go below."

"Certainly," said the captain; "we will retire if you wish it; surely you don't mean to attempt any resistance "

"I shall retain this vessel, sir," said the gallant-hearted Nelson, "while I have a man to carry out my orders."

"Do as you like, young fellow," said the captain of the Sandy Hook; "but if you are foolhardy enough to pit yourself against the Boston, all I can say is you are not the clever young chap I took you to be "

"I intend to do my duty, sir," said the prize officer, "and perhaps in the lucky chapter of accidents I may be fortunate enough to keep this vessel even against this——"

"Blue smoke and phosphorus!" exclaimed the American; "you are mad. Why the Boston carries twelve 18's and a crew of a hundred and fifty men."

"It is an unequal match I admit," said the lieutenant; "but I will abide the issue. Now, gentlemen, to your cabin if you please."

The American officers shrugged their shoulders, and looked upon the lieutenant in charge of the prize as little better than an escaped lunatic.

"Now my lads," said the young officer, when the Americans had gone below, "there's just a chance we may escape this fellow to windward, therefore let us make the most of it. Away there, sail trimmers, set every inch of canvas on the foremost."

The men ran and obeyed the order.

"Now, Jack," said Lieutenant Nelson, "I must promote you for the time. Take charge of the guns forward, and let us cripple some of his spars if we can. Remember if they once board us all chance of escape is hopeless."

"I'll do my best, sir."

"Ben Tompion," the young officer continued, turning to the coxswain, "fasten the hatch down over the prisoners; then run aft and see the braces tightly touched; we cannot afford to lose as much wind as would fill a lady's cambric handkerchief."

Ben Tompion touched his cap and went about the work selected for him.

These preparations completed, the lieutenant went to the quarter-deck."

By looking through the glass, Nelson saw the crew of the Boston were at quarters, and by the mass of heads visible near the forecastle, it was evident that Sandy Hook's consort meant to recapture the prize by boarding.

The young seaman understood the motive for this. The captain of the Boston did not wish to injure the spars or rigging of his friend's vessel.

"Cast loose a couple of guns," he said to Sheet-Anchor Jack, "and be ready to fire at my signal."

"Aye, aye, sir."

The sailing powers of the vessels were about equal. If there was any advantage, the Boston had it, in consequence of her extra light sails, which were now unfurled.

All that a clear judgment and a thorough knowledge of his profession could suggest was done by young Nelson to increase the distance between the vessels."

But owing to the few men he had to handle the ropes, the enemy, whose decks were crowded with men, was able, by the number of hands which were ready to go aloft, to execute quickly every manœuvre, and thus render the young officer's design fruitless.

With compressed lips, and the air of a man resolved to do and dare all that could be done in his desperate situation, the lieutenant stood upon the quarter-deck, speaking-trumpet in hand, his eye never, for a moment, leaving the Boston.

From time to time a low order left his lips, and, as it was obeyed, the pale face would glow over the momentary advantage gained over his skilful and ready opponent.

The time for action was rapidly approaching, for the Boston, by a masterly movement, shot suddenly ahead of the prize, then her yards were backed, the sails for a second fluttered as the wind was taken out; the next instant every inch of white gleaming canvass bellied out, the wheel was jammed down, and, like a sea fowl breasting its native element, the light craft dashed astern of the Sandy Hook, her larboard battery in a position to rake the weak-handed prize.

The young commander bit his lips with vexation, then called out to the helmsman:

"Luff, luff; steady, steady."

The bows of the Sandy Hook, obedient to the slightest movement of the helm, rapidly fell off, and brought the vessel nearer the wind.

At this moment fortune seemed to favour the young officer, for, owing to the haste in which the order was carried out on board the enemy's ship, the ropes fouled, and before the accident could be remedied, the Sandy Hook had shot rapidly ahead.

The advantage was soon lost, for the Boston was handled by a skilful seaman, who seemed to care more for displaying his seamanship than at once bringing matters to an issue by using his guns.

Quite twenty minutes were occupied by the Boston in trying to regain the commanding position she had lost.

A gentleman's yacht could not have been better handled than was the Sandy Hook, in spite of the feeble crew aboard; and owing to the exertion and skill of the young commander, she was enabled to frustrate every attempt made by the foe to regain the lost position.

At last, as though sensible that he had met his match, the American captain gave up manœuvring, and spreading every inch of canvas even to rigging extra topsails, he bore up, and was soon abeam of the Sandy Hook.

To have looked at these graceful vessels when they were clear of each other, it seemed only like the meeting of two beautiful fabrics to interchange the friendly courtesies usual when ships meet upon the ocean far far away from land.

True the stars and stripes of the Young Republic streamed proudly over the Boston's stern, and the Union Jack fluttered defiantly at the Sandy Hook's mast-head, but other signs of a coming conflict there were none, for both vessels had their ports closed, and the terrible engines of destruction were invisible from each vessel.

But looking downward upon the decks of the Boston the forms of their muscular men stripped to the waist might have been seen standing around the guns.

And on board the Sandy Hook the few men who could be spared from handling the ropes were collected around two only of the line of guns which belted the vessel.

There could not be a moment's doubt respecting the issue of such an unequal conflict, for the crew of the American ship were men who claimed the same lineage as the determined little band of British tars.

With their prows turned the same way, the vessels sped through the water until they were within hailing distance, then the form of the American captain was seen upon the bulwarks, one hand grasping a portion of the shroud, the other a speaking trumpet.

"Sandy Hook, ahoy!" came across the intervening space; "haul down your flag, or I'll fire into you."

The voice of the English lieutenant, sounding almost childlike in comparison to the stentorian tones which came from the broad chest of the American, replied to this summons:

"St. George's Cross will fly above this deck while there is a man left to defend it."

"Well spoken, young fellow," said the American; "but you must be mad to carry out your words. Now, down with your flag, and save me the sin of destroying brave men."

"You have my answer," said the lieutenant; "it is unalterable."

With the generosity of a chivalrous foe, the American commander hesitated before he made a gesture with his trumpet, which would cause the ports to fly open and a storms of missiles to belch forth upon the Sandy Hook.

"Listen to me, young fellow," he said; "and if you do not value your own life, think of the men entrusted to your care."

"The men are with me in the answer I have given; the stainless flag above us will never be struck while one Englishman remains to uphold its glory."

"I will treat honourably with you," persisted the commander of the Boston. "I want not your lives nor your liberty. Surrender the prize quietly, and you shall all be released and sent on board your frigate without as much as the loss of a side-arm."

"I am sensible of the humane motive which causes you to make these offers, but I must decline them; I have a duty to perform, and while I have life I will do it."

"Reflect; I give you another chance. I must also do my duty, which is to retake that vessel and I mean to do it, but would save unnecessary bloodshed, and you, unless you are mad, must see the inutility of contending against me with the small force you have."

"The issue of battle rests not always with the strongest."

"You refuse then to accept my conditions."

"I do."

"Be it so. Ready there—FIRE!"

Like magic the ports flew open, and a storm of fire was vomited from the apertures.

The young officer had foreseen this, and prepared for it by ordering the men to throw themselves upon the deck.

There was no occasion for this, for the Boston's guns had been trained to fire above the seamen's heads, and the shot whistled through the rigging, and finally disappeared with a sullen plunge beneath the surface of the water far beyond the prize.

After the roar of this discharge there was a stillness, so profound upon each hand, that the sound of water which was being dashed aside by their bows was plainly audible.

The concussion of the Boston's ordnance had caused her to fall a little out of the track she had been pursuing, consequently, the stern of the Sandy Hook now became parallel with the bowsprit of her enemy.

The opportunity was not lost by the young officer, who at once called the men from the two guns forward to cast loose the two sternmost carronades.

"Aim at the mast," he said to Jack; "our safety depends upon the amount of damage we can do to the enemy's spars."

A single flash had followed his words, but before those on board the Sandy Hook had time to ascertain whether that shot had done any damage, six guns from the Boston hurled their missiles at the captured vessel.

More than one shot told, for the crash of wood was heard, and a shower of splinters fell among the group on the quarter-deck.

"What's gone?" Nelson said. "Not a——"

"Only a shattered plank, sir," Jack answered. "No spars, thank heaven! Shall I try again, sir?"

Fire!"

The second gun from the prize blazed forth, then came the response from the Boston, and three men were struck down near the young lieutenant.

The groans of the maimed and dying were silenced by a hearty hurra from their messmates' throats, then came the cry ·

"Her bowsprit is gone! her bowsprit is gone!"

Shot off close to the stem was the Boston's projecting spar, and, held only by the cordage, the wreck hung down below the water-line, and impeded the vessel's progress.

As the Sandy Hook took advantage of this mishap, a dozen men ran forward and began to chop away the fastenings of the broken spars, while thrice that number prepared a new stick to replace the loss.

Although stopped in her career, the privateer's guns were not idle as long as the Sandy Hook remained within range.

Flash after flash came from her bows, and a long gun amidships began to open fire.

The practice was excellent, and though not a spar or sail had suffered so far, a few ropes had been cut in two.

The two sternmost guns kept up a rapid fire upon the privateer until the two vessels were out of range of each other.

The proud, exultant smile left the young officer's lips as the moans of the wounded and dying came upon his ears, and, stooping over the sufferers, he did all in his power to soothe their pain.

Gallantly the vessel cleft the waters as she glided onward, and just as the hope of dropping the troublesome pursuer began to beat high in every breast, the lofty pyramid of canvas began to rise higher and higher in the distance.

Another hour passed and with but little change in the aspect of affairs, and the only hope fer the handful of Englishmen to retain their prize was the coming of the frigate.

Ten minutes more and there was a line of boats to be seen leaving the Boston's side with their prows turned towards the Sandy Hook.

"Double charge the guns with grape," said the young officer; "keep steady, men—our hour of peril is at hand. Remember if these boarders once get a footing on our deck we are lost."

The oar-blades flashed in the sun as the boats came sweeping on towards the prize, and all on board, as they looked anxiously at the dark spots upon the water, knew their hour of peril had indeed arrived.

CHAPTER X.

BILL WEBB TURNS THE MATTER OVER IN HIS MIND, AND ARRIVES AT A STRANGE CONCLUSION.

ALTHOUGH for a moment or two surprised at the sudden manner in which he had been caught, as it were, upon the point of Hans Kleb's weapon, the soldier soon recovered his presence of mind, and, as though tickled at the affair, he began to laugh heartily.

"Come, Saul," he said, when this fit was over; "release this poor devil. I suppose he only keeps me here as a hostage."

"I bear you no ill-will, sir," said Hans Kleb; "but I think if you were in my position you would do as I have done."

"No doubt," said the Guardsman; and mentally added, "and when I got loose I would twist old Saul's neck."

"Hum!" said Saul; "a most unpleasant affair—hum!"

"Release this man, you old villain—do you hear?"

"Yes, Mr. Henry—yes; but if I do, he may take advantage——"

"I will answer for him; sheathe your sword, my man, and I will release you myself. But mind, no violence against this old man."

"I shall not attempt any, sir. I had no right to come inside this house, and should not have done so had I known it was a private dwelling."

Hans sheathed his cutlass as he spoke, and the soldier, stooping over the trap, loosened the jagged teeth.

"Thank you, sir," said the seaman; "I can hobble down to my boat, then I shall be all right."

"But you are bleeding, and——"

"Nothing to hurt, sir, the pain is worse just now than the wound." Then turning to Saul, he added, "look here, old man, you want to know what brought me here ——?"

"I know all about it," interrupted Saul; "but you can go back to your captain and tell him I am too much his friend to require a watch being set upon my actions."

Hans unbuckled his leathern belt, and, using his cutlass as a walking-stick, hobbled towards the beach, his face showing the agony of pain he suffered.

Hans Kleb spoke the English language with as much facility as a native; but, as he went towards his boat, he indulged in several soliloquies in the Dutch tongue, but whether they were blessings or curses upon Saul Mason, the reader is the best judge.

When he reached the Saucy Jane, the captain was lounging against the quarter-rail, and as

HANS KLEB AND THE PRIVATEER CAPTAIN.

Hans limped towards him he took the cigar from his lips and asked:

"What's the matter, Hans?"

"Matter enough, cap'en," said the captain of the afterguard; "my leg is well-nigh broken by that parchment-faced old mummy you told me to follow."

"Let me see the wound, Hans."

The seaman drew up the bottom of his trousers, and Anstey took a lanthorn and examined the wound.

"What is it, Hans?" he said; "are there any sharks in the Thames? or is this ugly place the mark made by the teeth of a spring trap?"

"That's just it, your honour, a trap, and I was caught in it before I knew where I had put my foot."

"How did it occur, Hans?"

The seaman gave his captain an account of the affair, and ended by saying:

"If it had not been for the soldier officer coming in, I should not have got out of limbo until the morning."

"Never mind, Hans, show your wound to the doctor. You've had many worse."

"That's true, captain; but not in the way I got this. Donner-und-blitzen, but I should like to twist the old mummy's neck."

"You shall have an opportunity, Hans, if he visits the ship again. By the way, did he say anything when you were released?"

"Yes, cap'en I'd nearly forgotten it. He bid me tell you he was too much your friend to require a watch put upon him."

"Did he?" said the privateersman, "Opinions differ upon that point. You may go, Hans."

"Yes, cap'en; but—but——"

"Well, speak out, man."

"This scratch makes me awfully dry cap'en."

"No doubt; well go to the purser and tell him to give you your fill.

Hans walked away, and the captain of the Saucy Jane lazily puffed his cigar as he watched the lights aboard the Mameluke line-of-battle ship.

During the time Bill Webb stood crouching in in the shadow of the bye street, he reflected over the unusual generosity displayed by Saul Mason on his, Bill Webb's, behalf.

"He may be a good sort," Bill kept mentally saying; "but if he is no one knows it. I can't think somehow that he would take all this trouble to prevent me being pressed on board that craft."

The yell Hans Kleb gave when he was caught in the spring-trap came upon the waterman's ear.

"What's that? Maybe it's that sailor knocking old Saul about. I can't stand that."

So Bill Webb turned up his jacket sleeves, and ran towards the door, and arrived there just as old Saul made his appearance with the light.

The waterman listened to all that passed, but he prudently stepped aside when the officer of the King's Guard made his appearance.

"It's a rummy go," thought Bill Webb, as he went back to the place where he had to meet old Saul, "a real rummy go; but the old 'un ain't doing all this for me. I'm not such a fool as to believe that. He's a deep 'un he is, and he wants me to do summat for that money he's promised—some dirty trick or other."

The shuffling sound of Saul Mason's footsteps caused Bill Webb to retire yet farther in the shade, from whence he did not emerge until he heard the cracked voice saying:

"Bill Webb! William Webb! Confound the thick-headed fool, where is he? He! waterman Webb."

"Hallo! is that you, sir?"

"Yes, come; I have no time to lose."

So Bill Webb came forward, and old Saul gave him a folded paper.

"You know the Mameluke, man-of-war, Bill Webb?" Saul continued. "It is there I want you to go, William Webb."

"Yes, your honour."

"And mind, Bill Webb, that you give this paper to no one else but the captain."

"I'll mind that, your honour."

"Now, off with you."

"What! to-night?" asked Bill Webb in astonishment; "and I been that distance——"

"To-night, yes. Why not to-night? If you do not choose to go, I must find some one that will. Plenty quite ready to go for five guineas, William Webb."

"Yes, your honour."

The waterman did not make any attempt to leave the place where he stood, so Saul asked, sharply:

"What are you waiting for, eh?"

"Nothing, your honour, only I thought—that is—I—I——"

"You what, William Webb? What is it?"

"I thought your honour said you would give —five——"

"So I will, but not until you have earned it, William—not until then. No, no, no. What! Saul Mason pay money before it is due? What a simple mind you have, friend William Webb, licensed waterman."

William Webb, licensed waterman, did not move even at this. He stood his ground, fumbling the folded paper Saul had given him until it became several shades darker under the manipulation of a dirty finger and thumb.

"William Webb," roared Saul, "what the d——l are you doing with that paper? Be off with you at once."

"I'm going, sir, I'm going. But you have forgotten my—my fare."

"Your fare," squeaked Saul, "I'm ashamed of you, I am indeed, what, ask me for your fare when I am about to make you rich—yes rich, William Webb? There—there, I don't want to hear your apology."

Profoundly touched by the boatman's ingratitude, Saul turned about and went to his home, and Bill Webb as he went reluctantly to his home, soliloquised.

"He need not have been afeard, I was not going to make any 'pology, it was my rights; it's always the same with that old cuss, he always manages to cheat everybody; but I know who he won't cheat, ha, ha! he won't cheat the old 'un, who is waiting for him—he—he—he!—won't he stir old Saul up that's all."

Bill Webb, the waterman, was wicked enough

to laugh at the prospective roasting of old Saul Mason.

"I'll pull down the stream a little way," thought Bill, as he placed the oar in the row-locks, "in case the old wretch is watching me."

He pulled down a little way and rested upon his oars when he heard the sound of a fiddle, and a sea-faring chorus coming from the open window of a water-side public house.

"I'll just have a wet at the Benbow," said Bill Webb, "and have a look at the paper that old sinner has given me at the same time."

The tap-room of the Admiral Benbow was full of tobacco smoke, the fumes of bad beer and dirty-looking, half sailors, half landsmen, who gained a livelihood upon the Thames.

Bill Webb retreated from the uninviting prospect the half-open door presented, and the landlord, who knew Bill Webb, graciously asked him to take a seat in the parlour, and at the same time politely inquired what he, Bill Webb, would take.

The waterman was pleased to order a pint of porter, which being served and paid for, Bill Webb retired to a secluded corner, and drew the paper Saul Mason had given him from the lining of his hat.

It was a sheet of letter paper folded in four, the loose corner held down by a wafer, which was quite soft in consequence of absorbing the moisture from Bill Webb's forehead.

"I wonder if he'll find me out," thought the waterman, as he turned the paper over and over, "if I open it, I don't see how he can. Oh the wafer ain't dry, so here goes."

Bill Webb opened the letter, then placing his back towards the door with some difficulty spelt out the following words:—

"To the Officer Commanding
H.M.S. Mameluke.

"Sir,

The commander of that vessel which lies at anchor near you is the notorious Parker Neville, the vessel is the equally notorious Wasp. There is a reward of £1,000 for the capture of this man and his ship; for the information I have given I shall expect £500, which amount I shall come forward and claim when you have captured the Wasp. Until then I must sign myself. "A FRIEND."

William Webb folded the paper, replaced it in the lining of his hat, drank his beer, and left the "Admiral Benbow."

"Old Saul," he thought, as he slowly pulled out from the shore, "is a villain. Why this Parker Neville, bad as he is, once saved the old rascal from being hung—at least so I've heard."

CHAPTER XI.

THE RESULT OF BILL WEBB TURNING THE MATTER OVER IN HIS MIND.

WHEN Bill Webb had gone a few boats' lengths further, he paused in rowing, and seemed for a moment undecided about continuing his journey.

"I don't like the job," he muttered, "old Saul is a vampire; here he wants to give up this young chap for the sake of getting the blood-money—he called me a fool this evening, too, then he wouldn't pay his fare, and if I do this dirty work for him he won't give me the five guineas. Don't you do it, Bill Webb; you can do better, much better; of course you can."

Whatever new project had come into his head he turned to put it into execution, for the boat shot forward at a tremendous pace, keeping the water up under her bows in a cloud of white spray

"I've turned the matter over," he said "turned it over twice in my mind, and I know the best thing to be done, and mean to do it."

Bill Webb pulled with undiminished vigour, until he reached the Saucy Jane, then as he ran his boat under the graceful vessel's quarter, he was much surprised at feeling the wherry driven slowly back in spite of all his efforts to prevent it.

Looking over his shoulder he saw this strange movement was caused by two seamen who stood upon the Saucy Jane's accommodation ladder armed with long boathooks.

"Hallo, mate," one of them said, when he saw the boatman's face, "trying to run us down."

"No," answered the waterman, "I want to come aboard."

"Do you? Come to-morrow, my hearty, we've locked up for the night, and lost the key till the morning.

"You'll have to find it then, for come aboard I must, for I want to see your captain very particular."

"Do you? then you had better go and whistle to him through the state-room window."

"Look here," said Bill Webb, "if I don't see your skipper at once there won't be much of a *sting left in the Wasp* by the morning."

"That's it, is it?" said one of the seamen, "you can come on board then"

Bill Webb went aboard, and no sooner had he reached the deck than the two sailors whipped out their cutlasses and took him prisoner.

"You know too much," one said, "so unless the skipper lets you go there will be a waterman's throat cut to-night."

"Oh, Lord!" gasped Bill Webb, "oh, Lord! what a fool I was to come aboard."

His captors laughed, and Bill Webb kept up his lamentations until the midshipman who had gone to report the waterman's arrival, returned with an order to bring him before tho captain.

The waterman opened his eyes with astonishment when he was taken to the magnificent state-room and saw the handsome captain, dressed in an embroidered dressing-gown and slippers, reclining at full length upon one of the gorgeous divans smoking a *nargili.*

The blue smoke curling through the perfumed water of the Eastern pipe, astonished the waterman more than the magnificence which surrounded him, for in those days the strange-looking Eastern pipes were but little known in England.

The captain took the jewelled mouthpiece from his lips, and seeing the waterman said :—

"Well, my man?"

Bill Webb looked first at one of his captors, then at the other, and in a voice anything but steady, said,

"I want to speak to you, sir."

"Very well. I am all attention."

"It's something, sir, I don't like to speak about but only to yourself."

A gesture from the captain's hand caused the two guards to leave the cabin, and Bill Webb felt much relief when he heard the cutlasses put back into their scabbards.

"Now," said the captain, "we are alone."

"Yes, your honour, I wants to ask you if you know Saul Mason, a ship-chandler, as lives at Blackwall?"

"I do. He is a friend of mine."

Something very like a sneer played upon the handsome lips, as he used the word friend.

"It's about him I come to speak, your honour."

"Pray proceed."

"I will, your honour. I brought him to your ship when he came to-day."

"Yes."

"And while he was going back he said he would give me five guineas to do something for him."

"Indeed!"

"I didn't know what that something was, your honour, until I went to have a wet at the Admiral."

"The Admiral?"

"Yes, your honour, the Admiral Benbow."

"Yes, I understand. A public-house. Changed one of the guineas my friend gave you?"

"No, your honour, he ain't give me a farthing yet; he wouldn't even pay me the fare or bringing him here."

"Mr. Mason is a prudent man. He never pays until the work has been done."

"No, your honour, not him, for he wouldn't pay me for pulling him——"

"So you have just told me."

"So I have, your honour. Yes, I came to the Benbow."

"Quite right; you went there to have a wet, I believe you said?"

"I did, your honour: and it was there I looked at the paper he gave me to take to the Mameluke."

"Ha!" exclaimed the privateersman, "have you taken it?"

"No, your honour, I thought it would be best to let you see it first."

The handsome captain's face was not pleasant to look upon, as he took the paper from Bill Webb.

Still less pleasant when he opened it and read the contents.

"The old viper!" he muttered savagely; "were I to have him choked I should——but no, he shall be paid in his own coin."

Bill Webb stood pulling the rim of his hat until that useful article was not at all improved in appearance, as he watched the angry privateersman stride to and fro.

Suddenly the officer paused, and joining Bill Webb, said :

"You shall take this to the Mameluke. Will you take another at the same time?"

"If your honour likes," said poor Bill Webb, pinching his arm with his thumb and finger nails to assure himself that he was awake: "but—but—"

"You think I must be mad to do such a thing."

"Your honour knows best," said the waterman; "I did not think you would send it, or I would not have come——"

"You have done me a service, a—a—what's your name?"

"Webb, sir; my old woman calls me Bill; lazy Bill Webb if I has had a bad day; but if I has had a good day she calls me William, and smacks all the young uns because they don't get out of the way quick enough when I comes in."

The privateersman laughed at his visitor's simplicity, and said,

"A wise woman, Bill Webb, this wife of yours; she regulates her conduct according to your pocket."

"Yes, your honour, I s'pose so."

You will be sweet William when you

go home to-night, Webb; take this for the service you have done me."

The privateersman gave the waterman 20 guineas in a small leathern bag, and Bill Webb's extremities trembled at the immense sum he held in his hand.

While penning a note, the privateersman said—

"It's all yours, Bill Webb, spend this well, and mind you get the five old Saul has promised you."

"I will try, your honour, but I don't want them now, I shall never be poor again."

The privateersman folded and sealed the letter he had written, and tossing it to Bill Webb, said—

"Wait for about ten minutes, then you can go aboard the man-of-war;" here's something for you to drink, help yourself while I go on deck.

The rich dressing-gown was thrown off, so were the slippers, the latter replaced by a pair of shoes, the former by a thick blue jacket; then the officer left the cabin.

Bill Webb ventured to sit upon the extreme edge of one of the sofas, and as he poured out a glass of the liquor he heard the privateersman say—

"Slip the cable at once, and have the sails bent; there is quite enough breeze to take us out of the river."

Bill Webb did not feel comfortable, although he was by this time perfectly sure of his state of wakefulness, for he kept feeling the little bag of gold which caused quite a good-sized lump to stick out from the pocket of his jacket.

"Oh, Lord!" he gasped; "suppose I was to be taken out to sea by this skipper; oh, Lord!"

For upwards of twenty minutes there was a scuffling of feet above his head, then he heard the splash of the cable as the end was pushed through the hawse-hole.

Then—and Bill Webb's hair stood erect with fear—he felt the vessel begin to move, and just as he had given himself up for lost the captain entered the state room.

"Come," he said, "be quick; the ship is under weigh, jump into your boat or you will have a long pull to reach the Mameluke."

Bill Webb did not require a second bidding; he went up the ladder three steps at a time, and when he scrambled into his boat and a seaman cast off the line which had held it to the vessel's side, he began to breathe freely.

Whether it was fancy or a reality, Bill Webb never felt certain, but he could almost have sworn the deck of the ship when he left had at least a dozen guns ranged each side, yet when he went aboard there was not, and he felt certain of this, one piece of artillery to be seen.

Faithful to his promise and very much confused by the night's events, he pulled to the Mameluke, and after a great deal of trouble he was allowed to ascend the lofty sides.

He was kept quite half-an-hour on deck before the captain gave him an audience.

"So you wish to see me, my man," the captain of the King's ship said; "pray what is the nature of your errand?"

"Well, your honour," said Bill Webb; "two different parties has stopped me on my way home, and asked me to bring you these letters."

He handed the papers to the captain, who opened that sent by the privateersman first, and much to his surprise, read these words:

"A few months since, the Alert, a merchant ship, was robbed of its cargo by a gang of river pirates; the cargo was bought by one Saul Mason, who lives at Blackwall. In a shed at the back of his house a portion of the goods are yet to be found.

"ONE WHO HELPED TO ROB THE ALERT."

The officer slowly folded the paper, and said, half aloud—

"If this is true, I shall perhaps discover the audacious gang who have so long infested the river. This shall be seen to at once."

His surprise was greatly increased when he read the second communication; for, without saying a word to Bill Webb, he ran on deck.

It was the second lieutenant's watch, and that officer was walking to and fro the quarter-deck, when he was startled by the captain confronting him.

"Read this, sir," he said; "read this, and tell me what you think of that audacious scoundrel who dined with us this evening?"

By the limited light the second lieutenant read Saul's letter, and his surprise quite equalled his superior's.

"I thought there was something suspicious about the fellow," said the captain; but I never could have believed he would have dared to have come on board my vessel.

So far from this being the truth, the captain had been charmed with Parker Neville; and when he left the vessel, the commander of the Mameluke was the loudest in praising the noble appearance and gentlemanly manners of their guest.

The lieutenant knew this, but he was too prudent to say so.

"You did, sir," he said; "and this has proved the correctness of your perception."

"It has indeed—the audacious rascal! Call away the cutter, Mr. Irvin, and go at once and take possession of the Wasp in the King's name,"

The cutter was soon manned, but when Mr. Irvin reached the place where the Wasp had been at anchor, she had gone and left no trace behind.

Bill Webb was questioned and cross-questioned, but to no purpose; he still adhered to the same statement—that he had been stopped by two men and asked to bring two letters.

The captain of the Mameluke chafed a little at the escape of the Wasp.

"I should not be surprised," he said, "if that bold rascal had not sent me the letters; he's gone, unfortunately. I hope we shall be more fortunate in the other case. Go to Blackwall, Mr. Irvin, and see what you can discover."

The cutter pushed off, and Bill Webb, finding no notice was taken of him, quietly descended the side, and pulled away from the man-of-war.

CHAPTER XII.

AN UNEXPECTED ALLY.

THE Boston's boats advanced in the form of a crescent: the cutter on one flank, the barge on the other.

Each of these boats carried a gun at the bows, and the young officer could see by the glass the gunners stood ready with a blazing port fire in their hands.

He had smiled a seaman's scorn of a foe when the light-heeled Sandy Hook left the Boston on her lee, but now the smile had passed away, and he stood silent and thoughtful watching his small crew who stood by their guns awaiting the coming of the foe.

There was a long struggle in his heart between the claims of humanity and duty.

He knew full well, unless the wind should suddenly rise, there was no chance of a successful issue between the small force he had and the well-manned boats of the American letter of marque.

Yet he liked not the thought of yielding while there was a possibility of keeping the prize which had been entrusted to his care.

"I will leave the issue with the men," he muttered after a long deliberation; "there is yet time to save much bloodshed."

Sheet Anchor Jack, stripped to the waist in common with the rest of the men, was raising the breach of a gun in order to sweep the advancing boats, when he was called aft by the young officer.

"Jack," said Nelson, "what are the opinions of the men respecting the approaching struggle?"

"They say we are a match for the boats, sir if we can only load and fire quick enough."

"They would not relish the idea of an unconditional surrender?"

"No, sir; the hearts of oak would sooner stand to a man."

"Be it so; away to your station, and be careful not to empty the three guns at once."

"I'll take care of that, sir."

The young seaman passed swiftly to the bows; then a deep silence pervaded the vessel—a silence which invariably precedes a battle by sea or land.

The enemy's boats swept onward, and by the regularity of their movements, it was evident the officer who sat in the stern sheets of the cutter, held his men in the most perfect discipline and control.

There was no hurry; each boat kept its allotted station, and if a young seaman whose nerves were not yet accustomed to row under a battery of shotted guns, turned his head towards the vessel they were about to attack, the deep voice of the officer in command of the boat could be heard, saying:—

"Look to your front; pull together, my lads! there is no hurry—we shall be aboard directly!"

The prize officer gave a keen and anxious glance at the enemy, noting well the admirable arrangements which, under the circumstances, precluded the possibility of the Sandy Hook's grape-shot striking more than one boat at a time.

All eyes being thus centred upon the boats, none noticed that the white speck which a short time before seemed like a sea-gull's wing, was becoming larger; and already by the glass one of the look-outs on board the Boston beheld the white sails of a vessel rising out of the sea, and beneath the lofty pyramid the sun glittered upon the long sweeps which propelled the hull forward.

The look-out saw all this, but as he knew there were many of the light-armed craft belonging to the young Republic in these waters, he closed the glass and contented himself by watching the boats from his vessel as they neared the prize.

"All ready, sir," came in the clear, firm voice of Sheet Anchor Jack, "all charged with grape, sir."

"Run up the Union Jack," said the young commander; then as the flag fell into lazy folds he added, "the cutter is within range—FIRE!"

One of the guns vomited its contents, and the cloud of smoke rising slowly above the blackened ports, hung among the rigging and shut out the view of the advancing foe.

One anxious face was visible for a moment peering out from the grey cloud of battle, then it disappeared and the voice of Sheet-Anchor Jack was heard saying—

"The cutter is crippled, they are stopping to take the crew in the other boats."

He had taken but one glance at the sunlit sea when he beheld this.

"One boat the less," said old Ben Tompion, should raise an almost impenetrable mist; but it is so, as the writer of these pages can testify, from having been engaged for nearly an hour with the enemy, and so dense was the smoke, that each party could only judge the other's position by the flashes of the guns.

The accident to the cutter was of more importance to the little band than they at the time knew.

The young commander, by passing fearlessly out upon the bowsprit, saw more than one

"GIVE WAY—GIVE WAY, MEN; RALLY ON THE QUARTER-DECK."

"if this smoke lifts we may be able to shut the other one up."

"It is our only chance," said Sheet-Anchor, as he placed his thumb on the vent of the gun which had been reloaded. "Use your hat, mates, and drive a little of the cloud away."

This suggestion was acted upon, and an opening made of sufficient size to enable the prize crew to see ahead.

To those who have not seen the smoke from a gun when there is no wind to carry it away, it may appear somewhat strange that the explosion of even a small quantity of powder

wounded or dead seaman taken from the cutter and placed in the gig which had followed in the wake of the "fighting boats" as the ambulance waggon follows a regiment to the field.

There must have been a person of rank crippled, for when the gig received her freight, she was put about, and the rowers pulled swiftly towards the Boston.

Nelson saw this, and was about to return when the crashing of wood beneath him, and a puff of smoke from the bow of the barge, told the attacking party had returned the fire.

He needed all his quickness to catch at a rop

above his head, for the projecting spar beneath him was broken by the round shot.

A groan came upon his ears as he jumped in among the men.

"What is the matter?" he anxiously asked. "Are you much hurt, Ben?"

Ben Tompion, despite the agony he suffered, touched his hat, as he answered:

"A bit of a splinter, sir. He's knocked a bit o' my bulwarks in."

Three of the old tar's ribs were broken, yet the young commander was compelled to repeat his order three times over for the old man to seek a place of safety, before the latter would allow his messmates to lead him away.

"I have fought in a liner," he growled; "I have worked the guns in a fight atween two frigates, and been hurt worse than this, so I thinks it hard lines I'm not allowed to stop and see this fight out. I ax your pardon, sir, but let me be stuck up in a corner, I can handle a firelock as well as an any jolly* as ever——"

"Take him away."

Old Ben was taken below, and as his head disappeared below the hatchway, Sheet-Anchor applied the match to his gun.

Simultaneously came the report of the swivel from the barge, and the round shot struck the muzzle of the carronade Jack had just fired, and ripped the metal open.

The gun was useless, and before another could be depressed, the shouts of their assailants were heard under the bows of the Sandy Hook.

"Stand by to repel boarders!" said the young officer, passing quickly to the threatened point; "use the pikes, my lads, and use them well; remember the Union Jack flying above us, and there it will remain until I am dead."

"Until we are all dead!" said Sheet-Anchor; "never fear for the honour of our profession—it is in safe hands; as safe, sir, as though the first, instead of the third, flag† was hanging at the main."

It was impossible to use the guns now—perhaps it were better so; for the prize crew were to few too be divided.

The head and bowsprit became filled with men, and the shout of the assailants was repeated by the prisoners, who were securely fastened below.

Twice the boarders were driven back by the pike and cutlass, and so great was the emergency, that Nelson fought with the men, until a strong-limbed boarder beat down his feeble arm, and would have cloven him to the chine, but for the sudden report of a musket far in rear of the combatants, and the bullet whistled past the young commander, and buried itself in the brow of tue foeman, whose arm was uplifted to strike.

The musket ball was fired by old Ben Tompion, who had crawled from the cot whereon he had been placed, and was crouched behind a gun which served as a rest for his musket.

"Retire, sir," Sheet-Anchor respectfully said; "remember, should you fall, our defeat must follow."

The friendly warning was unheeded, but not unheard. The young mariner had scarcely ceased speaking when the boarders made another and a more successful effort, for in spite of the devoted exertions of the defenders they were forced slowly back from the forecastle.

The momentary advantage caused the rear of the boarders to thicken, for those who had not before been able to obtain a footing now rushed on board.

The young commander had prepared for this. Having foreseen that numbers must necessarily for a time prevail, he had brought the guns on the quarter-deck, and so placed them that their fire would sweep the fore part of the ship.

The small crew had been fearfully weakened, yet those who remained thought but of selling their lives dearly.

There was a fierce rally near the fore-hatch, but the enemy, as though encouraged by the shouts of their imprisoned countrymen, drove back the gallant little band, until the ship, as far as the mainmast, was in their possession.

The crisis had now arrived, and the young commander, in a voice that was heard far above the shouts and yells of the combatants, called out:

"Give way, give way men; rally on the quarter-deck."

There was a hurried rush as the small party followed the officer to their last standing-place, and the enemy, as though conscious that the movement had not been made on the impulse of the moment, mechanically paused, when one of the lieutenants shouted,

"Down, down, all of you!"

The order came too late; old Ben Tompion only waited until his shipmates had made good their retreat, to apply the match to one of the guns.

The volley of grape-shot cut a lane through the closely packed ranks of the boarders, and several of the missiles striking the fastenings

† The first flag is the Royal Standard; the second is that of the Ensign; the third is the Union Jack; then follows the flags of the admirals in their order of succession.

* A marine.

of the fore-hatch, wrenched away the stout iron and liberated the prisoners.

They started through the opening, their triumphant yell sounding like a death-knell to the smoke-begrimed, blood-stained, and desperate band of Englishmen.

This addition to the already overwhelming force opposed to him caused Nelson's fortitude to give way to the utter hopelessness of any further resistance.

He checked Sheet Anchor, who was about to fire the second gun, and with quivering lips, said—

"It is hopeless; we must surrender."

"Fight it out to the last, sir," said the oldest of the seamen, "we can but try—death before a prison."

The remainder of the men gave a shout of defiance, and gripped their weapons yet firmer, and Sheet-Anchor, encouraged by these sounds, applied the glowing match to the vent of the gun.

The curses and yells that followed told how fatal had been the discharge, and before the thick grey mist had rolled away, the enemy gave a vengeful shout and rushed towards the quarter-deck.

In the next few moments events passed too rapidly for description, the English yet shrouded in the smoke could only thrust and cut at all came within reach.

But hopeless was their brilliant defence, for the enemy leaped upon the quarter-deck, and pike and cutlass were beaten down, and amid the cries of the exultant boarders the prize crew fell back inch by inch, determined when resistance was no longer possible to leap into the sea.

In their last moment of dire peril when there seemed but the blue waves or a prison for the little band, a mighty shout was heard in their rear, and those who turned their heads expect-to meet a fresh foe saw a swarm of men leaping over the taffrail, and a young officer in the uniform of the British navy leading his men forward to the strife.

"They gave no cry, but like the passage of a whirlwind they broke through the thin line of Englishmen, and hurled themselves upon the foe.

Unaware of the presence of these men until they broke through the smoke which yet hung pall-like over the stern of the ship, the Americans were taken at a disadvantage.

The new comers gave the assailants no time to recover from their astonishment, but went to work in a quiet, resistless manner, which told how used they were to scenes of carnage.

Like autumn leaves swept before the gale, the assailants were driven over the bows of the ship, and with the men who had been liberated from the hold they dropped into the boats and pulled swiftly away.

The leader of those who had come to the succour of the prize crew advanced towards young Nelson, but ere he could speak, Sheet-Anchor turned deadly pale, and exclaimed:

"The men who destroyed the Gloriana!"

CHAPTER XIII.

CAPTAIN HENRY JERVIS OF THE GUARDS.

Saul Mason returned to his visitor after he had started Bill Webb to the Mameluke.

Captain Henry Jervis had walked straight into old Saul's office, and there was an expression of pity upon his handsome but dissolute face, when he saw the grey-haired Edward Blendell at work among the heaps of paper which covered the table.

"Well, Blendell," he said, "you must be an invaluable amanuensis, for, no matter when I come here, you are always at work."

The pale face, so woe-begone and hopeless in their expression, was raised as the wretched captive answered—

"The work is nothing, sir—a mere trifle. Could I but breathe the fresh air when the day's labours are over."

"What! has not Saul relented yet? He told me you should have your liberty before this."

"He has said the same to me, sir, but I am as far from seeing the blessed sunlight as I was two years since when you so kindly interested yourself in my behalf."

"Saul is an old villain," said the soldier, "yet a useful ally at times."

This was muttered in an undertone, then he added aloud:

"Never mind, Blendell; the time will come when you —— What is that?"

"Rats, sir, we are surrounded with them, but what they find to eat I do not know. We keep but a poor table here, sir."

"Rats! I thought it was old Saul. Look here, Blendell, I want to ask you a question. Can you answer it?"

"Anything to you, sir, for you have been the only friend I have had among all the visitors who seek Saul Mason."

The gold-laced captain in the King's Guards leant forward in his chair, and in a voice audible only to Edward Blendell, he nervously asked—

"Can you tell me what has become of that boy Saul had for so many years?"

The tears started to the wretched captive's eyes, as he answered in a voice as low as that in which the query had been put—

"He has perished, sir—gone to the bottom of the ocean."

"Thank——

"Thank God," the Guardsman was about to say, but he knew how the wretched man's heart had clung to the handsome boy, so he paused and said—

"Thank you, Blendell, thank you; it was a sad fate for one so young."

"A sad fate, indeed, sir, but one to which many hundreds have been consigned who have had anything to do with Saul——"

The door opened, and the mummy-like figure of the ship-chandler entered the room.

Blendell went on with his writing, and the Guardsman played with the tassel which hung from the hilt of his sword.

Saul gave a suspicious glance at the pair; turning sharply to Blendell, he said—

"You can go, Edward, you have done sufficient for to-day."

The poor slave wiped his pen and placed the papers in order, then slowly left the room; his gait, through the long confinement he had suffered, was more like a man who had attained his threescore and ten than one in the prime of manhood.

"Saul," the Guardsman said, when Blendell had left the room, "why do you keep that poor wretch like a caged bird?"

"Because he knows too much, my friend," old Saul said, "too much for my safety and many more."

"He would not betray you, Saul, or I am much mistaken."

"He will not have the chance, captain. Oh, no—when people know too much, it is quite as well to look after them."

"You are a cruel old fellow, Saul."

"Am I? No, no—hum—hum—hum—you are so pleasant, always so full of your jokes. No, no. Now, Master Henry, what brings you to old Saul's dingy house?"

"The old business, Saul. I want some money."

"Again?"

"Yes; I lost the whole of the last trifle you advanced me two nights since."

"Trifle! Captain, trifle! why it was a fortune."

"Never mind, you will be repaid soon."

"Soon, that has been the cry for the last two years, yet your brother looks in as good condition as ever."

"How do you know? You have not seen him."

"Are you sure, Captain Henry? How did I come by this?"

He held the handkerchief he had taken from Bill Webb open in his hand.

"How, in Fortune's name, did you come by that? It belongs to my brother's wife."

"Hum, hum! I know that she lost it to-day when she visited the Wasp."

"The Wasp? Basil told me it was the Saucy Jane."

"The Wasp and the Saucy Jane are the same, Captain Henry. You knew of this visit then?"

"I did. Basil told me he had seen the captain of a letter of marque, and had offered him a large sum if he recovered the boy."

"He still believes the story you told him?"

"He does," said the Guardsman. "Why should he doubt it?"

"Hum, hum! I don't know. I thought, perhaps he might have become suspicious."

"No, Saul. His is the last nature to entertain the least suspicion of anything I may tell him, and at times I often wish I had not begun this business."

"Hum, hum! Let me see what cause you have to regret it. You are poor; your brother is rich. He has a son. That son stands between you and the riches you covet——"

"Covet! they are mine, Saul."

"Precisely so now the boy is out of the way; but let me alone, Captain Henry—no, no—hum, hum, hum—until I have finished my story."

"Have your own way."

"Very well; you persuade your brother to send his boy to sea; he does so, and I so manage it that the boy is kidnapped on his way to the ship——"

"Would it had ended there!"

"In that sense you would have been a beggar, Captain Henry. Well, I keep the boy, or child, for he was but a child, in my house until he grows nearly to manhood; then, fearing he would break his cage, I sent him off to sea."

"You have managed well, Saul."

"I always do manage well, if I am serving my friends. No, no—hum, hum. Well, during the time the boy is under my care you make your brother believe the ship he went away in was wrecked in the Mediterranean."

"Acting under your advice, Saul."

"Yes, yes, and good advice it was; now you see everything has turned out as I told you it would; the boy is wrecked in reality; and you have but to assist the working of the evident grief which preys upon your brother's vitals in consequence of the uncertain fate of his son. A master-stroke, that story of the boy being lost among the Algerines; it tells worse than an assurance of his death. In the latter case, your brother would know there was no hope, and in ime would get over the blow; but the uncertainty, Captain Jervis, is the thing, it is like slow poison."

"You are a cunning rascal, Saul."

"There, there, never mind joking; you are so full of pleasantry, Master Henry, that it quite cheers me up when you honour me with a visit."

"Does it? Well, I never felt less inclined to be pleasant in my life than I am now."

"Ho, ho—hum, hum! How is that, Captain Henry—how is that?"

"Empty pockets," answered the Guardsman, savagely, "and a lurking fear that this captain, whoever he is, may find Basil's boy."

"Ho, ho! is that all? Rest content, Master Henry, for this captain is the very man who put the boy out of your way for ever."

"I do not understand you."

"The man to whom your brother applied to search among the islands in the Mediterranean for the survivors of the Swiftsure, not long since, sent the Gloriana to the bottom of the sea, and those who did not die by the broadsides he poured into the vessel, were made to walk the plank."

"Do you think the fellow spoke the truth?"

"I am sure of it. Read this."

Saul handed Captain Jervis the copy of the *Shipping Gazette* which contained the paragraph relating to the loss of the Gloriana.

The Guardsman, callous as he was by nature, could not repress a shudder as he returned the paper to Saul.

"Everything is safe, so far," he said; "but the means to attain this safety have indeed been terrible."

"To the weak and nervous, yes; but those who play for a high stake, and have the courage to use the cards which fortune places in their hands, look upon the affair as one in which the means justify the end."

"We shall see," the Guardsman said, "I wish I felt as sanguine over the matter as you do, Saul."

"It is because you are not used to these things, Master Henry, that is all."

"God forbid that ever I should become used to them."

"Ho! ho! hum! hum!" purred Saul, as he took a quill pen from the table, and with a silent cat-like tread stole towards the door. "Ho! ho! take that."

He thrust the stumped end of the quill through the key-hole, and a faint cry of pain was heard on the other side of the door.

"Hum! hum! hum!" purred Saul, as he re-seated himself. "Ned Blendell will have the ear-ache to-morrow—ho! ho! hum! hum!"

The soldier could not forbear smiling at the little incident, so thoroughly in keeping with the man his profligate habits had compelled him to consort with.

"This captain of the Saucy Jane, or whatever the vessel is called," he said, "is not in your confidence, Saul?"

"Why do you ask?"

"Because if he was he would have known the boy for whom he was to seek was one of those on board the Gloriana."

"He knows nothing. He was paid to sink the ship, and did his work."

"You are acquainted with peculiar people, Saul."

I am, or I could not carry on my business. This Parker Neville——"

"Parker Neville! the famous or infamous pirate?"

"The same. What think you, Captain Henry? This man and his notorious ship are at the present moment beneath the battery of the Mameluke line-of-battle ship."

"He is taken at last, then?"

"Ha! ha! hum! hum! No, not yet. No, he dined with the officers of the Mameluke this very evening. But hum! hum! he won't dine with them again."

The Guardsman looked at old Saul, his fac expressing the disbelief he felt.

"You do not believe me, Master Henry?"

"I cannot."

"I will explain. This Parker Neville was formerly an officer in the Royal Navy, and distinguished himself so much in an engagement that upon the vessel's return to England he was presented at Court.

"He was a strange being, and having never before been brought face to face with royalty, had pictured the crowned head as something superior to the ordinary run of men."

"You know full well the unpretending appearance of the King, and Neville, when he left the royal presence, threw up his commission, and swore he would not serve a German farmer."

The Guardsman laughed.

"The most loyal, and they are the fat citizens, term the King Farmer George."

"Well, I lost sight of him for some time, and when next I saw him he was in command of the Wasp, and for the safer mode of carrying on his depredations, he managed when the war broke ont, to obtain a letter of marque.

"These papers he now holds; in them

vessel is described as the Saucy Jane; her owner as Anstey Phillips."

"I understand now how he can venture on board a man-of-war with impunity. But it is strange he has not been recognised in his double character."

"Not at all strange; for his vessel, like himself, is capable of the most perfect disguise."

"He must have a faithful crew, Saul, for the whole of them to withstand the offer of a £1,000 reward.

"He has. Now, Master Henry, as it is getting late, I should like to hear the sum of money you require for your present needs."

"One thousand five hundred pounds, Saul; not one penny less."

Saul Mason wheeled his chair round, and opened the desk, which had the peculiar lock, and took from one of the pigeon-holes a roll of papers.

He looked at the amounts marked at the foot of each slip of paper; then, after a few moments' mental arithmetic, he faced the captain of the Guards.

"Can't do it, Master Henry," he said. "The third share I am to have when your beother condescends to give over his property to you will scarcely repay me for the money I have already advanced."

"The seme old cry, Shylock," said the soldier. "Here, look over this paper. I have signed it, and you will find I have been more generous to you than you would have been to me under the same circumstances."

Old Saul read the document attentively, then said—

"All very well, as far as you are concerned, Master Henry, but suppose your brother does not die in the time specified?"

"He will—he must! We will buoy him up with the hope that his son has been found; then suddenly tell him that the cub has been killed and eaten by cannibals. If that does not finish him, the other mode you suggested must be tried."

"Hum—hum—well it is worth the risk, but you must remember, Master Henry, it has cost me large sums—very large sums—to get the boy out of the——"

"I know it. Am I to have the money?"

"Yes, hum—hum; but remember it is to be the last advance."

"I agree most willingly to that, Saul, for if the last trick I learned with the card proves a success I shall be a millionaire in six months; but come, Saul, hand over the notes, I have to attend at the table to obtain my revenge for losses."

Saul shot back a sliding panel in his desk with the peculiar lock, and drew therefrom two packets of crisp notes.

They were for fifty pounds each, and he counted the required numbers to make up the sum he was about to advance three times over to prevent any mistake.

The Guardsman sat watching him, a wolfish glare in his dark eyes, and when Saul rolled the notes tightly and handed them to his visitor, the latter clutched them with an eagerness that showed the excitement which burnt within his breast.

"Saul," he said, "you are a good fellow; I shall not forget you when I have the power to do you a good turn. I must be off; remember me to that pretty girl I have seen here—— Hallo, Saul, what is the matter?"

The old man had fallen back in his chair, his arms hung limp and listless by his side, his face was as white as that of a shrouded corpse, and the thin lips moved as though he was suffering the most poignant agony.

"What is the matter Saul?" the Guardsman repeated; "are you ill?"

"I am better now, much better: it was only a-a-spasm; there, there, good night, Master Henry, and, and don't, as a friend, mention a word about that young girl again, please don't."

The Guardsman touched the tip's of Saul's fingers, and felt they were clammy and cold; villain as he was, he liked not to grip the hand extended to him by the scheming old rascal.

"Good bye, Saul," he said; "I will send you word of the progress of my——"

"Open, in the King's name," said a stern voice outside, and the demand was followed by the noise of a dozen pistol butts hammering upon the doors; "open, I say, open, in the King's name!"

CHAPTER XIV.

SHEET-ANCHOR JACK DENOUNCES THE CAPTAIN OF THE WASP.

SHEET-ANCHOR JACK's words were scarcely understood by his shipmates, for the loss of the Gloriana was a topic upon which he seldom conversed.

The prize crew looked from the excited face of their companion to the calm features of the young officer, as though seeking, in a responsive look from the latter, a guide for their course of action.

The lieutenant was as puzzled as the men, for he was about to utter his thanks to the

BILL WEBB VISITS THE CAPTAIN OF THE PRIVATEER.

leader of the sturdy band, who had so well aided him in his hour of need.

The accusation made by Anchor Jack checked the words upon his lips, and leaning upon his drawn sword he gazed calmly at the man who had been so strangely accused of piracy and murder.

The latter's face, so far from betraying any alarm or confusion at the terrible charges, bore a look of pleased surprise, and as he motioned back his stalwart men he looked attentively at his accuser.

"The Gloriana!" he said, "this is news indeed. So you have escaped from the wreck, have you? Well, I am most happy to renew our acquaintance."

The young sailor's face flushed with indignation, and raising his cutlass, he sprang towards the speaker.

"Follow me," he cried; "seize this man, he is a pirate and murderer."

A few of the men followed their young companion, but ere they could aid him in securing the privateersman, Anchor Jack's cutlass was wrested from his grasp, and the blade point of the smiling Parker Neville was pressed against his breast.

"Come, my young springald," said Parker, "you must have a few more years' practice with a sword before you attempt to use it in such a hasty manner. Back, boy, back, or I may feel tempted to add to the red stain which is yet upon my blade."

The young mariner fell slowly back before the privateersman, and following the latter were three score strong-limbed men, who would at a word from their chief have cut down the very men they had but a few minutes before so ably succoured.

The lieutenant glanced at the graceful ship which rode athwart the stern of the Sandy Hook, and he saw the men who had towed the Wasp to the scene of action had by this time hoisted their boats.

He also saw the sides of the vessel were crowded with men, and one of the officers, as though acting from a signal from his chief, had manned the larboard battery, and a dozen dark muzzles were protruding from as many open ports.

His duty as a King's officer was clear, if Anchor Jack's words were true; yet in the face of the terrible odds that were against him, he felt it would be useless to attempt the seizure of the accused or his vessel.

He hoped there was a mistake, for he could not realise that the men who had come so nobly to the rescue of his crew could be as the young sailor represented.

These thoughts passed swiftly through his mind as he advanced towards the captain of the Wasp.

"There is, I hope," he said, "no foundation for this charge."

"Do not listen to anything this man may say," Sheet Anchor said, eagerly; "believe me, sir, I speak the truth; it was by his orders the Gloriana was destroyed, and by his orders her crew were made to walk the plank or serve on board his ship; there, sir, stand two of the men who formerly served on the Gloriana."

He pointed towards two of the seamen who were standing near Parker Neville, and they smiled grimly at his words.

"It is time to end this," said the King's officer: "therefore, I appeal to you, sir, to answer this charge"

"Quite time to end it," answered the captain of the Wasp; "I am Parker Neville; that vessel which lies in such a beautiful position to rake your decks, is the Wasp."

"I am grieved to hear," said the King's officer, "and lament that I should have to do my duty upon one who has proved himself a brave officer, when serving under the King's flag; one, who in spite of his misdeeds, has felt his old loyalty and saved the glorious annals of our country from being tarnished; perhaps to-day's action may soften your punishment. I hope it will. If my humble word can do you a service you can command it. Now, sir, much as I regret not being able to shake hands with my preserver, I must do my duty by requesting you to deliver up your sword, and surrender your ship to my keeping."

There was a smile upon Parker Neville's face as he listened to the lieutenant's words, and his followers were grinning, as though much amused at the idea of surrendering to a mere handful of men.

"Permit me, young man," said the commander of the Wasp, "to correct a few of your mistakes. I did not, I can assure you, feel any loyalty or affection for that rag; I thought it possible you were in a scrape, and as a fellow-countryman I could not help assisting you, but had your German master been aboard he might have become a target for the American muskets before I should have——"

"I cannot listen to this," said the King's officer; "give up your sword, misguided man, and throw yourself upon the mercy of the laws you have outraged."

The privater captain raised his sword, and in a moment the tops of his vessel were crowded with men armed with muskets.

"These men," Parker said, pointing with his sword to the topmen, "cover each of yours; they are true marksmen, and never miss. You wish me to surrender—I will, if my gallant fellows are agreeable."

The handling of pistols and the unsheathing of cutlassas followed these words.

"They are not, you see!" laughed the privateersman; then, looking towards his beautiful ship, he added:

"FIRE!"

The thunder of four pieces of ordnance shook the Sandy Hook, and the thick smoke rolled in volumes over the deck.

The guns were only charged with blank ammunition, or the prize would have gone to the bottom of the ocean.

Following the roar of the gun[illegible] the privateer captain's voice, as he sai[illegible]

"Seize that fellow!"

Amazed for the moment by the sudden discharge of the privateer's guns, and not being able to see anything of what took place as the privateersman and his men passed swiftly their vessel, the prize crew mistook the cry Sheet-Anchor Jack gave as he was seized and hurried forward, for the shriek of a man who had been shot down by one of the missiles from the guns.

They gripped their weapons, and with that dogged courage which has gained England so many victories, the little band closed round the young lieutenant, determined to sell their lives dearly.

A deep silence succeeded the roar of the artillery, and the half-stifled cry that came upon their ears, and when they expected to meet the onslaught of the privateersman's band, the silence was broken by Parker Neville.

"I wish you a pleasant voyage," he shouted through a speaking trumpet; "here comes the breeze, take advantage of it, but do not attempt to follow my vessel, or there will be something harder in the next guns I fire."

The breeze sighed through the cordage, as the daring fellow ceased speaking, and as the light top hamper filled out, the smoke rolled away to leeward.

The Wasp was the first to feel the breeze, and as she glided slowly forward the prize crew beheld Sheet-Anchor Jack struggling to escape from his captors.

CHAPTER XV.

BENARDIN ALLAH BEY.

FROM time immemorial until a few years since the beautiful creeks and bays of the Mediterranean were infested by Algerine corsairs and hordes of sea robbers belonging to the other States of Barbary.

These gentlemen were quite impartial in the distribution of their favours, for they captured English vessels with as little ceremony as they did the French, Dutch, and Spanish.

It was in vain the great Christian Powers made valuable presents to the Dey of Algiers and his principal officers to induce them to allow their vessels to pass unmolested over the blue waters of the Mediterranean.

The hardy Arabs accepted the presents, held great councils, and promised to be true friends to the country that had made them the richest presents, but—and this "but" the Western Powers found a great stumbling block—but they would not consent to forego their ancient privilege of searching all vessels that passed their port.

"For," the Dey would say, stroking his long beard, "although Allah has been pleased to make us friends from this day until the end of time, other countries who are not friendly with us may take advantage of our alliance, and endeavour to pass our port under your flag; therefore, you see, my friend, how utterly impossible it is for us to give up our right of search, which, under the pleasure of Allah, has been here enjoyed since the hour the faithful became masters of this land; but fear not, my good friend, we will be careful that no wrong is done to the ships of your nation."

So, after many salaams, the envoy would be conducted to his vessel; and no sooner had the ship sunk in the distant horizon, than out would sally the myriads of light-heeled proas, and, like the knights of old, go in search of adventures and profit; and again, like the knights, with whom chivalrous adventure was but another term for barefaced robbery, they would make all pay whom they overpowered.

The free and easy laws and mode of living in these States, as may be expected, drew many adventurers from all parts of the world.

Those who hated the iron hand of law—such laws as were in vogue in the days when the third George was King—left the land of their birth, and sought in other climes that liberty of action and a field for the exercise of their courage and line of adventure which were denied to them at home.

Thus it was that many of the fierce-turbaned Moslems who attacked and captured British ships were, much to the surprise of the captives, in the habit of addressing the latter in their native language.

Benardin Allah Bey, the commander of the Algerine fleet, and personal friend of the Dey of Algiers, was one of those adventurers, and in brutal ferocity and brilliant courage he far surpassed the bravest of the brave, and the cruellest of the cruel, among the myriads of fierce, untameable spirits he commanded.

To these men war was but a pastime, and a thrust from a yataghan or a shot from a silver-mounted pistol was pleasant recreation when practised upon the bodies of those who fell into their hands.

In the midst of a beautiful valley, where the tall cypress and sweet-scented myrtle grew in luxurious profusion, stood the dwelling of Benardin Allah Bey.

The exterior was of plain white stone quarried from the neighbouring cliffs, and was surrounded by a high wall, upon the summit of which paced a number of white-clad sentinels, upon whose shields and carved scimetars the fiery Eastern sun glittered and danced, and played around the long barrels of the matchlocks, which were slung across the Moslems' backs. Seated near one of the marble fountains which adorned his spacious garden, and surrounded by a bevy of beautiful women, was Benardin Allah.

There was but little trace left of those characteristics which proclaimed the land of his birth.

He way truly Oriental—in speech, manner, dress, and appearance; and no follower of the Prophet was fonder of Eastern luxury than was the Bey, when he found time to pass a few days ashore.

He had apparently just passed the prime of manhood; for among his dark locks a few threads of silver were perceptible, and the lofty brow, as white and polished as marble, showed, upon a closer view, those furrows which time alone can bring.

The Bey must have been a very handsome man in his early manhood, and one whose temperament was the reverse of gloomy; for the lower part of his face (what could be seen of it under his heavy and flowing beard), and the twinkle of his dark grey eyes, told that the Bey by nature was a jovial fellow, and the stories of cruelty, murder, and rapine, which were attributed to his name, were, if true, caused by the position he held rather than the result of his natural disposition.

Standing in rear of the Bey, and with upturned eyes and a most Puritan expression of face was Benardin Allah's favourite attendant.

There could not have been a greater contrast between two men than there was between the stout, jolly-looking Bey, and the tall, thin, repulsive, sanctimonious-looking Baba-da-Chuk.

Baba-da was, like his master, attired in full Eastern costume, and ne had suffered a few straggling hairs to grow upon his chin, but the most violent stretch of the imagination could not magnify Baba-da-Chuk's hirsute appendage into a beard.

There was no mistaking the nationality of the Bey's attendant; he was and looked every inch a Scotchman, and one upon whom a suit of seedy clerical-cut garments would have sat much better than the flowing Eastern robes and large turban which he wore.

Like his master, Baba-da-Chuk professed the true faith, and would not—so they affirmed—touch a vessel containing the wines or spirits of those infidel dogs who called themselves Christians.

"Death!" Benardin Allah was wont to exclaim, when envious tongues accused the great man of a fondness for the forbidden liquor, "before partaking of a draught of the accursed drink."

"Twenty deaths!" Baba-da, with upturned eyes and folded hands repeated, "before these pure lips should be defiled by the contact of the juice of the grape! Allah be praised for His mercy in opening my eyes to the true faith!"

Such were Bernardin Allah and his servant; having thus introduced these by no means unimportant personages, we will leave them to speak for themselves.

"Baba," said the Bey, taking the silvered mouthpiece of his chiboque from his lips; "has it pleased Allah to send a favouring breeze to fill the sails of our ships?"

"Allah is good," answered Baba-da; "most good to His children, for he has sent a favouring breeze to fill the sails of the true believers' ships; and He has given into His children's hands a vessel of the infidel."

"Allah is good!" said the Bey with a sidelong glance at his sanctimonious servant; "he is good indeed! tell me, Baba-da, of what consists the cargo of this vessel the faithful have taken from the infidel dogs?"

"Most high and mighty master of mine," said Baba-da; "my lips tremble and my soul turns white within me when I think of the contents of the vessel."

"Speak, then, O Baba-da-Chuk, thy master listens!"

"Know, then," said the Moslem-Scotchman, "the faithful followers of the Prophet have but met with a cargo of the strong waters used by the infidels, and the very smell of the forbidden liquor has made many of them so ill that they lie upon the decks of their galleys quite senseless."

"The rascals," muttered the Bey; "I'll bastinado every mother's son of them. How dare they smell the forbidden liquors?"

"The captains of the galleys," continued Baba-da, "have fled their vessels in dismay, and now wait outside the gates to know what is to be done with the subtle cargo."

"Call my black guards, Baba-da," said the Bey, "and I will give my faithful fellows an audience."

Baba-da-Chuk (*long and thin*) clapped his long hands thrice together, and the harem guards appeared and marched off the bevy of beauties to their chambers.

Then came the Bey's pipe-bearer and a crowd of slaves, who followed their master into a less private portion of the building than the harem gardens.

CHAPTER XVI.

BENARDIN BEY AND BABA-DA-CHUK SHOW THEIR HATRED TO THE FORBIDDEN LIQUOR.

AT a solemn pace, befitting such an exalted personage, the Bey and his follower passed through the myrtle and cypress groves until they reached the great audience chamber.

Here his effulgence was received by a body-guard—a band of richly-dressed and well-armed Arabs, who, unless their looks very much belied them, would as soon cut a throat or rob a church as they would partake of a rich, unctuous mass of pillau.

These worthies placed their scimitars across their shields when his mightiness entered the chamber, and an officer who held the Bey's standard, lowered the barbed point of the flag-staff until it touched the carpet.

The ceremony did not end here, for a band of musicians gave him a salute, and as the instruments were cymbals, bells, and drums, there was more noise than music, and the sound was not pleasant to the ear, as was testified by the manner in which the august Baba-da-Chuk plugged his ears with the forefinger of each hand.

The music ceased, and the scimitars and green standard were raised as his serenity the Bey squatted upon a rich divan, and his long attendant took post behind him.

The pipe bearers then came forward and filled the chiboque before their master, and the pipe-lighter, a Nubian boy, came with a red-hot piece of charcoal and placed it upon the bowl of the pipe.

The boy was new to his business, thus it happened that when the Bey made a vigorous pull at the amber mouth-piece, there was no smoke forthcoming, although the scented water in the crystal reservior boiled and bubbled under the pressure of the Bey's lusty pull.

His mightiness lowered the mouthpiece, and looking savagely at the boy, said,

"Come hither, thou imp, that I may thank thee for thy quickness."

The boy approached, the whites of his eyes rolling from right to left as his fear increased, and when he came within kicking distance, the Bey said,

"Turn thy face towards the curtains which guard our doors."

The boy wheeled round, and the Bey shot his right leg vigorously forward, and the poor culprit went at a remarkably swift pace towards the centre of the chamber.

"Baba-da-Chuk," said his loftiness the Bey (which means in the tongue of the infidel one long and thin of limb), "exercise thy right leg by kicking this careless slave thrice round the chamber."

Baba-da stalked solemnly forward and did as he was requested, but unfortunately the last kick which he meant should send the culprit through the doorway, missed the object aimed at, and Baba-da-Chuk's right leg flew upward with such force as to bring his long body in contact with the floor.

Baba-da gathered himself up and limped behind his master, uttering expressions in a strange tongue to the ears of those who saw the ignoble position the great Baba-da had so recently occupied.

"It becomes not one of my years," he muttered, "to make an *aith*, but * * "

The remainder of the sentence was lost in obscurity, as Baba-da slunk behind his master, and the latter, evidently amused by the accident which had befallen his servant, rolled about the divan as though he had the greatest difficulty in restraining himself from laughing outright.

"Let my captains be summoned," said the Bey, modestly hiding his face behind his white cambric handkerchief, "that I may hear the doings of the faithful followers of the true faith."

The major-domo, flourishing a white wand, backed out of the presence, and in a few moments returned at the head of about twenty swarthy Arabs, whose costume proclaimed them as officers in the service of the Bey.

They prostrated themselves humbly before the Dey's chief admiral, and his high mightiness the Bey condescended to raise his finger as a signal that the prostrate chiefs of the corsair galleys might assume the perpendicular in his presence.

The Bey took the initiative by saying:

"Allah has again been good to his children. The soft breezes of the west have filled their sails, and they have returned laden with the spoils of the unbeliever."

A grey-bearded Arab advanced and fell at the Bey's feet.

"Thy words, O Great Chief," he said "have sunk into the soul of thy servant, and he eats dirt in thy presence——"

"Arise, faithful friend," said the Bey kindly; "there can be no cause for one so true and brave as thyself to defile his beard before us."

"There is cause, a great cause, O Chief, for thy galleys have returned from a long cruise, and although they have, under Allah's favour, destroyed a war ship of the unbelieving English, and taken two vessels which the war ship was guarding; yet, O Bey, there is not in these ships any stuffs of silk, ingots of gold or silver; no, O Chief, there is nothing but the forbidden waters of the unbelieving dogs to reward thy servants for the fight they have fought with the English dogs."

"Dost thou not forget the guns and ammunition on board the war ship, O Achmet?"

"Thy servant forgettest not. The war ship in her last stand made against the galleys of the faithful blew up."

"Even so, good Achmet—there remain the hulls, sails, and cordage of the ships containing the forbidden liquor."

"Thy servant hearest; but, O Bey, dost thou forget that but one of these ships falls to thy share; the other to the light of the universe, the mighty Dey?"

"I forget not, O Achmet. To thee and thy followers I give the vessel which by our laws falls to my share. Go, and be content; but stay, what of the evil liquor? Hast thou consigned it to the bottom of the sea?"

"Thy servant has not; he would have done so, but the very contact with the barrels caused much evil among the faithful."

"It is just," said the Bey; "Allah is good to us; he teaches his children what is right. Now, O Achmet, let such of thy men as have not fallen beneath the evil spirits in these barrels work with a strong arm, and place the accursed liquor in the lowest vault beneath my dwelling. There I will go after fasting and praying, and exercise the evil influence in the barrels, and with Allah's help, will cause the contents to change into pure water, or to quit their receptacle and leave the barrels as dry as when they were turned from the workman's hands. Depart, now, and the peace of Allah be with you!"

"Thy servant obeys, but he would first learn what is thy pleasure concerning the captives?"

"Send them to the fields; there is work for them there."

"On my head be it; thy orders shall be obeyed. Yet, O master, I would ask thee about two of the captives we have made."

"Thy master listens."

"Know, O Bey, that among the many infidels who peopled the ships that held the forbidden water, thy servant found a maiden of rare loveliness, and a youth upon whose head had fallen the wrath of the God he worships."

"The maiden of rare loveliness," said the Bey, "can be sent hither when the evil and forbidden liquor has been consigned to the darkness beneath this dwelling."

"And the youth, O Bey?"

"He can accompany the maiden, and if we find he is as thou sayest, a bowstring can end his aimless life: thou art answered, O Achmet—depart, and forget not that the accursed waters be at once taken away from the faithful."

The grey-bearded corsair bowed with exceeding humility, and with his companions backed out of the Bey's august presence.

A few hours after this interview, Benardin Allah Bey and Baba-du-Chuk were seated in the Bey's private apartment, a chamber which was sacred to the great man and his body-servant; and the pair, who had thrown aside their turbans and much of their Oriental manners, were busily tasting the contents of three crystal drinking-cups.

"Whiskey, Sandy," said the Bey in English; "and uncommon good; what is in the other vessels?"

"Rum and brandy, or I am no judge," replied Sandy; "ho, ho, ho!"

"What the ——eh? what are you laughing at, you mummy? hand me the rum!"

"Laughing," said Sandy; "it would make the deil himself laugh to see how you have got the blind side of these Arabs. Aye, mon, but I think the evening will end in the barrels becoming dry."

"No doubt, Sandy, no doubt, especially if that beak of yours continues to draw so much from the——what's that?"

"Nothing but the galleys emptying the guns that were landed."

"Sandy," said the Bey; "have you forgotten how to brew a bowl of punch?"

"You shall taste of the success of my brew."

. . . . . .

Two hours later the Bey and his servant were bowing to each other and singing in a thick voice:

"Come, landlord, fill a flowing bowl," &c.

In the midst of their revelry there came a loud summons upon the outer door of the chamber, and as they ceased their song, their cheeks became deadly pale.

CHAPTER XVII.

EDWARD BLENDELL'S LETTER.

"HALLO, Saul, you old villain!" said the soldier; "what is the meaning of this uproar?"

"Open in the King's name," continued the voice outside; "open, I say, open!"

"Saul, you old villain——"

"Hum, hum, hum! Ho, ho, ho! How lucky to be sure!"

"Why the——don't you open the door, you old sinner?"

"Ho, ho, ho! Hum, hum, hum! It will do them good to wait."

"Who are they, Saul? what do they want?"

AT THE MERCY OF THE WAVES.

"Don't know, Master Henry; don't know ——"

A furious attack was made upon the shaky door, and Saul, to prevent the panel being smashed in, suddenly drew back the bolt.

"Well, gentlemen, well," old Saul bluntly said; "what is the matter? Come in; there is no one here able to serve the King."

Lieutenant Irvin, of the Mameluke, looked inquiringly at the officer of the Guards; then, turning to the mummy-like figure of old Saul, said:

"You are Saul Mason?"

"I am; but too old—much too old—for to serve the King."

"We are not a pressgang," the officer said, impatiently; "our business is of a very different nature."

"A thousand pardons," said old Saul, bowing; "pray step inside; there is a draught, and I am very susceptible to cold."

The lieutenant walked inside and followed Saul to the dingy chamber at the end of the passage.

Captain Jervis accompanied them; he was curious to learn the cause of the naval officer's visit with an armed boat's crew at his back.

"I have a very disagreeable duty to perform," the second lieutenant of the Mameluke said, as he took the chair old Saul offered him; "therefore, I had better get it over as quickly as possible."

"A glass of wine first," said old Saul; "I have really some very good—almost as fine as that which you naval gentlemen take a couple of voyages before tapping the barrel."

"Many thanks, but I would rather not."

"Allow me," said young Jervis, "to attest the good qualities of my friend's wine."

The naval officer bowed, and old Saul stepped between the pair, and said,

"Captain Jervis, of the 1st regiment of Guards, allow me to introduce you to—to——"

"John Irvin, second lieutenant of the Mameluke."

"Lieutenant Irvin," said old Saul, "Captain Jervis—Captain Jervis, Lieutenant Irvin—there gentlemen, I believe I have done my duty as a host; now allow me to bring you a sample bottle of such wine as you can seldom taste."

Before a denial could be given, the old man ran from the room, thus sadly embarrassing the lieutenant of the Mameluke, who felt that it was not consistent with the duty he had to perform to drink with a man whom he should in all probability be compelled to take prisoner.

"Really," he said, as these reflections ran through his mind, "Mr. Mason places me in a very peculiar position; I would rather he would allow me to fulfil my duty than he should insist upon treating me as a guest."

These words were addressed to the Guardsman, who shrugged his shoulders as he remarked,

"Saul is a peculiar fellow."

"You are a friend of his, I presume."

"No," the soldier answered frankly; "I find him useful in matters of a pecuniary nature. By the way, is it a breach of good manners to ask the cause of your visit?"

"Not so far as I am concerned," the naval officer said. "I have come to search his premises in consequence of the receipt of a letter by my superior."

"Indeed! An anonymous communication, I presume?"

"Yes; you can read it."

He handed the Guardsman the note Parker Neville had sent to the captain of the Mameluke.

"I do not believe the writer, whoever he may be," said the soldier. "It reads more like a malicious communication than anything else."

"Possibly; but as the Alert has been robbed and her cargo taken, the natural inference is that the thieves must have a ready means of disposing of the booty; therefore, we cannot do anything else than comply with the anonymous writer's request."

"Certainly not. Were I in your place I should do so at once: not that I think Old Saul could remove the stores in his shed while we are here, for the old man has not the strength of a boy."

The return of Old Saul put an end to the conversation, and as he placed a tray containing two bottles and a half-dozen glasses upon the table, the naval officer rose.

"Before I can avail myself of your hospitality," he said, "I must ask you to allow me to visit a shed in the rear of your premises."

"My dear sir," old Saul answered; "you are at liberty to search my house from cellar to roof."

"Thanks; but my orders only relate to the shed."

"Pray follow me; Captain Jervis will draw the corks while we are absent."

"With pleasure," said the Guardsman: and he spoke the truth, for the bottle was one of his vices, and had helped, with his love of gambling, to drag him down from the honourable gentlemen to a reckless cheat and a companion of the most dissolute scoundrels in London.

Saul Mason placed a candle in a lanthorn, and led the way to the shed in the rear of his house.

The place was about fifty feet in length, the ends and sides of which were black with age, and dirty, the roof was of slate, except here and there a hole had been stopped by cramming rags in to keep out the rain.

There was no lock on the shabby door, which swung to and fro in the wind; but had the officer from the Mameluke looked closely at the doorpost he would have seen that a staple had been recently wrenched out.

Pushing his investigations further, he would have found a similar hole in the door, thus proving that a staple and holdfast had been there at no remote period.

He saw nothing of this, in consequence of the manner in which Saul held the light, and when he came to the interior he found it empty, except in one corner, in which was piled up a few old boxes, the remains of a four-post bedstead, some pieces of old carpet, a broken chair or two, and other disused articles of household furniture.

"Thank you, Mr. Mason," he said, "I see we have been deceived, for by the dust and damp upon that heap of lumber it is evident that it has not been disturbed for months."

"Say years and you will be nearer the time," said Saul. "Now, sir, as you have fulfilled your duty, may I ask the reason of this visit?"

"Well, really," the officer said, "I feel almost ashamed, after this proof of the falsehood of the communication, to state the reason of my visit."

"Pray do not stand upon any ceremony, my dear sir—hum, hum, hum—pray do not, I beg."

They were walking back to the house by this time.

"Well," said the officer, "the captain of the Mameluke received a communication which stated that in your shed would be found a portion of the cargo of the Alert."

"The Alert!" exclaimed Saul in well-affected astonishment, "The Alert schooner!"

"Yes; the vessel that was so audaciously plundered while lying at anchor at the mouth of the river."

"Dear, dear!" said Saul; "why, sir, I partly freighted that vessel, and if you will have the goodness to look over the *Shipping Gazette* of the week before last, you will see that I have offered a reward of fifty guineas for the discovery of the gang of rascals who robbed the ship. Well, well, I must say I never heard a more absurd charge. The idea of a man robbing himself, and then—but never mind, it is only waste of time to dwell upon the matter."

"They were about to enter the room when the officer turned to Saul, and said:

"Excuse me, for a few minutes. I may as well send my men back to the boat."

"Certainly. Hum! hum! hum! Pray, allow me to give the brave fellows a drop of rum. They will be none the worse for it, I know."

The officer laughed at the idea of Jack being any the worse for a drop of grog.

Saul went to a cupboard, and brought forth a black bottle and a wine glass, and the smacking of lips which followed the distribution of a drop all round, proved how well Jack understood and appreciated the taste of a good glass of rum.

The midshipman who had charge of the men was invited inside by Saul, and the coxswain took command of the boat's crew, and marched them back to the cutter.

Captain Jervis was pretty keen, but he could not fathom the cause of old Saul's gushing generosity.

"The old villain," he thought, "has a motive in this, but for the life of me I cannot make out how he intends to make this hospitality subservient to his interest."

"This wine; hum! hum! hum! gentlemen," purred Saul, "has been three times to India, and I do not think for mellowness and rich flavour it can be surpassed by the best wine in London, and there is some good liquor in this dingy town of ours."

A glass proved the truth of old Saul's words, a second glass loosened the tongues of his guests, and Saul's ferret eyes were eagerly watching the change which took place in the severe-looking face of the second lieutenant of the Mameluke.

"Hum, hum, hum," he purred to himself, "I shall know all about it directly—hum—hum a glass or two more, and I shall see the letter if this fellow has it with him."

Captain Jervis had not waited the return of old Saul and the naval officer to begin the attack upon the bottles, and by the flushed face and thick voice it was evident he had done ample justice to the host's wine long before those astute gentlemen had returned from visiting the shed.

"Well," the lieutenant of the Mameluke remarked, as he toyed with his glass, "I am very grateful to the fellow whs caused me to be sent upon this errand, for I have never before known the taste of really good wine."

"It is passable," said old Saul, attentively refilling the lieutenant's glass, "in fact I may say it's good."

"It's magnificent, sir, and here's to the rascal's health who caused me to become your guest."

"I feel honoured," smirked old Saul, "and hope sincerely if you can spare time, no matter at what hour of the day or night, to have the pleasure of seeing you again."

"A thorough British welcome, eh, captain."

"Yes," Captain Jervis said, "old Saul's not a bad fellow when you know him thoroughly."

"He's not," said the naval officer; "so I accept your offer in the spirit in which it is given."

"You do me honour."

"Nothing of the sort, Mr. Mason, it is I who feel honoured. Now, gentlemen, one glass more and I must return, in case there should be anymore mysterious letters waiting to be answered."

"You are used to this sort of thing, then?" old Saul carelessly remarked.

"Well, no; but yours was the second communication received; and they both came by one messenger—a boatman."

"Indeed! Had the person to whom the first communication referred a shed for the reception of stolen goods?"

"Oh, dear, no," laughed the officer. "He was a new acquaintance of ours—a fellow who commanded a letter of marque; but to our skipper's disgust and annoyance, he turned out to be the notorious Parker Neville. Hang it! and we had expected a return invite to dine with him to-morrow."

"Allow me to replenish your glass," said Saul. "Then, I presume you caught the gentleman?"

"Far from it, for when I went to board his craft, she had disappeared."

Just a faint twitching was perceptible above Saul's mouth at this intelligence.

"That was unfortunate," he said, "for there was a heavy reward offered for the audacious scoundrel's capture."

"Yes, so your informant told us; but, had we captured him, we should have been compelled to have shared the reward."

"With the informant?"

"Yes," said the lieutenant. "Well, I am not sorry the fellow's escaped, for I hate those blood-sucking rascals who are always ready to denounce a man. For my part, I believe in most cases the witnesses are companions of the men they denounce."

"They are a despicable, cowardly lot," said Saul Mason. "Had I my way, I would hang them."

"Well spoken," said the officer, "I am of your opinion; there's something about these letters I cannot understand," he took them from his pocket and placed them upon the table, "and the more I think the matter over the more certain do I feel that the hypothesis I have formed is not far from the truth."

Saul's eyes glistened fiercely when he detected the well-known caligraphy of his friend Parker Neville.

He had too much control of his facial muscles to betray the volcano of passion which raged within his breast.

"I think," he said blandly, "you remarked that both of these letters were brought to your ship by one person."

"Such was the case."

"And you also said you had formed an opinion on the matter."

"I have, you shall judge whether I am right not; this letter," taking up Saul's, "was sent denounce the Wasp. Now it seems very feasible to me that the messenger thinking to make as much as possible out of the affair carried this to Parker Neville."

Saul drummed upon the table with his fingers and nodded approvingly.

"Neville, seeing the letter, and possibly wishing to prevent us following him, concocted this letter," taking up Parker's epistle, "knowing by our conversation at the dinner-table how much we wished to capture this gang of river pirates; as for the waterman's statement about being hailed by two men and each giving him a letter, I take it for what it's worth, and had I the rascal tied up to a grating I'd wager he would speak the truth."

Saul Mason quietly ground his teeth as a vision of Bill Webb came across his mind.

"I do not think it would be possible to drive nearer the truth," said Saul, "but as the rascal Neville has escaped, and the contents of the said letters turned out a hoax, the only thing now to be done is to look out for the fellow who brought the letters."

Saul clenched his hands so firmly that the long nails sunk deep into the yellow flesh.

"The rascal," the officer said, "will, I have no doubt, pass near enough our ship for a grappling hook to catch his boat; now, gentlemen, I must say good night."

He buckled on his sword, and taking the letters from the table, went to the door followed by the mid.

Saul and Henry Jervis accompanied them, but the latter shook hands with the naval officer in the passage, and old Saul accompanied them to the door.

Upon the threshold he lingered for a few minutes repeating the invitation he had given, and while his back was turned, Edward Blendell crept down the stairs and came to the Guardsman's side.

"Here," he whispered, as he gave Henry Jervis a letter; "hide this quickly, and when you are alone in your chamber and the door locked, read the contents—remember, when you are alone."

The soldier thrust the letter in the breast of his close fitting coat, and Edward Blendell crept stealthily back to his chamber.

CHAPTER XVIII.

BILL WEBB COMES FOR HIS REWARD.

"Hum, hum!—ho, ho!" purred Saul, as he closed the door upon his visitors. "Ha, ha, ha——" but he stopped suddenly and snarled, "Oh, Bill Webb—sweet William Webb, you precious scoundrel! I'll be even with you, my gentleman."

He had finished his snarl by the time he reached the chamber where the Guardsman was busy arranging the bottles upon Saul's dirty carpet.

"Why, Saul," you old rascal!" Jervis said; "what is in the wind? Do you expect to do a few little bills at cent. per cent. that you have been so generous?"

"Bills?" grinned Saul; "oh no, Master Henry. Don't you think the knowledge I gained to-night was worth the wine? Ho, ho, ho! Ha, ha, ha——"

"What's the matter with the old fool?"

"Ho, ho! Ha, ha, ha! Master Henry; that wine--ha, ha, ha!—was a portion of the stolen cargo of the Alert."

"You are a matchless old villain, Saul."

"Hum, hum! perhaps I am."

"Those river pirates, eh——"

"What, master Henry, what?"

"Are known to you."

"Known? yes—hum, hum—well, pretty well. I pay them regular wages, Master Henry, and give them a per centage upon all 'finds.'"

"You'll hang, Saul; as safe as possible your neck will be stretched at Tyburn."

"No, no, Master Henry; when the game is nearly played out Saul will retire to a sunnier land than this."

"Take care you are not strung up and dried before you have the chance of sunning yourself in a sunnier land."

"Quite safe from that, Master Henry, quite safe; for I have at all times a fast little cutter ready for sea, and so close that were I to be hunted to my street door I could escape by the back of the house and be away long before the limbs of the law could find out the back entrance."

"The most cunning have been trapped, friend Saul."

"Hum, hum! yes; but they did not prepare for the last move."

"Perhaps not; what was this affair of the two letters, Saul, the contents of which you took so much pains to discover?"

"The letters—hum, hum—curse that Bill Webb!—I always took him to be a fool!"

"Is that an answer to my question?"

"No, no Master Henry, no; one of those letters I wrote."

"I expected as much; that was the one denouncing Parker Neville."

"It was; and the rascal who took it must have found out the contents on his way, hang-dog looking thief! I did not think he could read; having done this he went to Parker, and Parker, the cunning villain, split upon me about the Alert; it was lucky, was it not, that I had the shed cleared out last week?"

"Very lucky for your neck, but what did you do with the cargo?"

"Sold it—hum, hum, hum!—to a Scotchman, who comes down the river once a month to buy what he calls 'sheep-goats,' and he generally manages to fill the hold of his brig with them."

"You must be acquainted with a great many rascals, Saul."

"There you are, again, Master Henry, always joking. Well, perhaps I am."

"Hallo! it's ten o'clock, and I'm for duty at twelve. Good night, Saul."

"The ship-chandler saw his customer to the door, then he returned to his office, and shuffled up and down, wondering whether Bill Webb would come for the five guineas.

"In the midst of his wonderings there came a knock at the door, and Saul chuckled and rubbed his hands gleefully as he went along the passage.

It was Bill Webb, and when Saul saw him, he said:

"Come in, William; come in, William Webb; come in."

And William Webb went into the little back room Saul called his office.

"So you've been to the King's ship, William?" Saul said, rattling a few guineas he had in his pocket, "and you have taken the letter, eh, William Webb?"

"Yes, sir."

"And what did the captain say, eh, William?"

"He didn't say nothing to me, your honour; only, when he reads it, he goes to his leftenant and says something."

"Yes, William, yes."

"And the leftenant takes a lot of men and a boat, and they goes away somewhere."

"Oh, oh! Hum, hum! Yes, so they goes away somewhere, eh, William? Where did they go?"

"I don't know, your honour."

"Shall I tell you, William?"

"If your honour likes."

"Well, I do like, William Webb. They went to find the ship you had left, but it was gone, Bill; it was gone, William Webb. Ho, ho! Hum, hum!"

Bill Webb looked round to ascertain whether the door was open.

"He's the very devil," thought the waterman. "How did he find out I had been there?"

"Nice ship, wasn't it, Bill Webb?" continued Saul, "very nice ship, and a very nice captain; how much did he give you for the letter I wrote, eh, Bill Webb?"

The waterman gasped like a fish out of water, and stood with staring eyes and mouth agape in front of old Saul.

Bill Webb," Saul went on, Bill Webb, to read my

letter, sell it, and then come to me for a reward."

Bill Webb felt there was nothing to be done except to brave the matter out, and stoutly deny the truth of all Saul Mason (as Bill Webb imagined) surmised.

"Your honour's very funny," he said, "to joke with me like this; you know very well I took the letter and you promised me five guineas for doing of it."

"True, Bill Webb, true William, but I did not tell you to read it on the way."

"How could I read it on the way, your honour, when it was quite dark?"

"Dark was it; if that is the case you went ashore and read the letter; don't deny it, Bill Webb, it's no use, for I know where you went to read my letter—in fact I know everything, William Webb; so mind what you are about or I will send for the watch and you will be hanged by the neck, Bill Webb, for aiding a notorious pirate to make his escape."

Bill Webb's knees knocked together, and his face underwent as many changes in colour as a dolphin when giving up the ghost.

"You've a large family, Bill Webb," his tormentor continued, as he rubbed his hands with glee at the sufferings of the unfortunate waterman, "and you've a wife, Bill Webb, a good sort of woman in her way, and just fit for you; a wise woman too, Bill Webb, for when the frost and snow of winter keep customers away from your boat, she forgets to get a nice warm tea ready for you when you come home, and allows your family of young 'uns to take up all the fire. A discreet woman too, Bill Webb, for when you are in luck's way she thrashes your interesting family and bids them make room for their poor father. Think, Bill Webb, of this exemplary wife, and the group of young 'uns all standing at the foot of the gallows because William Webb their father, who ought to have known better, is about to be hanged for aiding a notorious outlaw to escape from justice."

He gave the waterman time to realise this picture before he resumed.

"I can save you from this, Bill Webb, and will do so if you will truthfully and unhesitatingly answer all my questions."

Thoroughly subdued and frightened, the boatman gasped out,

"I will do anything your honour likes if you won't get me hanged. Oh Lord! oh Lord! I wishes I hadn't a come back here for the five guineas."

"I dare say you do, Bill Webb, but wishing will not do you any good now; you must speak the truth, not that I want to know, for, as I told you before, I know everything, but because I wish to know whether you are worthy of being saved from the gallows after the wickedness of which you have been guilty."

"Oh Lord!" gasped Bill Webb, "I wishes I had never seen them letters——"

"Ah! hum, hum, hum, these letters. Well William, William Webb, licensed waterman, with a wife and large family, you have the chance of speaking the truth or being hanged by the neck until you are dead, which you very soon would be, Bill Webb, if they once put the rope round your neck."

"Yes, your honour; oh, Lord! what am I to do?"

"Tell the truth, William, that's all, only the truth, and bear in mind as I know everything, you must speak only the truth."

"And if I does this your honour, I shan't be—be——"

"No, Bill Webb, you won't have your neck stretched if you speak the truth."

"I will try you. Now, Bill Webb, what is the name of the public-house where you read my letter?"

"The 'Benbow, your honour."

"Quite right, 'The Admiral Benbow,'" chuckled Saul. "Then you went to the Wasp and saw the captain?"

"Your honour must have been close to me."

"I was not far off, Bill Webb. Hum! hum, hum! You are a clever rascal, William, but not clever enough for Saul Mason. No, no, not for Saul Mason."

"No, your honour."

"No, Bill Webb, licensed waterman and arrant rogue. Mind what you are about, sweet William. Mind what you are about, or there will be a waterman hanged at Tyburn, and a woman and a lot of young 'uns howling because the waterman has been hanged—his neck stretched, Bill Webb."

"I hope not, your honour."

"It all rests upon your behaviour, Bill Webb all, mind that."

"Yes, your honour."

"Now, Bill Webb, tell me at once, and without the least hesitation, how much that rascally pirate fellow gave you for my letter?"

"I don't know, your honour."

This was the truth, for poor Bill had not yet looked into the little bag Parker Neville had given him.

"Don't know," said Saul, jumping from his seat; "don't know, I'll soon fetch somebody to make you know. Ho! ho! ho! One halfpenny each the last dying speech and confession of Bill Webb, who was hanged."

THERE WAS A KNOCK AT THE OUTER DOOR.

Saul made a movement towards the door, and the waterman overcome with terror fell upon his knees.

"Don't go, your honour," he pleaded; "I am telling of the truth, I am, indeed; for I ain't looked at the bag he gave me, yet."

"Ho, ho—that alters the case; but still I hink I had better fetch the officer, in case—"

"Please don't. I won't tell you anything wrong. You honour can ask me everything, and I will tell you all of it as it was."

"Very well. Hum, hum, hum! I will not fetch the officer yet. So you don't know kow much the bag contains, eh?"

"No, your honour."

"Where is it?"

Bill Webb shifted first on one foot, then the other; then he wiped his hat with the sleeve of his jacket, and looked so hot and uncomfortable that old Saul laughed and chuckled with delight.

"Where is it, Bill Webb?" Oh, I see; it is in your jacket pocket. Give it to me."

And before the waterman could help himself old Saul snatched the bag from his pocket.

"Oh, Lord!" gasped Bill Webb, "oh, Lord! he's got it."

"Yes, William, he's got it, and will count it when you have answered a few more questions."

"Your honour won't keep it, will you?"

"Keep it? Oh, no, Bill Webb. Keep it! What, Old Saul keep it? No, no, no—hum, hum, hum, hum. Now William, what took place after you received this nice, plump little bag of golden guineas?"

Old Saul shook the bag, and Bill Webb groaned aloud when he heard the chink of the yellow metal.

"After the captain gave me the bag, your honour," Bill Webb said dolefully, "he wrote a letter and told me to wait for a few minutes while he went on deck"

"And you waited, Bill Web?"

"Yes, your honour, aud when he came down again he told me to be off to the Mameluke or I'd have a long pull."

"And you went off, eh, Bill Webb?"

"I did, your honour."

"Sweet, cunning William. And you told the captain that two men had hailed you and each given you a letter to take to the liner. Cunning, deceitful, William Webb. Oh, you rogue, it is enough to make an honest man blush to know there is such villany in men's minds; look at me, Bill Webb, don't you see how I blush for you?"

Bill Webb looked at the parchment-like visage before him, and he thought if Saul blushed it was by a yellow tinge (a new thing in the way of blushes), but poor Bill knew it would not be politic to say so.

"I see, your honour," he said, "but I does hope you will think of my wife and little 'uns, and forgive me this once and I'll never do it agin."

"No Bill—no, William Webb, I'm sure you'll never do it again."

"No, your honour."

"Oh, no, no. I suppose when you take home this bag, and all the money, William, the young 'uns will have their ears doubly boxed if they don't get out of the way, and your wife will call you the best of Williams."

"Maybe so, your honour."

"But suppose you don't take it home, eh, Bill Webb?"

"But I will, I will, I must!" exclaimed the waterman, "I've been out a very long day, your honour, and if I don't take home something extra I——"

"You'll have some hot tongue—well, well, serve you right too. Now, William, what are you going to do with all this money, there must be at least fifty bright, yellow, golden guineas'"

"Yes, your honour, I hope so for I want a new boat."

"Yes, William, a nice light boat painted green and white, and your name on the stern in gold letters."

"Yes, your honour, and my number put underneath."

"Quite so, William—hum, hum, hum!—we will count the bright canaries and see how much there will be left after the boat has been paid for."

"He ain't such a bad sort after all," thought Bill Webb, "that he aint."

Old Saul emptied the money upon the table, and holding the mouth of the bag open, dropped the pieces in as he counted.

"That is fifteen, William," he said, when he had placed that number in the bag; "that will buy the nice light boat painted green and white, and your name and number in gold letters on the stern."

"Yes, your honour."

"Hum, hnm, num! five—that's twenty; now that will do to buy some new clothes for the young 'uns and yourselves."

"Yes, your honour."

Hum, hum, ten more, Bill Webb, in the bag, that makes thirty; the ten will be quite enough to buy you some new furniture."

"Yes, your honour."

"Now there's twenty left, which—ho, ho, ho! —you ought to have put away in a safe place Where do you keep your money when you save it, eh, Bill Webb?"

"Never has none to save, your honour."

"Ho, ho, ho! Hum, hum! you'll possess twenty guineas, and five I promised you—look here."

Saul took five guineas from his pocket and dropped them one by one in the bag, and Bill Webb's mouth watered and his palms tightened when he saw the extra pieces placed in the bag.

"Yes, your honour," he said, "I sees. I am much obliged to you for it."

"Don't mention it, William; now I will tie the mouth of the bag up for you; five and fifty guineas, eh, Bill Webb?"

"Yes, your honour, I am sure I am very much——"

"Yes, William, I know you are; but upon second—ho, ho!—thoughts—hum—hum, hum! —I think I will keep the bag myself."

Saul slipped the bag into his pocket as he spoke; and Bill Webb who was about to reply with the usual "yes, your honour," stood with mouth agape, staring at the chuckling old rascal.

"What's the matter, William? Ho, ho, ho! You don't—hum, hum, hum——"

"Give me my money," shrieked Bill Webb, rushing towards the ship-chandler; "give me my money. You shan't rob me. I'll have your life first."

Saul dodged out of the way; and Bill Webb, in his haste to clutch the old villain, lost his footing, and fell forward.

His temple came in contact with the fender, and in a moment he lost all knowledge of life.

Saul stood over the senseless body; and to make sure that Bill Webb was not counterfeiting insensibility, he held the flame of the candle close to the tip of the waterman's nose.

Not a muscle of the weather-beaten face moved, when Saul mercilessly singed the unfortunate man's flesh.

"Hum, hum, hum!" he purred. "Now what shall I do with him? Ho, ho! Fifty guineas in one night, and no risk. That's a good stroke. Now, let me see. Ah, hum, hum! Yes, that is the way to dispose of Master William Webb."

With a show of strength that seemed impossible for his stunted form to possess, old Saul seized the collar of Bill Webb's jacket, and dragged him to the street-door.

He propped poor Bill in a sitting posture against the front of the house; then he ran inside and brought out a large rattle.

Standing in the centre of the road, old Saul sprang the rattle, and shouted—

"Watch, watch, watch!"

Windows were opened with a bang, and men appeared at the doors of their houses; but old Saul heeded them not. He kept up the whirr-whirr of the rattle, accompanied by the words,

"Watch, watch, watch!"

So well was old Saul liked by his neighbours, that none came beyond their doorstep to ascertain the cause of the disturbance.

"I hope," said one charitable individual who lived opposite old Saul, "that some one has robbed the old scoundrel."

"So do I, neighbour," said the party next door, "and I wish they had cut his throat at the same time."

Hurrying forward as quickly as age and infirmity would permit, a couple of "Charlies" made their appearance at the end of the street; and to inspire the person who screamed thus with courage, the old fellows used their rattles as they came along, and many an indignant mother, enraged at having her children awakened by the din, seized their water-jugs and would have given the watchmen a sousing had they not luckily for themselves kept in the centre of the road.

"Watch, watch!" Saul yelled, raising his voice as the "Charlies" came nearer. "Help, help, help! Watch! Hi! Watch!"

Saul was panting and hot in consequence of the labour attendant upon his frantic calls and the swinging of the heavy rattle.

"What's the matter, master," demanded one of the guardians of the night; "you ain't killed anyhow."

"I might have been," answered Saul, "had I depended upon you for my safety."

"Well, what's up? we come as quick as we could, and we couldn't come any quicker, 'cos some young blades for a lark nailed my mate up in his box, and I had to get him out. Now what's up?"

"Look here," said Saul; "do you see him?"

The watchman held his light close to Bill Webb's feet, and spoke as a modern policeman would have spoken had the case come under the notice of one of those active and intelligent officer's observation.

"Drunk," he said, "beastly, speechless drunk. I s'pose he's been 'saulting you, sir?"

Old Saul adroitly passed a silver coin to each of the watchmen, as he answered:

"Assaulting me, yes; and would have killed me had not the drink overcome him."

"The wagabone. Here, Jack, catch hold of his feet, we'll soon find a place for him."

"Stay a moment," said Saul, "I only want you to lock him up for the night, for the poor fellow has a wife and family, and I don't want him punished."

"I'm sure, sir, you is a wery good gentleman, to be so kind."

"We must not be harsh to each other, my friend. No, no, now mind what I say, let him go in the morning, for although the poor fellow did in his moments of intoxication accuse me of robbing him of fifty guineas, I will not have him punished."

"That's a good 'un, too," said the Charlie. "Fancy, Jack, this here gentleman a-taking fifty shiners from this here dirty creature; why I don't suppose he has had fifty shillings all at one time. Now then up with his heels. That's it, off we goes."

Off they went, and old Saul called out to them:

"Be gentle with the poor fellow. Don't be harsh, he's only had a drop too much."

He watched Bill Webb's limp form as far as he could see it, then he went in doors chuckling like an old demon.

CHAPTER XIX.

THE CONTENTS OF NED BLENDELL'S LETTER.

WHEN the Guardsman reached his quarters at St. James's, his soldier servant gave him a letter.

"From Basil," he muttered; "I will read Ned Blendell's first. You can go, William."

The man saluted and left the room.

Captain Jervis was not given to thinking as a rule, but as he sat in his chair, holding the letter between his fingers, he pondered over the inevitable result of his connection with old Saul.

"I don't like the old villain," he thought, "and if I do not keep a good look out ahead, as the sailors say, the old mummy will get the best of the bargain. Now what I want is to get him in my power, and unless I am much mistaken Ned Blendell is the man to put me up to the needful knowledge. Now let's see what is in the letter."

"Sir,—I was a witness," so the letter ran," of the confusion your question respecting the young girl caused the arch villain Saul Mason. He desired you not to speak of her again. I will tell you the reason. She was his brother's child her father was for many years an officer in the Royal Navy; but unfortunately his ship struck on a rock, and he was tried and cashiered in consequence. Thus disgraced, he left England, but before doing so he gave the child to Saul's care, also a sum of money, the savings of his pay and prize-money. What became of him was never known; but Saul having reason to believe his brother dead, and wishing to obtain possession of the money, sent the poor girl as a passenger on board the Gloriana. You are aware of the loss of that vessel. I have not time to write more. Peter Quills, lawyer of Aldgate, can give you every information upon the matter if the fee is high enough to open his lips. "E. BLENDELL.

"P.S.—Peter Quills is no friend of Saul's. They are both rogues; but there is neither honour nor love between them."

The Guardsmen pondered for some time over this strange epistle.

"Peter Quills will speak," he soloquised, "if the fee is high enough. I will call upon Peter, and instead of using Saul's advance at the gaming table, I will grease Master Peter's palm, and oil his tongue with it. Now, my friend Saul, if I can only prove you sent the girl away with the fore-knowledge that the vessel would never reach its destination. What a fool I am! Of course he told me Parker Neville destroyed the Gloriana."

He soon came to the conclusion that the knowledge he had thus obtained was valueless unless he found Parker Neville, and could persuade that gentleman to go hand-in-hand with him against old Saul.

"Still," he reasoned, "it may be worth while to see this Peter Quills; something may be done if I can make this limb of the law——Come in."

"His servant entered the chambe r.

"There is a servant from Sir Basil's, sir."

"Well, what does he want?"

"He says your brother is getting worse, sir."

"Worse," repeated the guardsmen, turning pale. "Give me that letter, William."

The servant handed his master the three-cornered note, and with trembling fingers the heir expectant broke the seal and read—

"Dear Harry,—Basil's lowness of spirits, consequent upon the uncertain fate of our boy, has at length affected his mind, and he is now in a state of delirium. "CONSTANCE."

The Guardsman jumped from his seat, and was about to leave the room when his eyes fell upon the uniform his servant had placed ready for him.

"Confound this guard," he said; "here, William, run to Captain Wood's and give him my compliments and tell him my brother is dying; ask him to go on this turn of duty for me."

"Yes sir."

"Woods will do this for me," thought the soldier. "Should Basil die I must have leave of absence from to-morrow. This is very sudden. Poor Basil, now the hour has come for which I have so long plotted, sinned, and waited, I feel the affection which has so long been stifled by my desire to inherit his wealth re-asserting its sway; but it is too late now, even if the knowlege I possess respecting the boy would restore his shattered health—too late, for I dare not impart it to him—dare not, for Saul would bring me to the gallows. Curse him, he has taken his measures too well for me to escape.

He had just finished donning a plainer suit of clothes than the gorgeous uniform of the Guards when the servant returned and said,

"Captain Woods will do as you wish, sir."

"Thanks, William; now fetch me a hackney coach."

Sir Basil Jervis's town residence, was in the then aristocratic neighbourhood of Golden-square, and thither the Guardsman was taken as fast as the jaded hack could be induced to move.

He found the knocker muffled, and in the sockets outside the door two links burning; beyond this no lights were visible, in consequence of the whole of the shutters being closed.

The soldier's heart sank when he surveyed the gloomy-looking house, but the pang was but momentary, and it gave place to a feeling of exultation as he pictured himself master of his brother's wealth.

"He is gone," was the thought which came to his mind. "I should have liked to have seen him, yet it is better as it is, for bad as I am I could not play the hypocrite."

The door was opened before he could knock, and when he saw the troubled face of the domestic, he felt his surmise was correct.

"Your master," he said, "surely——"

"He's gone, Mr. Henry, gone; and so sudden, too, that we can't believe it yet. Poor Sir Basil, we shall never get such a master again."

"Not flattering to me," thought the Guardsman, as he passed the old man, "but I suppose the old fool does not know I am master now."

He was met at the top of the first flight of stairs by the Lady Constance, and so deep was her grief that she could not speak.

He took her hand, and led her to the dressing room, muttering something about the loss being very sudden, and doing his best to console the afflicted widow.

Captain Henry Jervis was an eligible frequenter of the best houses in town. He could dance, and flirt with the young ladies, play a game at whist with the old ones, and, in fact, earn for himself the name of being a charming young man.

But in cases of this description he was as awkward as a country clown, and, to save his life, he could not make any attempts to console the poor lady.

She became calmer all the sooner in consequence of his silence. and withdrawing the white handkerchief from her face, faltered :—

"He wanted to see you, Henry, but it is too late, now. He passed away from us half an hour since."

"My poor brother!"

"You are now master here," she said; "but I pray you to allow me to see that my poor husband's funeral is arranged."

"I shall not interfere in any way with arrangements," he said, "I am not master here yet."

"Thanks. Would you like to——No, you had better not at present. Another time, unless you insist. Yet it would not——"

Here she burst into a paroxysm of tears, and the soldier said—

"I will be entirely guided by your wishes in this."

"Thank you," she sobbed, and again covered her face, "thank you, Sir Henry."

The sound fell pleasantly upon the Guardsman's ears—"Sir Henry!"—and for the time the mention of his new rank startled every sting of conscience—he felt, and felt keenly in spite of his hardihood.

"Sir Henry!" he thought; she has soon acknowledged me; but Constance is a clever, sensible woman, and as Basil has no doubt died without making a will, I shall not forget to be generous to his widow."

He took the earliest opportunity of leaving the house of sorrow, and jumping into the hackney coach which still awaited him, he was driven back to St. James's.

The further he went from the house in Golden-square, the higher his hopes for the future and his wish to escape from old Saul became.

"One can stand a little twinge of conscience for this," he thought, "a title and over £40,000 a year—no, not forty, for that old vampire, Saul, by our bond, is entitled to one-third. Curse him! but for his subtle counsel I should never have sinned as I have sinned."

He thought of Peter Quills as he paced to ar. fro his room, and grinding his teeth savagely he resumed—

"I shall be even with him yet. If this fellow will but speak and place old Saul in my power, it will go hard if I do not make him hand over every paper he holds which gives him such uncontrolled command over me."

When the hackney coach was carrying the Guardsman back to St. James's, it passed a cart drawn by a single horse.

In this vehicle two men were seated, and both were in high glee.

"It don't matter," one said, "to us what the people at that house wanted with the stiff—do it, Tony?"

"Not a bit," answered Tony, "we has been well paid for it, but the job was a little bit particular like."

"It was; I have lifted many a stiff," said the first speaker, "but I never had such a job to find one to suit a customer."

"He was mighty particular, and no mistake, but he paid well, that's all we cares about."

"In course, but as I says afore, it's a rummy go, and I can't make it out at all why the stiff should be so high and such a size, and such a colour about the head of hair; a stiff's a stiff in my way of thinking, and it don't matter as I can see whether the hair is red or black, or whether it's five foot ten or five foot four."

"Perhaps they wants to make a skiliton of it."

"Perhaps they does, but then it wouldn't matter about the colour of the hair."

These men were resurrectionists, and the "stiff" they spoke about was a corpse taken from the quiet graveyard.

Two days after this, and about the same hour that Henry Jervis went to take a last look at his brother's body, a well-armed and swift schooner sailed from the Thames.

The vessel was owned by a gentleman, and no expense had been spared to make her worthy of the mission she was intended for.

Henry Jervis took but a momentary look at his brother's quiet face; he felt a coward in the presence of the dead, and was glad the Lady Constance did not open the shutters and throw more light upon the form which lay so awfully still in the cerements of the grave.

CHAPTER XX.

THE DEY MAKES A REQUEST.

BENARDIN ALLAH BEY, although a trifle the worse for the amount of the forbidden liquor he had indulged in was perfectly well aware that only one person in the whole of the States of Barbary dare knock at the entrance to his private chamber.

That person was the Dey of Benardin Allah. Although he stood high in the favour of the terrible old Moslem, he knew his head would pay the forfeit were he detected in the act of imbibing the forbidden drink.

"Hide the bottles, Sandy," he said to his servant, "Hide them, you long-legged, narrow-backed, porridge-bred thief, hide them."

Baba-da-Chuk would have done so, for he valued his head quite as much as his effulgency the Bey did that very useful part of his anatomy, but unfortunately he had not time to do so before the Dey and his attendants pushed open the door.

The old infidel raised his hands in pious astonishment at the scene, and his slaves, as in duty bound, also gave unmistakable signs of horror at beholding two of the elect of the faithful, waving short-necked, stumpy bottles, and singing in a tongue that was quite unknown among the followers of Islam.

Benardin Allah Bey was sobered by the appearance of his august master, and dropping the black bottle behind the divan he advanced to welcome the Dey.

"Most illustrious master," he said, "thy servant prostrates himself in all humility before thee."

The Dey stalked into the chamber, and looked very much as though he would like to call the chief executioner to execute summary justice upon the offenders.

His grisly beard bristled with wrath, and his small bird-like eyes shot revengeful glances—first at the Bey, then at his servant.

"Allah, be good to us!" he said. "Is it thus I find my most trusted servant?"

"Light of the world," said the Bey, "upon my head be the punishment of thy just wrath. Yet, O Dey, I have but done, or tried to do, thy faithful followers a service."

"Speak; thy master listens."

"Know then, O Dey, the spirits of evil which have for so long fought against the true faith have come in the guise of seductive drinks, and the chief of the evil spirits willed that our galleys should receive multitudes of his demons."

"It is so," said the Dey. "Speak on, O Benardin Allah Bey, and prove thy face white in my presence, and I will be unto thee the master of yore."

"My soul drinks thy words," said Benardin humbly, "as the tongue of the parched traveller laps the clear waters of the desert."

"Thy master listens."

"Know, then, O mighty Dey, before whose power nations tremble, when my captains brought me word of the evil they had brought amongst us—when, O my master, several of the faithful were prostrate through having the spirits of evil aboard, I had the accursed waters brought here to my house to wrestle with the evil they contained——"

"Humph!" muttered the Dey.

"I fought with them, my master, but they were too powerful; then I called into my assistance Baba-da-Chuk, and we both fought with them, and had well-nigh gained the mastery, when thy summons came to the door. I did not then, O master, seek to hide from thee the accursed bottles of the fiends, but kept up with the enemy. I have spoken, O mighty Dey. If thy servant has done wrong, let him be punished."

The Dey stroked his beard, then turning to the attendants bade them begone; and to the surprise of the effulgent Baba-da-Chuk, he said to that individual—

"Leave us, good Baba, I would have private speech of thy master."

The infidel deftly concealed the two bottles under his robe, and staggered from the chamber.

"Well, well," he muttered, "this master of mine has the gift of speech, and it would be nae wonder to me if he made the Dey drink of the forbidden waters."

Baba-da-Chuk retired to his chamber; and when his black attendant came to dress him in the morning, he found the great Baba had gone to bed without undressing, and with his heels on the pillow.

"Thy face is white," said the Dey, when he was alone with Benardin, "for the good thou wouldst have done us we forgive thee. Rise, O Bey."

The Bey kissed the hem of his master's garment, and arose, then stood with bowed head and folded arms before the Dey.

The latter seated himself upon the divan, and placed the mouthpiece of Benardin Allah Bey's chiboque to his lips.

The Bey did not move from his respectful attitude, until his master, having taken a few whiffs of the scented herb, motioned him to be seated on the divan.

"The honour is too great, O Dey," said Benardin; but he took the seat indicated nevertheless, "too great for one so humble."

"Be seated," said the Dey, "I would have speech with thee touching this liquor of the infidel dogs; also respecting the captives Allah has been good to send thee this day."

"Thy servant hears, O Dey."

The commander of the faithful crossed his legs, and the Bey assiduously arranged a pile of cushions for the commander of the faithful's back to recline against.

"Thanks, good Benardin, we feel more at ease now."

"Thy servant is glad."

"There is among the captives," the Dey said, "a girl of surpassing loveliness, O Bey."

BROADSIDE FOR BROADSIDE.

"Mine eyes have not yet beheld the captives, O Dey."

"So much the better," thought the Dey, "if thou had'st, well; but no matter, if the dog refuses my request I will bowstring him."

"But," continued Benardin Allah, "if your mightiness has seen this Frankish girl which the captain of my galleys has taken captive, you must know if she's of surpassing loveliness."

"I have seen her, good Benardin," replied the Dey, "and she is most lovely. I would she graced our harem."

"Allah be praised," said Benardin. "But is

the infidel girl, O Dey, fit companion for those in the harem of the faithful?"

"She will soon be converted to the true faith, Benardin," replied the Dey, "under the instruction of my eunuchs. Set a price on thy captive, and I will see thee paid it at once."

"O, mighty Dey, thy goodness is unbounded," said Benardin; "thy servant is but too happy to give her to thee without one sequin of money."

"Thy master will not forget this, O Bey. Now, touching this fiery liquor of the Franks. What is thy intention respecting it?"

"With Allah's permission, great master, I, the humble follower of the true faith, purpose to keep the evil juice of the grape within my cellars until, by prayer and fasting, I turn the contents of the bottles into water, or cause the evil liquor to leave them."

The Dey looked out of the corners of his eyes at his admiral, and the expression of his face implied as plainly as though he had said—

"If you continue as I find you, there will not be much difficulty in causing the liquor to leave the bottles. Does the taste of this accursed drink excel our clear water that the Franks freight their vessels with it, so that others may taste of the juice of the grape?"

The Bey drew the back of his hand across his mouth as he answered—

"It is of a sweet taste. Will my master have one of the bottles, that he may judge whether these Franks are any better than asses to spoil the fruit which Allah has sent them?"

"I would taste of this drink, O Bey, but for the edicts of the Koran, which sayeth it is a sin."

CHAPTER XXII.

THE EVIL SPIRIT OVERCOMES THE DEY.

"NAY, but my master, did not the Great Mahomet often sin when it was to benefit his faithful followers? And the sins he thus committed were looked over by Allah when he saw they were for a good purpose."

"Prove to me, Bey, that I shall be doing Allah, or the Prophet, or the faithful a service, and I will defile my lips."

"I will try, O my master," said Benardin. "Is it not said by the Koran that kings, princes, and rulers shall be always ready to sacrifice their prejudices, aye, even their lives, for the good of those they govern?"

"It is so, but of what avail is this in the present instance?"

"Much O Dey, as the tongue of thy servant shall prove."

"Do so, good Benardin, for I have affairs of moment to attend."

Benardin opened his eyes; it was not often his Moslem master gave the most momentous affairs any consideration.

The Bey, like most renegades, had attained his position quite as much by intrigue as personal bravery and skill in the management of the Corsair fleet.

He knew his appointment had given offence to a host of lawless Arab chiefs, and he knew also that they would use every means in their power to bring him into disgrace.

Thus when the Dey spoke of having to attend to matters of an unusual kind, the Bey's suspicions were aroused, and he resolved if possible to learn the nature of the pressing business.

"I will not keep your highness long," he said, "as a man may at times learn wisdom from a child, so may the great and mighty ruler of Barbary learn much from his humblest of slaves."

"Thy master listens."

"It is this, O Dey, the Koran forbids the faithful the use of certain drinks, a wise law, Allah be praised; but, my master, does not the book of laws expressly lay down a rule that all chiefs and elders are to know that which is good and that which is bad for their followers?"

"It is so."

"Well, O Dey, forbidden as the drink of the infidel is amongst us, it has one virtue, and may be used even with the Prophet's sanction for the purpose of healing the sick."

"Say you so? By my beard, but I never knew of such an article in the holy book."

Benardin produced a copy of the Koran, and placing the tip of his finger upon one of the passages, read—

"Should the cleansing and prayer not heal this sickness, go forth into the fields and cull the herbs which Allah has placed there for the use of those who suffer; should these again fail let the faithful use other remedies, aye, even to the burning waters used by the infidel dogs, for at such times there will be no sin in casting away the uncleanness of the body, if after there is prayer and fasting to carry off the contact with the unclean water."

"By the beard of my father," said the Dey, "the words are plain and so is their meaning."

"They ought to be," thought Benardin, "for I have twisted the sentence pretty well out of its original sense."

"Allah be good to us!" continued the Dey; "now I bethink me I have felt but weak of late; close the door safely, Benardin, and I will even try this remedy the Prophet has allowed us to use."

The Bey placed a bar across the doors, then drew the heavy curtains closely together to prevent any of the attendants peeping through the chinks, for the woodwork of even the best houses were not remarkable for the closeness of their joins.

"This bright liquid," he said, holding a bottle in front of the Dey's eyes, "is called by the infidels brandy, and is much used by them for sickness of the body."

"By the head of the Prophet," said the old fellow, "it has a hue pleasant to look upon; haste, good Benardin, haste, for the sickness is coming fast over me."

The Bey knocked off the top of the bottle with one sharp tap with the back of his yataghan.

"It has a pleasant aroma," said the Dey, picking up the cork and placing it against his illustrious but snub nose; "a perfume, Benardin, that feels refreshing to the nostrils."

"It is a much-prized drink by the unbelievers, O mighty Dey, and they ascribe many virtues to it."

The Dey looked roguishly at his companion, and said:

"Be sure, O Bey, to cast out the evil spirit that so overcame thee and thy servant."

"Water," said Benardin, "is the best for the purpose, my master; shall I fill this glass with the pure stream."

"I will taste the liquor in its pure state first; then if the evil spirit begins to assume a mastery, I can use the clear water to drive him forth."

Benardin watched the Dey sip a little of the brandy, and his effulgence seemed to like it, for he smacked his lips, and muttered:

"Truly, the infidel dogs are skilled in the preparation of strong waters; blessed be the Prophet's name for allowing the faithful to partake of it when sickness comes upon the body."

He was about to empty the glass, but paused as it touched his lips and asked:

"You are sure, O Bey, that prayer will remove the defilement my lips are about to ustain."

"On my head be it, good master."

The Dey gulped down the dose, and the tears ame to his eyes, for the spirit was very strong."

"It is a powerful medicine, Benardin," he said; "for already I feel it warming my body and driving away sickness."

He held the glass out, and the Bey re-filled it, saying:

"Will my lord take a little of the clear strea with his medicine?"

"Not yet, good Bey, not yet."

Glass after glass was drunk by the Dey, and the effect soon became visible by his thick speech and inflamed face.

Bernardin had a purpose in view or he would not have diluted his drink with a plentiful supply of water.

Watching his opportunity, he said:

"Thy slave asks pardon for reminding thee of the matters of importance thou hast to attend."

"Fill up, Bey, fill up," said the Dey, "there is ample time for that; let the dogs wait, they seek an audience to state their grievance against thee, my faithful friend. Fill up."

Bernardin filled up, and while doing so asked:

"Will my gracious lord tell me the names of those whom I have had the misfortune to offend?"

"Aye, that I will, good Bernardin, it is the three officers next in command to thyself; but may a jackass sit upon my grave if I do not bowstring them for grumbling about one who is the light of his master's eyes."

Bernardin Allah Bey made no comment, but the flush of anger which spread over his face augured ill for the three officers next in command to himself.

An hour later the Dey was prostrate, the spirit had done its work, but ere he fell back upon the soft cushions he said:

"Good—and—hic—faithful servant—hic, hic, let me have, hic—some of the—hic—wonderful medicine—hic—for I am often taken—hic—with this—hic—hic—sickness."

"On my head be it," answered the Bey; 'to-night my master shall have many dozen bottles of the infidel's medicine."

Early the next morning one of the captains brought the captives before the Bey.

They were but two. One a fair young girl, perfect in form and feature; the other a youth of about twenty years of age, whose lack-lustre eyes and heavy forehead told that he was deprived of those reasoning faculties which make man superior to the brute creation.

The remainder of the prisoners were the common seamen of the captured vessel, and, chained wrist to wrist, they were marched to the interior to work in the fields.

The Bey fixed his eyes upon the young girl, and a strange thrill ran over him as he gazed into her face.

The features seemed familiar—so much so

that her presence recalled the face and form of one who had long since been dead.

"Impossible," he thought, "utterly impossible; it is the few English faces I see causes this strong resemblance."

He tried to shake off the strange feeling which had come over him by reasoning in this manner, but it was useless, and when the girl spoke he felt as though a knife had been passed through his heart.

"Well, my lad, he said, speaking to the youth, "what can you do? Are you any trade? Mechanics are useful here."

"The young maniac stared at the speaker as though he was surprised to hear his natural tongue spoken by one in such a strange garb; but beyond this, he showed no sign of reason, for his answer to the query was—

"It was fine—all alone on the water—it was fine, and Dick would like to go there again."

"Has this any meaning?" the Bey asked, the young girl, "or only the babblings of an idiot?"

The girl kept her eyes fixed upon the carpet, as she answered:

"He refers to the many days we were float-about an the ocean, upon a broken spar."

The voice troubled the Bey:

"You were wrecked then?" he said.

"We were attacked by wicked men, sir, and our ship destroyed; and after clinging to a wreck for many days, we were picked up by the vessel which has fallen into the hands of your countrymen. Oh, sir," she suddenly exclaimed, clasping her hands and looking full in the Bey's face, "you speak our language, and you are not so cruel as those men who took our ship. Pray save us, save me from them."

"The voice, the attitude, the expression of the girl's face touched a chord in the Bey's heart, and as he clutched the cushions nervously, he said:

"I will do all in my power. One question, and answer it truthfully as you wish to escape from the horrors of slavery. What is your name?"

"MILLY MASON."

Th Bey breathed very hard, and his face became pale, as he gasped:

"That is your mother's portrait in that locket which hangs from the chain around your neck?"

The girl's blue eyes were filled with astonishment and tears, as she answered:

It is, sir."

The Bey sprang from his seat, and reeling forward like a drunken man, moaned:

"My God! and I have given her to the Dey."

He fell back senseless into the ready arms of Baba-da-Chuk.

CHAPTER XXIII.

PARKER NEVILLE NEARLY PLACES HIS HAND IN THE LION'S MOUTH.

THE Bristol, the flag-ship of Rear-Admiral Sir Peter Parker, was one of the finest built ships in the British navy, and, despite her majestic proportions, the liner could sail as swift as many of the smartest frigates afloat.

One lovely eve, soon after the hammocks were piped down, old Ben Tompion, Bill Jinks, and Tom Cox were seated on the forecastle, enjoying their pipes, and talking over the qualities of the various ships they had served in, and the commanders they had served under.

"It do seem strange like," said Bill Jinks, "to see you in this here craft, Ben—werry strange, for with all the shifting about we gets from ship to ship now-a-days, it are a wonder we ever meets a person we knows."

"That's true, Bill," said old Ben, "but I don't think I should a come hadn't it a been for young Leeftenant Nelson, who says, when he was 'pointed to this ship as third luff, you come with me, Ben; so I comes, and I ain't sorry, for arter being shut up in a little bit a privateer with a wardroom——"

"The barky had a wardroom, Ben."

"No, Tom Cox; you, who has as much jaw as a batch of new middies; no, I had the wardroom, and a devil of a one it was too."

"It ware a ugly place, Ben," said Bill Jinks, "but howsomdever as it have ceased, I don't see you need grumble, for there is more room in a craft like this than you'd get in a old tub like the Lowestoft."

"You're right enough, Bill, you're right enough; so, arter all, I suppose I must think it was for the best that I got that tack."

"I wonder what became of that young chap," Tom Cox said, "that we picked up in the Lowestoft?"

"Don't you know?" old Ben said, "if you don't you ought, for his name is almost as ocular as——"

"Popular, Ben, popular."

"Well, popular, then—not that I can see it makes much difference when you understands what I mean."

"No, it don't. Twist away, old hoss."

"Ah," said old Ben, "there warn't a better man aboard any craft than that Anchor Jack was; no, not a cleverer chap or a smarter from stem to starn; and though he was but a young un he know'd a seaman's duty, and more he didn't purtend to know; not like your capering youngsters we sometimes gets aboard, and pretends as they can do unpossibilities."

"Steady to the tack, old Ben," said Bill, "small helm steady, old hoss, and let's hear what's come of the young fellow; pay it out, and don't go yawing about in your course."

"Let him alone," said Tom, "don't you know old Ben is something like this craft, give her a foot of the sheet and she'll go through the water like a swan; but for all that she lays on a bowline to leeward, so does Ben when he——"

"Avast there, Tom Cox, captain of the foretop," said Ben; your jaw goes like the tail of a westerly hurricane. May I never bowse my jib again if I tells the story if you ain't quiet."

"Then, I'll be quiet," said Tom, "as quiet, old hoss, as a marine in the lee mizen chains."

"Well, that's settled then," said old Ben, "I've told you about the way we beat off these Americanisers, and how the young chap, Anchor Jack, when he sees the officer who led the boarders to our help, ups and tells as how he was the chap as sent the Glory something to old Davy."

"Gloriana, Ben."

"Yes, that were the name, although for what I could remember it, it might have been the Glory Polly as the Glory Anna. Well, there was our young luff here, him as is third on this bark, has some palaver with the officer about surrendering; but the young chap only laughs at our luff—a fine clean-built young chap he was too, about as clean as ever shipped a pair of swabs. Well, howsomever, there was a lot of guns went off all of a sudden: the werry polite, nice-spoken young officer takes Anchor-Jack up under his arm, and flies right up over the blue smoke as come from the guns aboard his craft, and when the breeze lifted the smoke, they were all gone, ship and all."

"What!" exclaimed the incredulous Tom Cox; "d'ye mean to say the young officer flew up among the rigging with Anchor-Jack under his arm?"

"Do I mean to say so?" said old Ben; "well, consarn your carcass, of course I do! Why, didn't I hear the young chap cry out, and when I looked there they was flying up like a pair of seagulls! and Anchor Jack was a kicking out like as though the young officer's fingers was hot, and burnt him through?"

Tom Cox looked at Bill Jinks and whistled, and Bill Jinks looked at Tom Cox and likewise whistled, and old Ben, scrambling to his feet, left the forecastle, growling:

"May I be stationed astarn a lumbering convoy, may I never see grog for a week, or have a run ashore for five years if ever I tells another bit about that young chap and Anchor Jack! *Why, they don't believe it!* when I seed it——hallo!"

Old Ben tumbled over one of the watch, who was asleep on the deck, and the man, siting up, rapped out a few blessings upon old Ben's eyes and limbs.

Ben heard him not, but went on his way muttering—

"May old Bedgerbag* marry me to a maremaid if I ever tells them a word again. Why, *they won't believe me.*"

It was the third lieutenant's watch, and as he paced to and fro in the soft morning light and gazed alternately from the surface of the ocean to the towering sails and cordage of the majestic battle-ship, who can say but the enthusiastic young fellow's mind already felt a glimmering of the great future which was to reward his ceaseless study and enthusiastic love for the noblest profession in the world?

A young lad was by his side—a fair-haired, ruddy-cheeked, laughing youngster, whose light form seemed more fitting to be under a mother's care than to brave the rough hardships of a sea-boy's career, and the chance of meeting the foeman's steel and bullet.

They had been relieving the tediousness of the last hour of the watch by talking over the singular events which befell young Nelson when he had charge of the Sandy Hook.

The boy listened to his companion's words with the deepest interest; and when the story was finished, he looked up into his companion's face and said—

"You must be very brave, or you would have felt afraid when you were placed in such peril."

"Afraid!" said the third officer; "I never knew the meaning of the word fear."

"I hope I never shall," said the boy; "it must be nice never to know what fear is."

The young officer placed his hand upon the boy's shoulder, and kindly said—

"Wait a little time, Oram. You are brave enough for your years, or you would not have chosen the life you have. Listen to me, young gentleman, and follow my advice, and you will do well."

"I will try to follow any advice you may please to give me, Mr. Nelson."

"There are three things which you are constantly to bear in mind—first, you must implicitly obey orders, without attempting to form any opinion of your own respecting their propriety; secondly, you must consider every man as your enemy who speaks ill of your King; and

* Neptune

thirdly, you must hate a Frenchman as you do the devil."

"I will bear these things in mind, sir."

"Do, and you will not regret the profession you have chosen."

One of the look-outs gave notice of the approach of a sail to windward of the Bristol, and the midshipman handed the lieutenant the glass.

A white speck soon rose above the distant horizon, and in less than an hour the seamen who were gathered at the vessel's side could make out with the naked eye a copper-built vessel approaching the man-of-war.

"She are a beauty, she are," said Bill Jinks, "or she wouldn't have come up with us in this style."

"No," said a seaman, "it ain't every craft afloat as can do much with the Bristol in the way of sailing; but this one will soon pass us like a hare passes a tortoise."

Ben Tompion kept his eyes fixed upon the stranger, and moved away from his messmates, in order, as he mentally observed, to take his "observations on the quiet."

"Hallo, Ben, my hearty!" said the captain of the after-guard, "what do you think of her? She are a witch on the water, eh, old hoss?"

"She do go pretty quick," said Ben slowly, "but if I hain't seen her afore somewhere, I'm not Ben Tompion."

"Where have you seen her Ben? She looks to me like one of the lavender and rose-water crafts what hangs about Spithead, and waits on the admirals and all them big fellows; tell you what, Ben, that's where you've seen her."

"No, Bill, I'm not one of your fair weather sailors; rough and smooth, man and boy, I've been afore the mast for nigh a lifetime, and but little of the lazy holiday vessels has come to my share; it's out in the salt waters I've seen this craft, or else I've never seen her at all."

"She are a easy one to remember," said Bill Jinks, "if she always carries that white duck aloft. I've seen some queer fancies in the way of dressing a barky, but——"

"There goes the private signal," said old Ben, "so belay your jawing tackle, and see if she answers the private signal."

The flag officer was by this time on deck; and while chatting with his subordinate, he gave the signal-man brief directions, and watched the ready way in which the stranger replied.

"What name and number?" Sir Peter asked; "surely not forty; why that is the Chloe."

"Yes, Sir Peter," said the quartermaster, and he asks permission to come alongside, for last night's gale has started the water barrels I expect."

"Have the ship brought to," said Sir Peter to his lieutenant; "come quartermaster, hoist the answering signal, and let the Chloe know we await her pleasure."

"I understood that the Chloe was on secret service," said the doctor, addressing the admiral, "somewhere off the coast of Sierra Leone."

"Danby may have a roving commission," Sir Peter answered; "otherwise he would not be in these parts—what for goodness' sake has he been doing with his canvas?"

"Trying to imitate the rig of a light ship," said one of the lieutenants, "if I am any judge."

"What's the matter with the Chloe's figure-head?" laughed a young mid to one of his messmates. "It seems as though her captain was afraid it would take cold, for he has wrapped it well up in canvas."

"A bit of Bond-street gilding and painting, I expect," said another mid; "I remember the figure when the Chloe lay in the roads, the whole fleet used to laugh at the queer-looking old woman, and our captain—I was aboard the Zealous then—used to say Commander Danby had had his figure-head painted from one of those sixpenny china ornaments."

"Very likely," another young gentleman remarked, "as we have nothing over our stern except a coat of arms, the captain of the Chloe does not like to show all his paint and gilding for fear of making us feel jealous."

The subject of these remarks had by this time come abeam of the Bristol, and her graceful proportions and high rakish masts formed a strange contrast to the large man-of-war.

Her sails were smartly taken aback as she brought to, and as the English colours floated over her stern a boat was seen to fall from the davits.

"Hem," said Sir Peter, "Danby keeps his men in good order—pretty smart—pretty smart."

"The boat was soon near enough the Bristol for the officers and men to see the faces of those who were seated on the thwarts.

"I don't see Danby," began Sir Peter. "Who is that fellow who sits in the stern ——"

"Him as flew away with Anchor-Jack," shouted old Ben Tompion; "—— my toplights if it ain't!"

The words were heard by the officers on the quarter-deck, and Lieutenant Nelson jumped upon a carronade, and turning to Sir Peter, said:

"The man is right; this is Parker Neville."

ANCHOR JACK MADE PRISONER.

"The audacious scoundrel!" said Sir Peter. "Call away the marines; we'll teach him to play his tricks with a line-of-battle ship."

But for the third lieutenant standing upon the gun, and thus rendering himself perfectly visible to the boat's crew, the daring privateersman would in all probability have been captured.

The desperate games Parker Neville used to play caused him to be always on the alert, and when he recognised the prize officer of the Sandy Hook, and saw the gleam of the marines' bayonets as they were mustered at the side, he gave the rowers orders to pull the boat back to the vessel as quickly as possible.

"For your lives," he said, "pull, or we shall have a lump of iron in the midst of us."

The seamen pulled like men who where used to sudden emergencies; the strokes of their oar blades were not hurried, neither was there any apparent confusion amongst them as the boat sped towards the low-hulled vessel.

"Give him a shot—capture the boat. Quick men, quick," said the admiral angry; "aloft, sail-trimmers—attend to the guns, Mr. Nelson,"

The orders were given hurriedly, and were obeyed in the same manner; so when the gun was fired the shot went wide of the mark.

CHAPTER XXIV.

THE WASP FALLS INTO BAD COMPANY.

"THANK you," said Parker Neville, as the shot from the Bristol plunged into the water about half a cable's length from his ship; thank you!"

He ran nimbly up the side, and the next in command, as soon as Neville and the boat's crew reached the deck, gave orders for the yards to be squared, and the vessel's head, swinging slowly off as the breeze began to fill the sails, was soon gliding through the water.

The sail-trimmers had stood with their hands upon the ropes they were to handle; thus the Wasp, although she had to wait for the return of the boat, was in motion quite as soon as the line-of-battle ship.

The captain of the long gun, which stood upon a circular transverse amidships, was at his post directly he saw the boat about to return; and by the time the privateersman got on board, the gunners had loaded the long tube, and were standing with ramrod and sponge in hand, ready to obey the orders of their desperate and fear less leader.

The captain of the gun stood match in hand, and as a second shot came from the Bristol and cut away part of the shrouds he looked towards his leader.

Parker Neville made a slight gesture with his hand, a loud report, followed by a grim laugh from the lawless crew, told how well the shot had been aimed.

"You've scattered the group on the quarter-deck of yonder elephant, Thompson," said Neville; "give them another before it is too late, and hear, you Anchor Jack, haul down the flag."

Sheet-Anchor made no attempt to obey this order.

"Harkee, my lad," said Parker, "you can go too far. Were I to do my duty I should have you started upon that job with a rope's end."

"You forget," Jack said, "that I do not belong to your ship. I am a prisoner here, and you can scarcely expect me to disgrace the flag under which I have served and still belong to."

Another hand lowered the English colours, as the privateersman turned angrily upon his heel and walked aft.

"If you were not destined to become very useful," he muttered, "I would take the rebellious spirit out of you or flog the flesh from your back. The whelp! I saw the disappointment he felt because I was not captured."

"A narrow escape, sir," said the first lieutenant of the Wasp, as his superior stepped on the quarter deck; "was it one of our old friends?"

"Not the ship, Grant, but there was a fellow on board I did not expect to have the pleasure of meeting."

"But you did not——"

"Go on board? No, Tom Grant. I saw the prize officer of the captured American standing out in such a capital relief against the vessel's canvas that I knew it would be quite as well to pay my respects to another of his fat Majesty's ships."

"It's very provoking," said Grant, "for we cannot be far from the convoy."

"Not far, but there is a chance of falling in with another man-of-war; from her officers we obtain all the information we require. What's that gone?"

"Only a backstay; those fellows fire too high; well done, Thompson, that shot has broken the trap boats of the sucking admirals."

The privateersman laughed as he said—

"What! has it gone through the gun-room?"

"Yes, and among the crockery, for I saw the youngsters rush below."

A 32-pound shot whizzed over Neville's head as his lieutenant, Tom Grant, ceased speaking.

"They will break something besides crockery," the privateersman said, "unless we get out of range. That liner sails very well."

"She does," Grant answered, "but she would be the devil's craft to overtake us now."

He looked aloft as he spoke, and saw every inch of canvas was bellied out by the wind.

"Cease firing," he said to the captain of the long gun, "and wish them good-bye."

The majestic line-of-battle ship was a beautiful sight as she bore down towards the Wasp, for there was not an inch of her spars, from deck to truck, that was not covered with snowy canvas.

The English flag streamed out gallantly above her huge stern, and the rear-admiral's bunting was floating above the lofty pyramid of sail.

Now and then a puff of smoke came from her bows, and as long as the ships were within range, the Wasp answered her big adversary's guns.

By degrees the shots from the Bristol fell far astern of the light-heeled brigantine; and finally the bow chasers ceased as the rear-admiral saw there was no chance of coming up with the matchless but spiteful Wasp.

A smart run of six hours brought the privateer to the classic waters of the Mediterranean.

"Grant," said the privateersman, "I think it would be as well now to give up all thoughts of that convoy, especially as we are nearing a place where much business may be done."

"The convoy," Grant said, "has become a thing of the past. Your suggestion, I suppose, refers to the Algerine galleys."

"Yes, we may capture one or two if we are careful."

"We may," Grant said, "but the reward is scarcely worth the risk."

"We have always our heels," said the privateersman, "and I doubt very much if the rascally Dey has a galley that could out-sail the Wasp."

"These Arabs," Grant said, "build remarkably fast boats, yet their country does not produce either sails, anchors, ropes, tar, iron, or wood."

"They manage matters very well under these somewhat difficult circumstances," said Neville, "for they find the materials all ready for use."

"How?"

"How, blockhead? why they break up the prizes they take, and make their galleys from the materials thus cut and dried for use."

"Clever fellows," said Grant. "Well, captain, shall we go in towards the coast?"

"Yes, take charge of the little beauty, I shall go below for an hour or so; send that Anchor Jack down to me in a few minutes from this."

The officers saluted each other, and Parker Neville went below, where he was soon after joined by Sheet-Anchor Jack.

"You wished to speak to me, sir," the young sailor said.

"I do—be seated."

"I prefer standing in the presence of my superior."

Parker Neville bit his lip.

"Do as you like," he said, "but answer my questions truly or you may repent it."

"I am not in the habit of telling lies."

"I am glad to hear it, and hope you will adhere to this very commendable habit for the next few minutes. Now, look here, I warn you for your own sake hereafter to tell me as much as you can about your connection with Saul Mason; there must be more than I have heard."

"I have told you all I know," Jack answered; "more I cannot tell."

The privateersman looked full at the young mariner as he said:

"It is for your own interest I ask these particulars."

"And," Jack said, "were you to make me an admiral I could not tell you more than I have already."

The privateer tapped the table with his fingers for a few moments.

"You never knew any other name than that of Jack?"

"No other."

"Saul never by chance applied a surname to it?"

"Never; if there was any reason to keep my surname a secret, Saul Mason is about the last to betray himself."

Tom Grant knocked at the cabin door and put an end to the conversation by saying:

"There is a large galley bearing down upon us, sir."

The privateersman snatched his sword from the table and ran on deck, and when he saw the Algerine galley coming towards his vessel with the speed of a sea-bird, he ordered the drummer to beat to quarters.

The green flag of Islam was flying at the galley's stern, and her low bulwarks showed a host of turbaned desperadoes ready and eager for the fray.

They waited not to open fire from their few guns, nor did they notice the shower of grape which the Wasp poured into them, but taking advantage of the smoke which hung over the vessel the galley shot alongside, and despite the desperate resistance on board the privateer, they swarmed upon the deck.

Their leader carved a passage right to the foot of the mainmast; there he was met by Parker Neville.

Sheet-Anchor Jack folded his arms and watched the conflict between Benardin Allah Bey and the captain of the Wasp, and the lad felt that the triumph of the Moslem would alter his destiny as far as Parker Neville was concerned.

CHAPTER XXV.

THE SULTAN'S TRIBUTE.

THE DEY, although absolute monarch, of that portion of Barbary called Algiers, was compelled, according to ancient usage, to pay an annual tribute to the Sultan.

This tribute consisted of twenty well-grown youths and ten young girls (Christians preferred) and to keep up this yearly tax often caused the Dey, his admiral, and his chief bashaws a deal of trouble.

Benardin Allah Bay had under his control the whole of the Dey's navy, which consisted of about twelve small frigates, about the same number of xebecs—small three-mast vessels peculiar to the Mediterranean—and between thirty and forty swift war-galleys.

This fleet being used solely to collect the dues from all ships that came to hand, or, as ill-natured people assert, for piracy, are seldom or never idle, but are always scouring the seas.

When near the time for the Sultan's tribute to be paid, the whole of these vessels would be out day and night until they had collected the requisite number of fine-grown youths and handsome girls. And fine grown youths and handsome girls not being very plentiful upon the seas, it often took three or four months to accomplish the end in view.

The august Baba-da-Chuk was much perplexed at his master's emotion, and when the Bey recovered his senses, the great Baba learnt the reason of Benardin's peculiar indisposition.

The beautiful girl had been given over to the care of the Bey's many wives by Baba, and they, regarding her as another acquisition to the harem, were particularly kind and affectionate to her, as may be supposed they would be—for the gentler sex, as a rule, are so loving to strangers—especially as they imagine the young stranger was about to become their rival in the affections of their lord and master the great—the strict—the mighty Benardin Allah Bey.

"What think you, Sandy?" said his master when he had opened his mind to the great Baba; "what can I do? Come, you have helped me out of many a scrape with that long head of yours. Tell me what I can do for the best."

They were in the Bey's private room; therefore both spoke in their native tongue, and without that reserve they were compelled to use when in the presence of the guards or the captains of the Corsair fleet.

Baba-da shook his sage head, and rubbed his nose, as those that were the seat of wisdom, before he answered—

"Well, it is awkward—very awkward; but something may be done if we are very careful."

"Careful? Surely I will be as careful, Sandy, as a thief robbing a hen-roost is careful not to disturb the old rooster. Come, Sandy, tell me your plan, for I see you have one by the expression on your honest face."

Baba-da-Chuk smiled at the compliment, and cast a sly look at the reflection of his long visage, which was shown in an oval mirror, set into the panel of the room.

"I've two plans," he said: "one is to substitute another girl for yours—for the young leddie."

"Yes, yes," said the Bey eagerly; "but how is the substitution to be made?"

"Well, easy enough," said Baba; "suppose you send the young Spanish girl one of your galleys captured last week."

"You are a fool, Sandy."

"Eh—a fool?"

"Yes, an arrant ass."

"How is that?"

"Why, has not the Spanish girl eyes as dark as sloes, and hair as black as the raven's wing?"

"Well, what of that?"

"Everything. Has not the Dey seen Milly, and noticed her golden hair and blue eyes? Think you I can so easily deceive him?"

"Well, you might try; if he noticed it, say her hair and eyes had changed colour, because she has been greeting so."

"No, Sandy, that will not do."

"Well, there is another plan. The time is close nigh to send the youths and girls to the Sultan; you might persuade the old sinner to send Miss Milly to the Commander of the Faithful."

"Why that would be worse—ten times worse—than giving her to the Dey."

"Yes," Sandy said, "if she got as far as Constantinople."

"Go on, Sandy, speak out; but first reach me that short-necked bottle."

"Suppose," Sandy said, handing his master the bottle, "he consents to send her to the Sultan—and he can well spare her from his harem—you could not, I suppose, overtake the ship she would be in, and take her——"

"You must be mad. What would be the consequence? The captain would make the affair known, and I should taste the bowstring. No, Sandy, depend upon it, the captain would not run the risk of losing his head through me."

"I should not give him the chance."

"How would you manage?"

"Just this," said Sandy. "I would board his vessel at night; take the young leddie away and send a shot into the craft just below the water line."

"Ah! that sounds better. Well, but about my own men? It would never do to trust them."

"Man your vessel with negroes: they would not chatter—at least, if they did, it would not matter, for you could send them to Berea—there they would be well out of the way, for the Bereans would soon seize upon them and sell every mother's son for slaves. A lot of rascals these Bereans, master."

"Yes, Sandy, great rascals. Well, I will think over your plan, and see if I cannot manage it; that is, if the old vagabond will consent."

"I think he will, especially if you back your

request by a present of a case of that particular drink we have set aside for our particular use."

He helped himself to a glass of that particular liquid, and watched the face of Benardin, who had sunk into a deep reverie.

"With a little modification," Benardin said at last, "I think we shall be able to save the poor child. Give me my sabre, Sandy, and have a horse ready. I will at once to the Dey."

Sandy assisted his master to dress, and, while doing so, excited Benardin's ambition by his wily words.

"Suppose," he said, "the rascally old man should insist upon having the little leddie, what shall we do then?"

Baba-da-Chuk invariably coupled himself with the Bey.

"Do?" Benardin said fiercely, "do not ask me. The bare thought drives me nearly mad."

"Still, it may come to that, and it is as well to be prepared."

"He shall not have her," Benardin said, breaking away, and pacing the chamber. "I would sooner slay her with my own hand."

"Yes, and get bow-stringed for doing it. That won't do, Bey."

"Life would be bitter without her, Sandy."

"Aye, it would be unnatural if you did not think so, after finding her so strangely."

"Her appearance was indeed strange, and the story of the wreck still stranger. Sandy——"

He caught his man by the arm as he stopped in his hasty walk, then as suddenly released his grip, and strode forward, muttering:

"No, he could not, would not, do such a villainous thing."

Baba heard the muttered words, and drily answered:

"When a man has been wicked all his lifetime, he does not improve as the years roll on."

"Good, Sandy."

"Well, well, I hope it is so; although he was always a canny hand, and would not stop at trifles—but about the Dey, master, what is to be done if he will stick to his bargain?"

"There is but one thing."

"That, master, I read in your angry face—you will resist."

"Aye, and from the deck of my ship batter the town about his ears."

"That is but a rash thing to do—very rash."

"Am I to see the child—but there I am a fool to talk thus; I should await the end of the coming interview."

"Which will be as I prophesy," said Baba-da-Chuk, "and as it would not do for us to return to England yet, it would of course not do to oppose the Dey's wishes, and as for using the guns of your vessel when you have the little leddie aboard, that would not do."

"Why?"

"Because your ship would be soon taken, if not by some of your own captains who are jealous of your power, it would by the English or French cruisers."

"What are you drifting at, you long-legged thief?"

'Just this," Sandy said, "the best and easiest of all things would be to depose the Dey."

"Ah?"

"And just now is a good time, for the chia bashaws and the basheldas are getting tired of the old man, and many of them like you very well."

"He has been good to us, Sandy."

"That's true, but you cannot give up the blue-eyed little leddie for all that."

"I do not intend to; but we will talk of this when I have spoken with him. In the meantime, you can try and ascertain how it should stand with the chia bashaws, and whether a growl or Allah Bemish would be my reception if circumstances came to the worst with the Dey. Of course," he added "I am sure to be elected, and the great Baba would have to be made prime vizier."

"We could do the business of Dey and chief minister of state between us," said Baba, "and do it well, too."

They were walking towards the gates of the Bey's house as Baba spoke; at the gate Benardin mounted on a white Arab steed which was waiting for him, and followed by a train of attendants and a score of his mounted bodyguard, he rode slowly towards the Dey's palace.

The meaning of the words used by Benardin needs a little explanation.

At the elections of the Dey a body of officers called the douwan or common council, gather the votes, and the chief Aga proposes to the assembly the name of the man they wish to elect.

The name is taken up by the chia bashaws, a rank equal to our colonel; the name is again echoed by four men called basheldas, and by them the question is repeated to every member of the council, whether they will have the individual proposed for a chief.

Now these basheldas, if they do not like the man who is proposed to fill the vacant office, or to depose a reigning Dey, make a loud grumbling noise as they put the question to the members of the douwan.

The Aga, the President, soon ascertains by the loudness of this grumbling noise how much chance the individual proposed has of being the elect; but should the majority be in favour of the election, the new Dey is saluted with the words "Allah Bemish," which means, "God bless and prosper you."

The new Dey, immediately upon taking office, strangles all the members of the douwan who opposed his election, and fills up their places with those who were most zealous in his cause.

Under such a form of government, as may be expected, the Deys all reach the throne by intrigue and bloodshed, and as a rule they are deprived of their power by the same means' for scarcely one Dey in a dozen ever dies a natural death.

Baba-da Chuk had long aspired to seeing his master on the Algerine throne; and, unknown to the Bey, he had been waiting for months to gain the goodwill of those upon whom the elevation of a new ruler mainly depended.

CHAPTER XXVI.

THE FOLLOWERS OF THE FAITHFUL GET THE WORST OF IT.

Benardin Allah Bey found his brilliancy, the Dey, in a most unpleasant humour. The old gentleman had partaken very freely of the forbidden liquor on the previous night, and in consequence of his august legs forming the letter X when he endeavoured to reach his bedchamber, his effulgency had tumbled backward down the marble stairs, and grazed the skin off his superlative back.

In addition to the disagreeable sensations about the region of his spine, the Dey was afflicted with an intolerable thirst, a disagreeable headache and a general seediness of feeling, which gave his brillancy's not usually good temper a turn for the worst.

He kicked his slaves right and left; threatened to bowstring his ministers, and swore he would put all his wives in sacks, and throw them into the sea.

A slave who brought him a cup of sherbet had the glass vessel broken over his head for his pains, and fled howling from the presence; then the Dey executed a *pas seul* indicative of the mood he was in. At its conclusion he sank upon a cushion and cursed the Bey for sending him the fiery liquor, and the Franks, for making it, and himself for drinking it.

He had arrived at this point, when a trembling slave announced the arrival of Benardin Allah Bey.

"Show the dog in," growled the Dey, "show him in, and by the beard of the Prophet, I will teach him to throw dirt in my face."

The Dey's language was a figurative one, but how he could reconcile the metaphor he used with the cause of his present disagreeable sensation is a matter for proposed research.

From the vizier, from the pipe-bearer, from the captain of the Dey's body-guard, Benardin heard of the unpropitious frame of mind his most excellent master was in; and to the surprise of those functionaries, the Bey, instead of turning pale, and retreating from the palace only smiled and bid the vizier lead on to the presence.

Benardin shrewdly guessed the cause of the Dey's ill-humour, and, so far from it deterring him from facing the old savage fellow, he looked upon it as one of the luckiest things that could have happened.

He entered the chamber alone, for the grand vizier having tasted the Dey's slipper more than once during the morning, prudently kept in the rear.

Prostrating himself humbly, first touching his breast, then his forehead, and uttering the usual Oriental salutation of "Allah Bemish," he waited in the lowly attitude he had assumed until the Dey spoke.

His high serenity saw the cause of all his trouble before him, and his little bear-like eyes blazed with anger as he looked around for some thing portable to hurl at the Bey's head.

There was nothing suitable in the chamber in consequence of the crusty old fellow having thrown all he could conveniently lift at the skulls of his attendants and ministers of state before the Bey's arrival.

"Well, dog," he spurted out at last, "have you come to laugh at my beard?"

"On my head be it, my master," answered the Bey, "if I came but to ease thy mind of the trouble that is upon it."

"Ha, dog! What knowest thou of my disorder?"

"That which those who love thee can read on thy face."

The Dey tugged at his grizzled beard for a few moments, as he debated whether or not the Bey was merely playing the hypocrite, or was sincere in his profession.

"And what," he growled, "canst thou do to give my mind ease, and my body free from pain? Thou art no hakim."

"I am not, as thou sayest, a physician," said Benardin; "but I can ease thy mind, if not thy body. Here, O light of the universe, drink of this, and my head shall answer for it if thy mind is not the better."

"Your head shall answer for it," growled the

Dey; "if this drink does not allay my burning thirst, and give my head freedom from pain."

"So be it, O Great Master of the Universe."

Benardin gave the Dey a flask filled with the particular liquor set aside by Baba-da-Chuk for their private use.

Tho Bey guzzled the contents of the flask then smacked his lips and said:—

"This drink, O Bey, is of a strangely similar taste to that which you sent me."

"Your mightiness is mistaken," said the Bey, "the flavour of the wine is still in thy mouth. No, great Bey, this is a draught the secret of whose preparation I learnt from a Christian slave, and lest others should enjoy the nectar that I have prepared solely for thy use, I caused the rascal to be sent into the interior."

"Then you have none of this drink?"

"But little, O Dey, for the time taken in perfecting its flavour, and the difficulty of obtaining the materials, render the possession of but a small quantity quite impossible."

"By my beard," said the Dey, "I would give the fairest and best of my wives for a supply of such goodly drink."

The Bey's eyes brightened.

"It might be obtained, O Bey," he said, "if we could but traffic with a certain Jew of Oran, who alone possesses the materials for the manufacture of the coveted drink, and he," the Bey added, "will only take fair-haired and blue-eyed maidens in exchange."

"He shall have them, O Bey. Have we none that will answer the purpose?"

THE MOSLEMS GET THE WORST OF IT.

"But one," the Bey answered, in rather a shaky voice, "and she has been chosen by your highness to send to the Sultan as a portion of the tribute now nearly due."

The Dey stroked his beard and reflected.

"My faithful Benardin," he said, after a pause, "has erred. I said not that the maiden should go towards the tribute. I have willed it that she should become one of our wives."

"I am humbled in thy presence," the Bey said, "yet I could tell your highness the hour and the night when you gave me the orders to guard her for the Sultan. It was at the time thou first tasted of the Frank's liquor; nevertheless, if it is thy pleasure she should be sent to the Jew of Oran, thy servant has but to obey thy wish."

"That would be of the two the better," said the Dey; "for the possession of the maiden would but cause some jealousy among my wives, and the bartering her for a supply of the liquor I have just tasted would be a joy such as the faithful seldom possess."

"Thy wishes are law. To-night she shall be sent to the Jew of Oran, and by the hour when the sun glows on the minarets, thou shalt have a plenteous supply of the liquor; for now I remember the dog of a Jew has the secret as well as thy servant, and he will, at my bidding, send thee a small cask. But touching this tribute," he added, suddenly changing the conversation for fear the Dey should alter his mind—"this tax to the Sultan?"

"A thousand curses upon the Sultan!" said the Dey, "and may a jackass sit upon his father's grave."

"The tribute is unjust," said the Bey, falling in with his master's humour; "yet it must be paid, and we have not at this hour one youth or maiden to send."

"To sea, then, Benardin," growled the Dey, "and collect the tribute; let me see all thou mayest get before sending them away."

"On my head be it!"

"But do not forget the Jew of Oran, Benardin."

"I will not, most gracious master."

"And," said the Dey, "if thou hast a little more of the goodly liquor, send it at once, for one draught has cured my throat of its consuming fire; therefore, it is not too much to hope that a second would replace the skin I have lost off my back by slipping down the accursed steps."

Benardin Allah Bey had to bow very low to hide the smile upon his face.

"It can but be tried, O great master," he said; "thy servant will see that the Jew of Oran sends a bountiful supply, and, in the meantime, any of the goodly liquor that I possess shall be yours. I will send it by the hand of my faithful Baba-da-Chuk."

"Do so, O Bey, and thy face and the face of thy servant will be white in our presence."

Benardin backed out of the chamber, and the Dey reclined upon the soft cushions of the divan, and closing his eyes, muttered:

"A useful and good servant is this Benardin Allah Bey, but if all my faithful ministers tell me is true, the dog would aspire to our throne. If once I have good proof of this, there will be one renegade the less."

"So far, so well," thought the Bey, as he rode slowly homeward. "I have baffled the cunning of this old villain, and Milly is mine—mine—mine."

He laughed hysterically, and much astonished the grave pipe-bearer who followed in his rear.

"Baba, the long throated thirsty thief, will not be over well pleased at the agreement I have made," muttered Benardin, "for I must give up all the rich old port Sandy has set aside for our use. Well, it cannot be helped. Lucky for my poor girl that the Dey took a wee drap too much last night; still luckier he does not understand the nature of wines or spirits, or my ready lie about the Jew of Oran would not have been of much use."

Arrived at his house the Bey was met by Baba, and much to the long gentleman's surprise his master ordered him to take as many bottles as he could carry of the rich wine to the Dey.

Baba lifted up his eyes, then rubbed his chin, where a few hairs stood out defiantly, and said:—

"Good Lord!"——

"Well, you growling porridge-bred son of a sea-cook, what is the matter?"

"Naething—naething. Oh Lord! six or or seven at the very least of the good old ——"

"Be off with you."

"Well, well, don't be in a hurry. What about——"

"Everything is all right. I will explain another time. Do not be away long, for I must be off to sea at once. Where's Milly?"

"Among the women, and a fine life they are leading the wee lassie."

"Are they?" said Bernardin fiercely. "Send Aztuff the eunuch to me."

Baba shambled out of the chamber, and soon after a powerful black, dressed in a rich costume, entered.

"My lord sent for his slave," folding his arms across his breast; "he is here."

"Listen, Aztuff," said Bernardin, "there is a young maiden of the Franks in thy charge."

"It is so, master—one of the fair face—yet she pines as the caged dove that has lost its mate."

"Place her apart from the women," said the Bey; "there is a suite of rooms facing the sea, let her have them, and place slaves at her command. On thy head be her safety and seclusion from the women of the harem."

"On my head be it, great lord."

The Nubian backed out of the chamber, then Benardin struck a small gong, and a boy answered the summons.

"Hie thee to the captain of the Fezi Baria (Pride of the Sea), and tell him to prepare for my coming; we must to sea before the sun sinks beyond the west. Tell him also to have ten row galleys and four xebecs ready to accompany my ship."

The boy went upon his mission, and the Bey paced to and fro the apartment, his face expressive of the most intense joy.

"Shall I," he thought, "make all known to the poor girl before I leave? No, I may never return, therefore it will be but rendering her wretched should an unlucky shot put my life out. No, the best plan will be for me to leave directions with Sandy; he can take her to England should anything happen to me."

For the guidance of Baba-da-Chuk, the Bey made out a long list of directions respecting the money and other valuables he had secreted away, and how the wealth was to be placed for the use of the young girl who had so strangely fallen into his hands.

By the time he had finished writing, Baba returned, looking very red in the face, and his gait anything but steady.

"Why, you guzzling thief, could you not take those bottles to the Dey without breaking one on the road?"

"Look here," said Baba, "the Dey is a jolly old chap, a brick, and a man made of the right stuff."

"Hallo," said the Bey, "what has worked this change, Sandy? Why, it is only a short time since that you were advising me to depose him."

"Well," Baba answered, "I may have said that, but when a man asks you to share such stuff as that with him it makes a great difference."

"It does. What was the old fellow's opinion of the wine?"

"I left him finishing the last bottle but one, and he invoked the blessing of Mahomet upon our heads for the present."

"Did he? Now get me my Damascus sabre and silver-mounted pistols, and when I have gone aboard look at this paper, and should I not return, follow the instructions you will find written out for you."

An hour later and the Bey was on board his ship, which soon stood out from the land, followed by the light-heeled row of galleys and xebecs.

The Fezi Baria was a swift sailer, and soon distanced her attendants, and long before night set in she ranged alongside the Wasp.

The Algerine corsairs, although led by their redoubtable leader, were unable to keep a footing upon the deck of the privateer.

Thrice they were beaten back, each time to return to the charge with a determination to vanquish the privateer.

Once the two leaders stood face to face and crossed their blades. What the result of that fierce combat would have been it is hard to say, for both were men who understood the weapon they carried, and both fought well, for they knew the fate of the day rested upon the fall of one of the leaders.

When they were putting forth every known cut and guard, the sudden rush of the Algerines as they were driven back by the privateer's crew, separated the leaders, and Benardin Allah was carried back in the tide of fugitives to the deck of his own ship.

Enraged at his defeat and anxious to take the vessel, he raved and swore at his men like a lunatic.

He had caught sight of Sheet-Anchor as the lad stood with folded arms watching the combat, and he rushed to capture the young sailor, no matter what the cost might be.

Sheet-Anchor and a young officer of the Wasp Benardin saw, would be most acceptable presents for the Sultan; and as the collection of the tribute was a matter of more import than plunder, he rallied his men for another attack.

The grapnels were yet fast, and the sides of the vessels rolling together prevented either of them using their guns, or the superior weight of metal carried by the Algerine would have soon settled the matter.

"Followers of the faithful," the Bey said, "you have got the worst of it so far. Bring hither the green flag, quartermaster, and let all true Moslems follow the sacred banner; and remember, those who fall will together sup in Paradise, attended by dark-eyed houris more beautiful than even the Frankish maidens."

The speech was not much, but it suited the purpose, for the Moslems, with a yell, dashed forward and leaped upon the privateer's deck.

CHAPTER XXVII.

SHEET ANCHOR JACK MADE PRISONER.

The swarthy-visaged corsairs were received by a close volley, which sent many of them to taste of the joys promised by the Bey.

The volley of small arms was followed by an advance of the privateteersmen, armed with boarding pikes and cutlasses.

The Moslems were checked for a moment, but Benardin cheered them onward. He was savage at the loss of life his men had sustained, and to arouse the ferocity of his followers, he shouted, "Allah, Akbar! follow me here, and one half of the value of this ship is yours."

"Rally, men," Parker Neville shouted; "meet them, meet them, and give the scoundrels a taste of an Englishman's steel."

The hardy crew, obedient to their leader's voice, stood shoulder to shoulder, and met the savage Arabs upon the points of their weapons.

"Remember Paradise and the dark-eyed houris," roared Benardin, "and down with the Christian dogs."

The Bey set a good example to his men, for he leapt from the Wasp's bulwark right in the midst of the privateteer's men.

His blade of tempered steel struck their pike-stuffs as though they were reeds, and many fell beneath his sinewy arm.

For some moments the Moslems had the advantage, and the crew of the Wasp were forced to retreat to raised the poop.

The thirst for plunder was stronger than even the high authority of the Bey, for his followers began to disperse and run below, each man wishing to be first to handle the riches supposed to be below deck.

A few stood only by their leader, and with these Benardin followed up his advantage, but before a Moslem foot could touch the quarter-deck a light gun crammed with grape was fired amongst them.

The discharge of the gun struck down the greater portion of the men who had stood by the Bey, and the latter seeing his perilous position sprang back in time to escape a volley of small arms the privateer's men poured in from their advantageous position.

"Cast off the grapnels," said Parker Neville. "Cast off, and we have them in a trap."

With the ferocity of a wounded tiger, the Bey stood and opposed his single blade to the men who ran forward to execute this order.

He would have held his ground against a host at that moment, for he heard the excited shouts of the men in the row galleys and the zebecs as the light craft swept towards the Wasp.

Parker Neville saw his peril; he knew if the swarm of Arabs once reached his deck capture or death was certain.

"Follow me," he said, "follow me!"

He sprang from the quarter-deck as he spoke, and his hardy crew were at his heels, and in spite of the Bey and a few men who had run up from below, the grapnels were cast off, and the ship, feeling the breeze, began to move slowly through the water.

"To your ship," said the Bey; "up, up from below there, or you are lost."

His voice was heard above the groans of the wounded, the curses of the dying, and the sharp reports of matchlock, pistol, and musket, and the eager plunderers who were below came swiftly to the deck.

They were too late to regain their vessel, for the light wind had already separated the Wasp from the Fezi Baria.

There was a gulf between them of more than twenty yards, and as the Arabs stood for a moment confused by the sudden change in affairs, four of the privateer's men were seen busily reloading the light gun on the quarter deck.

There was no time for hesitation; in another moment the charge of grape would sweep the deck from the mizenmast to the bowsprit.

The Bey uttered a few words in Arabic, and, followed by his men, he jumped to the bulwarks, and from thence into the sea.

Sheet-Anchor Jack stood in the Bey's path, and before he could save himself he was clutched by the hair and toppled overboard, and when he arose to the surface, Benardin stretched forth his hand and gripped the young sailor by the collar.

The men on board the Fezi Baria edged in towards the swimmers, and the matchlock men on board the row galleys and zebecs poured in a volley of balls to cover the escape of their countrymen.

Luckily for the Bey and his party this volley gave the privateers enough to do to reply to the guns of the Fezi Baria, and the swivels in the zebecs and row galleys opening fire, caused Parker Neville to use the better part of valour, for he knew a stray shot might cripple his rigging, and leave him at the mercy of the corsair horde.

Impelled forward by every art in handling the sails, the Wasp glided away, and when at a safe distance from her swarm of foes, her long brass carronades began to reply to the fierce fire she had sustained.

The scene had been so exciting, and had passed so quickly, that Sheet-Anchor scarcely knew what had occurred until he found himself upon the Fezi Baria's deck.

The Bey raged like a demon when he regained his ship, and tried by every means in his power to come up with the light-heeled Wasp

The swift vessel defied his utmost attempts to get closer. Eager to use his guns and as though delighting in having the Bey's anger, her stern-guns sent a shot every now and then through the Fezi Baria's rigging.

An hour had passed in this manner. Then the Wasp, as though tired of tantalising her enemy, spread additional canvas, and soon after her beautiful outline sank below the horizon.

The sun was sinking when the Fezi Baria gave up the chase, and Benardin hoisted a signal for the attendant craft to close in around the Fezi Baria, and while this manœuvre was being performed he caused the officers of his ship to assemble on the quarter-deck and the men to gather below.

There was an evil glitter in his eyes as he looked around at the group of men, and many of their hearts sank when he advanced to the edge of the poop, and said—

"This day have I been disgraced by those who should have stood by me in fair or foul weather. Stand forth, ye dogs, who forgot your duty, and went below in search of plunder and left but a few of the faithful to combat with the dogs on board yonder vessel, whose masts are now sinking below the water's edge."

His searching eye singled out the chief delinquents, and in a peremptory gesture they stepped out to the front, and stood with blanched faces and quivering lips before the stern merciless admiral of the Corsair fleet.

He regarded them savagely for a moment, then striking the hilt of his sabre vehemently, he exclaimed—

"Tie them to the shrouds and bastinado, every dog!"

Six only of the culprits had been singled out by the Bey, and they were tied, feet uppermost, to the shrouds.

"Begin," said the Bey to the men who clung to the rigging by their feet and left hands, their right hand grasping a thick bamboo cane; "begin, and may Allah, the prophet, and the devil, give you strength, or I will have you tied up afterwards."

The hint was sufficient; the men found strength, and every blow that fell upon the naked feet of the miserable culprits was followed by a howl of agony.

Thirty strokes were administered upon the soles of the poor wretches' feet before the Bey gave the signal for the men with the bamboo canes to desist.

When the culprits were taken down, three out of the six had fainted, and to the remainder, as they limped away, the Bey grimly said—

"You dogs, your feet will not be so ready to take you out of the fight in future."

"Allah is fair," murmured one of the sufferers, "and his servant repines not."

"Well," thought Sheet-Anchor, who leant against a gun and watched the fearful punishment, "if this is Arab flogging I would prefer the English mode."

Anchor-Jack's reflections were cut short by the Bey calling out in English—

"Come here, youngster."

The young mariner obeyed, and Benardin continued:—

"What is the name of that vessel we so unceremoniously left?"

"The Wasp."

"Hum! Her captain's?"

"I do not know."

"Mind what you are about, my lad; we have plenty more bamboo sticks left."

Sheet-Anchor's lips were about to give utterance to an angry retort, but a moment's reflection told him the folly of angering a man like the Bey.

He had a natural dread of undergoing the fearful punishment of the bastinado; therefore, with less bravado than was usual with him, he answered—

"I am speaking the truth, for I did not belong to the vessel."

"Explain yourself," the Bey said sharply, "and be quick about it."

"The fellow," Jack thought, "is an Englishman; no Arab could speak our language so fluently as he does."

He told the Bey the story of his connexion with the Wasp; and Benardin, dallying with the amber and jewelled mouth-piece of his pipe, became interested in the lad's recital.

"There must," he said, "have been a special and powerful reason for this."

"There was," Jack said, "a very powerful reason."

"What was it?"

"The captain of that vessel was a scoundrel, and his crew a gang of rascally cut-throats."

"A nice character. Well, what did he do to you?"

"He sank the vessel I was aboard of, and made all who would not join his crew walk the plank.'

"He must have been a scoundrel. Well, what was the name of the vessel?"

"The Gloriana."

"The devil!"

"No; the Gloriana."

"Yes, yes, I know. Was there any others besides yourself saved from the wreck?"

"None."

"Are you certain?"

"So far as this," Sheet-Anchor said, "there were but three of us left when the shattered hull went down, and I only saved myself by clinging to the broken bows."

The Bey sucked his mouthpiece for a few moments, then said:

"Who was the owner of that vessel?"

"She belonged to a Mr. Mason, of Blackwall."

"Ha! Do you know the gentleman?"

"I do. I have good reason to."

"Why?"

"Because I was for many years in his house; in fact, he kept me, as he said, because I had no friends; but from what I know of the man, I do not think it very likely he would do so."

"Indeed! You do not think him generous?"

"Far from it. The man would sell his soul to Satan for money."

The Bey shifted about uneasily upon the soft cushions; then he looked out upon the quiet waters, and from thence to the rigging and sails above him, and, finally, his gaze returned to their starting point, and was fixed upon Anchor Jack's handsome honest face.

"Do you," the Bey asked, and his question caused the young sailor to utter an exclamation of astonishment, "know anything about the young girl who was on board the Gloriana?"

"Do I?" Jack said, and his face flushed crimson. "Do I?—but why do you ask?"

"Because I have reason for so doing."

"But—how?—you cannot have seen her. She went down—down—down—to the depths of the ocean, and I, who would have given my life to have saved hers, was unable to help her."

"She did not require your help, young man."

"Then she is saved?"

"She is not drowned, or I should not have been able to have spoken to you about her."

"True, sir, true. Then she has fallen into—that is, she has been saved by you——"

"Not exactly; yet she is safe and well, and under the care of one whose life will have to answer for her welfare."

"Thank heaven—thank heaven!" said the young sailor, gratefully raising his eyes and clasped hands heavenward, she is saved! Now half the bitterness of that terrible hour has passed away now that I know of her safety."

The Bey watched the young fellow very closely, and mentally remarked—

"Sincere, at any rate. I wonder who he is? he seems a cut above the common seamen of his country."

Sheet Anchor Jack was lost to the position in which he stood as he dwelt upon the joyful intelligence imparted by the Bey—a delicious trance, from which he was awoke by Benardin's sharp voice saying—

"Now will you be good enough to answer my question?"

"I beg your pardon, sir. What was it?"

"Respecting the young girl who was saved from the wreck of the Gloriana?"

"What do you wish to know?"

"All that you can tell me; how she came on board, by whom she was placed there, and to what port or place she was consigned?"

"I knew Miss Mason," Jack said, "to be one of the best and gentlest of her sex. Oh, sir, had you seen, or could words of mine picture, what she suffered at her uncle's hands, you would think as I do."

The Bey clutched the hilt of his scimitar, and drew the blade out a couple of inches, then pushed it back with a snap, and nodded for the young sailor to proceed.

"Her uncle, for such I believe was the relationship that existed between her and the hard cruel man in whose house we were," Jack continued, "never gave either of us a moment's respite from our miserable condition, as recipients of his bounty."

The Bey gave a stifled howl.

"When the Gloriana was ready for sea," Jack said, "I was sent on board as one of the crew, and the young lady as passenger. She was consigned to a Senhor Acides at Santa Cruz ——"

The howl the Bey gave this time was not stifled, far from it, for the fierce sound had such an effect on his obsequious slaves that they bolted down the steps leading from the quarter-deck, and finally disappeared below, as though nothing but instant annihilation could follow the Bey's exclamation of anger.

"I have little more to add," Sheet-Anchor continued. "We were boarded and taken by that vessel from which you escaped by jumping into the sea."

The Bey seemed not to heed the young mariner's words, for he sat with his eyes fixed upon the water, and his face betokened the raging of a volcano of passion in his breast.

From this position he started suddenly, and began to stride to and fro the deck, uttering curses and vows of vengeance against old Saul Mason, but as he used a great many Arabic expressions, the young mariner was not able to glean much from the Bey's strange behaviour, which as yet was an enigma to him.

SAUL MASON IN DIFFICULTIES.

CHAPTER XXVIII.

KORA AILEY, THE APPLE OF LOVE.

The Algerine fleet were four days at sea before they had collected sufficient of the Sultan's tribute to warrant their prows being turned homeward.

From the first day of Jack's captivity, the Bey had not spoken to him, but as he was not placed in confinement, or in any way interrupted by either officers or crew, the young sailor did not find his captivity very irksome.

The strange habits of the Moslems, the many exciting chases he witnessed when the Fez-Baria was in chase of her prey, all tended to beguile the hours, and if these failed, his mind had plenty of employment in endeavouring to solve the connection between Benardin Allah Bey and the rascally old ship-chandler of Blackwall.

When the vessels returned to the harbour, the sun sparkled upon the brilliant arms of the Arabs who had assembled to welcome the return of the Corsair fleet.

Guns were fired from the forts, and all the piratical vessels were gay with flags, for the return of the great Bey with his flotilla was always an object of interest to a population who subsisted chiefly on piracy. The Bey was known as the most successful "collector of duties," and cunning Jew merchants from the adjacent towns stood ready to barter their gold for the conqueror's prizes.

Slave-dealers, too, were there ready to give the Dey a good price for either male or female slaves, for the market for the commodity was large and not over-well stocked.

The Dey was at the landing place, surrounded by his body-guard, and in rear of the white Arab steed he rode there was a silken palanquin containing half-a-dozen of his favourite wives, who were permitted by their gracious lord to satisfy their curiosity by peeping through the curtains at the prisoners.

Amid the clashing of cymbals, the rattle of drums, and the firing of matchlocks (loaded), much to the danger of the crowd, the Bey landed and prostrated himself before his master.

"Rise, O good and faithful servant," said the Dey, "thanks to Allah for sending a favourable wind to bring thee and thy treasures home. Has there been much despoiling of the unbelieving dogs, O good and favoured Dey?"

"Gold and silver stuffs, O my master," said the Dey. "Cloths, spices, tin, iron, brass, sail-cloth, bullets, and lead in bars."

"Allah is good to his children."

"Lemons, rice, sugar," continued the Bey, "quicksilver, cordage, damasks, and the youths and maidens for the Sultan's tribute, together with three vessels, my master, which have fallen to the share of the faithful."

"Allah is great, O Bey. Is there none of the liquor of the grape?"

"Enough, O my master, enough for thy desire until the winds are favourable to waft thy ships again out to sea."

"There is but One God, and he is Allah," said the Dey, and we are his children, and he is good to us—send the youths and maidens ashore first, O Bey, that we may judge of their excellence."

"Thy servant hears, and will obey."

The slave-dealers passed to the front to examine the human merchandise, and when the Christian captives were led and driven to the landing place, the dealers there, not satisfied with looking at the unfortunate creatures, ran forward and drove their fingers against the flesh of those who had any portion of their body exposed.

As ill-luck would have it, Sheet-Anchor was nearly in front of the string of captives, and having his broad muscular chest exposed, one of the Arabs poked his fore-finger against Jack's white chest, and exclaimed:

"Beard of the Prophet, but here is a youth of great price!"

Jack did not understand the Arab's motive nor his words, but his face flushed at the indignity; with one blow of his clenched fist he knocked the Algerine head over heels against the palanquin containing the Dey's favourite wives.

The Arab was a short fat man, and the palanquin only being supported by four slight props, was overturned in a moment, and its fair occupants were tumbled out, a misfortune they did not bear well, considering the shrill cries they raised.

The Arab slave merchant knew the danger he had incurred by overturning the Dey's wives, for according to Moslem law a man must not look upon the face of another man's wife, especially if she or they are the wives of of a Moslem of rank—therefore he took himself quickly out of sight, and left the half dozen to scream and the Dey to rage and belabour the palanquin-bearers with the flat of his scimitar.

Sheet-Anchor knew nothing of Moslem laws, therefore his first impulse was to rush forward and raise one of the fallen ladies in his arms, and as his choice fell upon the handsomest and youngest of the bevy, a yell of horror burst from the assembled Arabs; and, as for the Dey, he was so "taken aback" at the audacious act, that he could only sit over his horse and howl like a hungry hyena.

The youngest and most beautiful of the Dey's harem, Kora Ailey, or the apple of love, did not seem to think the support of the young sailor's arms a place to flee from with horror, for she allowed her head to drop upon his breast as she swooned, or pretended to do so.

By the time the palanquin was raised the Dey had finished a splendid howl, and flourishing his scimitar over his head he spurred forward with the evident intention of taking Jack's head off at one slice.

Sheet-Anchor was unaware of his danger, for the lady was very beautiful, and the diamonds and precious stones with which her dress was enriched was in itself a sight sufficient to take away the breath of a European whose eyes had been wont to gaze upon the cotton and silken-clad dames of his native country.

As the Dey advanced, a couple of the harem guards ran suddenly in front of his effulgence, and without the least tenderness or respect for the jewelled lady, snatched her from Jack's close embrace, and tumbled her inside the palanquin.

The Dey turned his eyes for a minute to

watch the youngest and most beautiful of his numerous houris, as she was placed in safety, and that moment was sufficient for a tall gaunt figure, who stood foremost in the crowd, to clutch Jack by the arm and pull him away from before the horse's head.

"Get among your companion," said the man in English, slightly tinged with the accent nearer north of the Tweed. "Get back, for you have committed a crime punished with death."

Jack fell back more in obedience to the jerk he received from the stranger than of his own free will, for he had clenched his hands preparatory to making an attack upon the pair of blacks who had torn the vision of loveliness from his arms.

The Dey was not to be so easily baulked of his vengeance, for he rode after Jack who had taken his place in the ranks of the captives; but ere he could be reached, the stranger who had done Jack such a signal service, prostrated himself humbly before the mighty and wrathful Dey.

"Most gracious master," he said, "this infidel has but sinned in ignorance; it would be better to give him time to——"

"Out of my path, Baba-da-Chuk!"

"Thy servant hearest; but, O master, listen before thy sword drinks his life. There is but the number of youths for the Sultan's tribute, and——"

"I care not. Yet stay, Baba; let him be brought before me; I will adjudge his punishment when the fire of anger has cooled. On your head be it, Baba-da-Chuk."

"On my head be it, Light of the Universe."

When the nproar occasioned by this incident had subsided, the living portion of the Corsair's booty was marched to a stone building across the palace, and there being a few young girls in excess of the number required for the tribute, they were reserved for the harems of those who could afford to purchase them from the Dey.

The goods were then landed, and a just distribution made.

All the warlike stores went to the Dey, also one third of the booty; another third was Benardin Allah's share, the remainder was given to the officers and men of the fleet, and as ready money was more an object to them than the richest cloths, they were soon busy bartering with the Jews.

The value of the plunder put the Dey in a good temper, for as he rode away, he showered a handful of copper paras (twenty make a penny English currency) among the ragged crowd of rascals, who shouted themselves hoarse with praises of the great, the magnificent, the generous Dey, whose life they hoped would continue for ever, and his shadow never grow less—a circumstance not likely to occur, for the effulgent was growing stouter every day.

When the Dey and his escort returned to the palace, he found Baba-da-Chuk in an ante-room with Anchor Jack.

The young sailor's arms were fastened behind his back, and to render aid in case of need, half-a-dozen of the Dey's spearsmen were near at hand.

From Baba-da-Chuk Jack had learned the enormity of the crime of which he had been so unintentionally guilty, and the great Baba here chimed in by saying:

"I don't know my lad, but you will be better off if the Dey orders your head to be cut off, for there is no knowing what may befall you when you become the Sultan's slave."

Sheet Anchor's life had been one of trouble and but little happiness so far; therefore, he felt less dread of death than many youths of his age would have felt.

"Well," he said, "I have known little worth living for yet, so the Dey's sentence may be as you say, a merciful act."

"It may be so, young man, it may be so; but still, a young fellow like yourself, ought to make a way in the world, especially in this part, or the part where I expect they will be for sending you."

"Who was that beautiful girl I saw to-day?" Jack asked, turning the conversation; "she is very young to be the wife of an old man like that old vagabond."

"She is very young," said Baba; "but that is not much here, for the Dey has about forty wives, and some younger than Kora Ailey."

"The old vagabond!"

"Nay, my young man, rail not at the customs of the country! for who knows—if your head is not taken off by the Dey—but you may rise in the world, and become a man able to keep a dozen wives?"

"The Lord forbid."

"So I said once upon a time, said Baba, "but now—although I am not such a bad-looking fellow as the Dey—I have a dozen handsome lasses—very handsome."

Before Jack could reply, the musical beat of a silver gong was heard.

"It is the Dey's snmmons," said Baba, "so mind, yonng man, what I have told you. Be very humble and obedient, and you may get off, for having the head once taken from your shoulders is not the way to make a young fellow's fortune."

Anchor Jack had read a well-thumbed copy

of the "Arabian Nights," and when he entered the Dey's chamber he fully realised one of the exciting scenes he had been so fond of picturing to himself.

There was one drawback to the harmony of the picture: that was the presence of a gigantic Nubian, who stood in the centre of the chamber with a broad-bladed naked scimitar across his arm.

"The chief executioner," whispered Baba, as they passed the curtain which descended from an alcove.

The Dey was reclining upon a thick Persian carpet; near him knelt a black boy, whose duty it was to keep the imperial pipe alight, and the dexterous manner in which he placed a piece of live charcoal upon the sweet-scented herb was quite a feat of skill, which, to acquire, must have caused many a blister upon his finger and thumb.

To the right of the Dey was a pile of eider-down cushions, covered with blue damask and silver cloth. Upon this reclined the lovely young Kora Ailey, whose employment was shown by the fan she held lightly in her right hand.

The cushions upon which she lay being much higher than her lord and master's carpet, she was considerably above him, and the *arch*, mischievous look she bestowed upon Jack was unnoticed by the savage old Moslem.

She seemed an adept in the use of the fan, for while keeping the flies away from the Dey's face, she so well concealed her own features that she was enabled to bestow upon the handsome sailor many unmistakable glances of admiration

Glancing from the yellow wrinkled face of the old Dey to the frank, honest, boyish features before her, there can be but little wonder the lovely young Arab girl should form conclusions as to which of the two she would prefer.

Jack had been told by Baba that Kora Ailey possessed more influence over the Dey than the whole of the other thirty-nine beauties who filled the harem. This, it may be, accounted for her presence in the audience chamber.

"Baba-da-Chuk prostrated himself so lowly that Jack felt an almost uncontrollable impulse to kick the great Baba.

"Rise, Baba-da-Chuk," said the Dey; "your face is white in our presence. Come behind me that I may hear through thy lips what this dog has to say that I do not kill him."

Baba translated as much of this speech as was necessary, and Jack answered—

"Tell the ugly old thief he can do as he likes, and be ——."

"Keep thy tongue within bounds, young man," said Baba; "keep it while you have one to use, and above all keep your eyes from that pretty face, or it will be the worse for you. The old fellow is in a good temper now, and all may yet be right."

The caution was quite necessary, for the Arab beauty's black eyes were almost too much for the susceptible youth's firmness.

"Gracious lord," said Baba to the Dey, "this infidel has sinned through ignorance of the customs of a country so far above his wretched land, that his eyes were ——"

"But, Baba," interrupted the Dey, "of what avail is this to his unclean hands touching the body of this our wife?"

"The dog says," answered Baba, "that it is the custom in his benighted land, where, would you believe it, O Dey, they believe that women have souls and rights! Master, the unbelieving asses allow their wives to appear before men with their faces uncovered."

"Shade of the Prophet," said the Dey, taking his pipe from his lips in sheer astonishment, "Allah be good to us for opening the eyes of his children. Go on, good Baba."

"I will, O master. This infidel, this eater of the flesh of unclean animals, says it is the custom of his land to aid any women they may see are in want of aid ——"

"What! Baba, if she is the wife of a pacha or chiak bashaw!"

"Even so, mighty Dey, therefore when he saw the lovely Kora Ailey, the light of the harem and the sunshine of thy life, struggling beneath the palanquin, he ran forward and rescued her, thinking by so doing he was making a friend of one at whose frown the thousands that people this land tremble."

"It may be as thou sayest," said old Achmet, "but if I let the dog off I shall have the faithful believe I show favour to those who are not fit to live; but tell me," he added, turning to Kora Ailey, "what is thy wish, sun of my soul, concerning this dog?"

"I had hoped," the beautiful Arab readily answered, "to have seen his head taken off by Mirza, but as the offence is passed I would that he were punished every day he stays here—a punishment that I could see and rejoice at."

"In the name of the Prophet," said the Dey, "How, O Kora, sweet flower of loveliness, can this punishment be carried out?"

"Easily, great lord of my heart," said the Arab beauty, chasing a mosquito from the Dey's nose with her fan, "from the lattice window of my chamber in the Serai, my eyes dwell upon a garden overrun with weeds: let this dog—for these Franks understand the art of gardening full well—be set to work from sunrise till noon-day. Let him clear the garden of all that is foul, and I can feast my eyes upon his sufferings under the red fierce sun. O, lord of my heart, this will be indeed a sweet punishment for me to behold, but a terrible one for the unbelieving dog whose filthy hands have dared to touch Kora Ailey, the apple of her lord's eye, and the sun of his soul."

The bitter emphasis which accompanied these words had their weight with the Dey, and he gave way to her wishes, and Baba-da-Chuk, who watched the beautiful girl's face glow with undisguised pleasure when the Dey gave his permission, felt there was a motive in this that would either lead Jack to fortune or death.

Baba's sage opinion was confirmed when he looked suddenly back as he was marching his prisoner from the room, and saw the look of admiration with which Kora Ailey followed Jack's form.

CHAPTER XXIX.

SAUL MASON BECOMES AN OBJECT OF POPULAR INTEREST.

The Lady Constance, after her husband's funeral retired to a country house in Sussex, and left Captain Henry Jarvis to enjoy his fortune.

The Guardsman was glad to be rid of her presence, for her pale face was a source of discomfort to him, and marred the enjoyment he would otherwise have felt at the position he had so suddenly attained.

He had not yet seen old Saul, and truth to tell he was not in any haste to meet the old rascal who was to receive one-third of his income.

True he had repaid the various sums of money the ship-chandler had advanced, and accompanying the cheque he forwarded to Saul, Henry Jarvis had promised to call soon and arrange about other matters of a more private nature.

As Saul made accumulating gold the chief object of his life, he was glad to receive the money, and as he purred and rubbed his hands over the cheque, he mumbled:

"Hum—hum—hum—can wait for the rest, master Henry—can wait for the rest!—you must pay it—oh! oh; or else old Saul will pull you down faster than you have risen—much faster."

Henry Jarvis knew full well that Saul would claim to a penny-piece the amount of his bond, and the knowledge deprived the possession of his wealth of much of its charm.

"If I could get rid of the old scoundrel I should feel happy," was the thought that crossed his mind twenty times a day, "but how is it to be managed?"

The excitement and the multiplicity of business attendant upon his accession to his brother's title and wealth had driven all recollection of the respectable Mr. Peter Quills from his mind.

One day when he was in hourly expectation of receiving a visit from old Saul, he chanced to turn over some papers, and to his joy, found the letter Ned Blundell had given him the last time he saw that hapless being.

"The very thing," he exclaimed, half frantic with joy; "the very thing. I will at once to the office of this limb of the law; and if matters can be so arranged that I can rid myself of this incubus, it will be a profitable day for Mr. Peter Quills and a joyful one for me."

Sir Henry still retained his commission in the Guards; the duties were very easy and the uniform very attractive to the fair sex. The latter circumstance was alone sufficient to make a vain man suffer a little inconvenience at times, for his duties at the palace of St. James's often interfered with his private engagements.

He had but just come off duty when Ned Blendell's letter fell into his hands, and so eager was the desire to disarm old Saul of the power he possessed, that the handsome Guardsman waited, not to change his suit of scarlet and gold, but sent for a coach and was driven to the office of Peter Quills, attorney-at-law.

"Your name, sir?" inquired a clerk, when the Guardsman passed the green-baize door.

"It is of no importance," said Sir Henry; "you can say on important business; that will be sufficient."

"Thank you, sir; will you take a seat?"

The clerk disappeared through a dingy passage, and after a few minutes' absence, returned, and begged the gentleman in scarlet and gold to walk in.

Mr. Peter Quills was a stout, clerical-looking man; he had the mildest of blue eyes, a high forehead, small mouth, and his teeth, like his linen, were of spotless white.

He looked an honest man—a kind, humane, gentle, tract-distributing sort of gentleman—except when he smiled, then his face lost its pleasing expression, and the aspect of the man underwent a total change.

"Important business, I believe," he said, politely handed his visitor a chair; "most happy, I am sure, to give it the best attention."

The soldier took the seat near Mr. Quills' table; he scarcely knew how to begin the business, for Mr. Quills' benevolent countenance seemed but the reflex of a just and virtuous mind.

"Ned Blendell," he thought, "has formed a wrong estimate of this man's character, for, as far as I can judge, he seems about the last man in London I should suspect of having any dealings with a scoundrel like old Saul."

"We have had some remarkably fine days of late," said Mr. Quills, nibbling a namesake, "very fine days indeed."

He smiled as he spoke, and the soldier, who was a good physiognomist began to alter his opinion of the lawyer.

"Very fine, indeed," said the Guardsman, "I have, that is——"

"Decidedly. Pray do not hesitate to confide in me; a lawyer's private room, you know, is, I may say, like the confessional. So pray, do not hesitate."

"Well," Sir Henry Jervis said, coming bluntly to the point, "my object in visiting you was to ascertain whether you know anything of a person called Saul Mason, of Blackwall."

"Yes; I have a slight acquaintance with him, in fact, have managed very difficult affairs for the gentleman; for, as you may perhaps be aware, he is very speculative, and at times matters do not altogether take the smooth course."

"He is not a particular friend of yours?"

"By no means. I will be candid with you. I have seen him this very morning, and our interview did not end so amicably as it began."

"I am glad to hear it, Mr. Quills, for I have come to ask a favour of you, which you could not grant if you were on friendly terms with Mr. Mason."

"I shall be most happy, I am sure, to do anything to oblige, that is, if the matter will not interfere with any conscientious scruples. We have all our weaknesses, sir, and my conscience is mine."

"A lawyer with a conscience," thought the soldier. "I shall hear of the men in my company, refusing to get drunk when they have an opportunity next.

"I have no doubt I can serve you in any matter," continued the lawyer. "Of course, unless it is interfering in the manner I have explained. Now, as a preliminary, I must beg you will deal with me as though I were your friend; that is, be candid, hide not the slightest trifle likely to bear upon the matter at issue, and I shall then be able to form my opinion upon its merits, and act accordingly."

Part of this speech was the usual mode of address he adopted to his new clients; therefore, it did not mean so much as the words implied.

"Thanks for the hint," the Guardsman said; "I will be candid with you; of course, I may rely——"

"My good sir," said the lawyer, showing his white teeth, "were you to give me the details of a case which would injure my best friend, I should regard it as sacredly as the priest does the crimes that are unfolded to him in his capacity as a minister of religion."

"Quite sufficient," said the soldier; "therefore, I will begin by telling you the most essential features of the case. Until a few days since I was a penniless man; my brother's death has altered my position, but it was during his lifetime I did as many others have done—borrowed money to supply my needs."

"Exactly—a common occurrence."

"Saul Mason was the man who supplied me with enormous sums; and as an extra inducement for him to do so, I signed a bond to give him in return, besides the money and interest, one-third of my income when my brother died; of course," he added, "I did not expect this event would so soon come to pass, for my brother was a man who, from appearance and general health, I looked forward to outliving me."

"Quite so," the lawyer said, and Sir Henry thought there was a touch of irony in the tone he used; "quite so, my good sir."

"His death happened very suddenly, and my first duty was to send Mr. Mason a cheque for the whole of the money and interest due."

"Very thoughtful indeed; pray continue."

"This done, I ought, in the natural course of events, to be free from any obligation to Mr. Mason; but, owing to the power I have given him over me, I am not safe until I can glean something that will turn the tables, that is, to speak frankly, I wish you to place him in my power, if you have the means of doing so."

The lawyer reflected for a few moments, and then asked—

"What do you estimate your income at per annum?"

"Fifteen thousand pounds."

"Mason's share would be five thousand as long as he lived."

"It would; therefore you can easily understand my motive in seeking you."

"I can; and, to be plain, you could not have sought one so able and willing to assist you."

The soldier stretched forth his hand in the eagerness of his joy, and exclaimed:—

"I am overjoyed to hear it, and as an earnest of my intentions towards you, here is a blank cheque. Fill it in with the sum you think a fitting recompense for the service you are about to render me."

"I am not sure: but never mind, we shall see—we shall see. Now, Saul Mason, I should imagine, will live for some years to come. Suppose I fill this in for the amount you would have to pay him in one year, I think that would be a fair estimate for my services. You need not sign it, you know, until I have done that which you require."

The sum was rather heavy, and made the soldier wince when he saw Mr. Quills writing on the cheque; yet he made no remark, for he justly argued that it was better to pay one year's money and be free than have old Saul "bleeding" him as long as he lived.

The pair talked low and earnestly together for nearly an hour after this, then the Guardsman left the lawyer's office, and as he passed the threshold he came face to face with old Saul Mason.

"Hum! hum! hum! ho! ho!" purred Saul. "So glad to see you, Sir Henry; so glad, Sir Henry; should never have thought of seeing you here; this lawyer is a great rogue. Don't trust him, don't trust him."

Sir Henry Jervis wished his old acquaintance at the bottom of the sea, but he controlled his feelings sufficiently to give Saul a civil greeting.

"Just the very man I was about to visit; jump into the coach."

"Hum! hum! how lucky! I wanted to see you to——"

They entered the coach, and when the lumbering vehicle reached the corner of the street in which Saul resided, the pair alighted, and the soldier desired the driver to wait.

They had not gone many yards towards Saul's house, when they met a crowd of boys; it seemed as though the whole of the rising generation of Blackwall had turned out *en masse.*

"Yah!" they shouted, and some threw stones at old Saul, "who robbed the boatman? Go home, you old cheat. Yah! yah! Give poor Bill Webb his money!"

"Pleasant this," said the Guardsman; but I wish the stones they use were softer."

"Hum! hum!" said Saul: the fruits you see, Sir Henry, of being a popular man."

The shouts came louder and stronger in expression, as they neared the house, and the stones came in greater number, as old Saul fumbled with his latch-key at the door.

"The reptiles!" growled Saul. "I'll make them smart yet for this, I will, by all that's ——"

A three-cornered piece of granite struck him on the back of the head, and the boys, when they saw the old rascal fall, raised a shout of triumph.

CHAPTER XXX.

SHEET-ANCHOR JACK IN THE PRIVATEER'S HOLD

In the garden of the Serai there was a summer-house covered with the odoriferous climbing plants indigenous to a warm climate.

The building was constructed with stout branches, and so interleaved, that neither sun or rain could penetrate the interior. The place had long fallen into disuse and become a receptacle for a heap of garden tools, bags of seed, and roots of bulbous plants; but as these did not occupy much space, there was sufficient room left for a piece of carpet, a few cooking utensils, and such articles as were necessary for the accommodation of a person residing there.

Sheet-Anchor, in his capacity as gardener, was brought to the summer-house by one of the harem guards, who, by signs, explained that the young sailor's dwelling would be henceforth the summer-house.

Jack sat upon the carpet and watched the guard take a position near the small gate that ormed the only outlet from the garden.

From the Nubian's figure Jack's eye wandered to the high wall, and he saw there was but little chance of escape in that direction.

The prospect before him was not a pleasant one. He had heard strange stories of the cruelty exercised against the Christian prisoners. He had also heard that a European, once in their power, never returned to his native country.

The future seemed but a dreary, hopeless blank; for, although he was not chained in a dungeon, still he was none the less a captive; and his prison, though filled with the most gorgeous flowers, would be none the less hateful than the walls of a cell.

While thinking moodily over these matters, he raised his eyes, and saw the gaunt form of Baba-da-Chuk approaching the summer-house.

He had heard from the worthy Baba sufficient to understand that his captivity in the harem gardens would in all possibility be changed for a life of bondage in the country of the Sultan.

He hoped the latter would be his fate, for Jack justly thought there were many chances of escape during the voyage to Constantinople.

The ship might be wrecked, or overhauled and taken by an English cruiser, or he might possibly incite the Christian captives to rise upon their Moslem keepers; in each of these there was a chance of escape, but while imprisoned in the harem gardens there was none.

Jack observed that Baba-da-Chuck kept his eyes fixed upon the ground as he advanced towards the summer-house, and coupling this with the insight he had already had of Eastern manners, the young mariner looked upon it as a point of etiquette that Baba must not look up towards the latticed window of the Serai.

"I am glad," Baba said, when he entered the summer-house, "to find you are so comfortably settled in your new quarters, and have come to give a few useful hints for your guidance in the rather difficult position you will soon find yourself in."

Jack looked up inquiringly at the speaker, as he repeated:

"Difficult position I shall find myself in?"

"Yes, young man; but first I will tell you all that has transpired since you were brought here after you left the Dey's house."

"The yellow-visaged old ruffian!"

"Perhaps you are right, but you know we who value our heads, do not tell him so; far from it, we call him the Light of the World, Sun of the Universe, Great and Mighty Dey, and all that sort of thing; it does not cost much to say, and it goes a long way to the keeping of one's head in the proper place."

"I'll see him——" Jack began savagely.

"You'll do just as I tell you," Baba said, "and not make a fool of yourself; for if you play the game properly, you will soon be in a better position than ever you could have aspired to attaining in your own country, or in your profession."

"I don't understand you."

"Very likely not; you make room for me on your carpet, and I will explain."

Jack made room for the Bey's confidant.

"Benardin, my master," Baba said, "has interested himself in your behalf, and therefore, in place of your being sent to Constantinople with the Sultan's tribute, you will be kept here, providing my master, the Bey, can find another youth to make up the number, and he will find one, I have no doubt."

"But," said Jack, "I would sooner go to Constantinople ten times over than remain cooped up in this garden."

"You would sooner go to the devil," said Baba; "you don't know what you are saying, young man, not a word."

"I know this," Jack answered, "there would perhaps be a chance of escape during the voyage; but as long as I am hear, there will not be any."

"Quite as much as you will want."

"What?"

"Quite as much as you will want," Baba repeated: "for take my word for it, you will not care about escaping, when you know all."

"The sooner I know it the better, for at present my mind is filled with nothing but plans for getting safely away from here."

"And when you get safely away, where do you intend going?"

"Anywhere—on board ship, if possible."

"Silly boy," said Baba; "if you passed the gates of the palace you would be caught—perhaps by a slave-dealer—who would send you to the interior; as for the ships, suppose you reached them, there are none in the harbour but those who are in the Dey's interests."

"I care not, I will make the attempt."

"Nonsense; listen to me—you saw that pretty girl who sat close to the Dey."

"I did, she was the one I picked up from the affair that upset."

"She was; now do you know, young man, that beautiful girl has taken a violent fancy to you?"

Jack thought of the Arab beauty's black eyes, as he said—

"Has she?"

"Yes, she has, and had it not been for her, your head would have been taken off by the executioner."

"She was very kind, and I feel obliged."

"You ought to; for under pretext of punishing you, she has persuaded the Dey to appoint you chief gardener, and unless I know nothing of the tricks of these women she has done this for no other purpose than to have you near her, for the windows of the Harem overlook this garden, and there is a private door that leads from the staircase to the ground."

"How, sir," Jack said, "how shall I be benefited?"

"In every way; that girl has a bold mind, and she is as crafty as she is beautiful. She hates the Dey, and if I am not mistaken, admires you. Well, do you not see anything in this?"

"Yes," Jack said, "plenty of danger, for if I am caught speaking to her, my life would not be worth much with the black fellows."

"If she wishes to see you," Baba said, "she has Eastern drugs potent enough to send all the Dey's army to sleep, much less the few guards."

"Taking your view of the case," said Jack, "I don't see how my condition will be bettered, unless a constant danger added to it will improve it."

"You're in a strange country," the great

Baba said; "the Dey has immense treasures. He trusts her entirely, and she possesses wonderful power over him. Now, what is easier than for her to poison the guards, seize the treasures, and with her Christian lover seek another land?"

Jack laughed at Baba's words, and continued,

"How are they to get to another land?"

"A ship. There are plenty in the harbour, and plenty of their commanders would not hesitate to transfer their services to you for a consideration. In fact," Baba added, warming with the subject, "there would be nothing to prevent your having a fleet of your own. You could make your home one of the lovely islands down the coast between here and Santa Cruz, and there, with a beautiful wife, or a dozen if you wished, a fleet of galleys bringing you in the produce of the whole world, you would be richer and more absolute than any European monarch."

The picture was as dazzling as it was romantic, and for a few moments Jack's heart beat quicker, and in fancy he saw himself at the head of his corsairs sweeping the seas, to enrich his island stronghold, but this feeling soon passed away, and he said:

"The life you have pictured certainly seems as agreeable as it is adventurous, but taking into consideration the distance it is from here, the enchantment is perhaps better than the reality."

"You may possibly find the reality, even more enchanting than the perspective."

"No doubt," Jack said, "especially as I cannot speak one word of the lady's language who is to do all this for me?"

"Ah!" Baba said, fumbling in the folds of his turban; "I had almost forgotten. Here's something for you."

To Jack's astonishment, Baba placed in his hand a small book, having on the back the impression in English, "Arabic and English Vocabulary."

"There," Baba said, "with the aid of that book and the guards, not to say anything of the Dey's favourite Odalisque, you will soon be able to converse. Now I must leave you. Good bye, success attend you; now be careful, you seem to like the task imposed upon you. Begin to put the garden in order; the sooner you do it the more favour you will gain in the Dey's opinion. Lastly, should the Dey ever walk out here accompanied by any of his wives, for your life keep out of sight; it was to tell you this I was admitted to the gardens. Good bye, what assistance you may require, the slaves are ordered to furnish."

"Good bye," Jack said. "Good bye."

Sheet-Anchor pondered over this interview, and the conclusion he came to was not flattering to the illustrious Baba-da-Chuk.

"This renegade Scotchman is an awful liar," muttered Jack, "I suppose the truth of the matter is the Dey wants a European to keep his garden in order, and this precious rascal has been paid to humbug me in order that I may not make any attempt to escape—but I shall do so, and that as soon as the day closes."

"I'm very glad," thought Baba, as he left the palace, "I saw the youth, and put these things in his head, for he will be sure to fall into a mess over it, and have the bowstring; it will be a good riddance, for it will never do to let the Bey ransom him from the Dey; if he does, I know my chance with the little lady, Milly Mason, will be very small, for she likes the fellow, there's no doubt about that, after what she said to the Bey when he told her he had seen this strip of a lad."

Baba chuckled and grinned the more when he thought over his policy and became so buried in thought, that he noticed not a porter, heavily laden, coming down the street.

Baba's eyes were turned towards the ground as he thought over something very pleasant; the porter's eyes were in the same direction, in consequence of the heavy load he carried.

In consequence of this, they cannoned, and the porter being the heaviest, he stood his ground; while the great Baba measured his length in the road, and covered his august person with the accumulation of filth the inhabitants of the East deem so necessary for their welfare—at least the traveller would imagine so, for the writer of these pages when in an Eastern town, has been compelled to plug his nostrils to escape the vile effluvia, while the natives sat cross-legged on their carpets, and seemed to enjoy the odour of the stagnant filth in the gutters.

Baba did not enjoy it, for he scrambled to his feet, and after saluting the porter with a choice bouquet of the flowers of abuse, he belaboured the poor fellow with the thick stick he carried in virtue of his office as major domo of the Bey's household.

"Son of a dog," he said, "reptile of the most filthy swamp, may your shadow shrivel up, and a jackass sit on your father's grave."

The porter bore his punishment like a man who felt it was his kismet to be thus thrashed, and when the by-no-means fragrant Baba-da-Chuk had exhausted his speech and the strength of his long arm, the porter picked up his load and went quickly onward, muttering the usual:

"Allah is good, Allah is great."

Such of the youthful population of Algiers as chanced to see the great Baba ornate with his coating of filth, gave silent manifestations of delight at the sight.

The few hours that intervened between the time Baba left Sheet Anchor and the darkness, the young sailor employed himself in looking over the vocabulary, and learning some of the most useful Arabic words by heart.

He was not sure of the pronunciation, but that would come to him, for as a rule a native of a foreign land, if asked a question by a stranger, in nine cases out of ten repeats the inquiry by pronouncing the words, and sets the questioner right in the pronunciation if he is intelligent enough to profit by the lesson.

When the darkness set in, Sheet-Anchor quickly left his Arcadian dwelling to put into execution a plan he had commenced during the afternoon.

He took with him a thin but strong cord, to the end of which he had fastened a large rake.

The top of the high wall was overgrown with thick vegetation, so Jack knew if he did not fail in his first throw there would be no noise when the teeth caught on the top of the wall.

If he missed it the noise of the rake striking the ground would alarm the harem guards, and—— Well, he did not like to speculate upon the result, fearing it would make him nervous and spoil his aim.

Placing his right foot upon the end of the rope in case the throw might be too powerful and the weight of the rake if it passed over the wall carry the rope with it, he raised the loose coils over his head, and with all his strength jerked rake and rope upward.

There was a slight rustle as the iron teeth caught in the foliage. Then Jack, who could scarcely refrain from shouting hurrah at his success, went close under the wall and hung upon the cord to test the grip of the teeth, and no sooner did he find it would bear the strain than he went up hand over hand.

Arrived at the summit, he sat across the wall and pulled up the rope, reversed the teeth of the rake, in order that it should grip the other side.

This done he turned his face towards the Dey's dwelling, and placed the thumb of his right hand against his nose and worked his extended fingers about something after the fashion of a flute-player executing a quick tune upon his instrument.

To slide down the rope was the ocupation of a few seconds, to jerk the rake from the wall and make off towards the sea did not ocupy very long.

Sheet-Anchor had chosen a very good time for his escape, for at that hour the faithful were kneeling on their carpets, their face towards Mecca, and praying as hard as they were able.

Jack passed some of them thus devoutly engaged, and prudence alone prevented him from giving them a hearty kick upon the part of their anatomy so conveniently elevated for the purpose.

Arrived at the water's edge, Sheet-Anchor threw the friendly rope and rake into the sea, then looked around at the vessels.

He saw some of European build and rig, but whether they were prizes to the Moslem's knife and matchlock, or Mussulmans, come there for the purpose of trade, he was in doubt until from a clumsy-looking brig came the well-known sound:

"Turn up, there, turn up."

"The watch is being roused. That's an English ship, at any rate, and the voice seems familiar, but that I suppose is my fancy, or else all bo'sens' voices are very much alike."

He went close to the clumsy-looking brig, and saw she was fastened to one of the rings by a single hawser.

He also saw it would be possible to reach an open port by means of the thick rope, but before attempting this, Sheet-Anchor held a mental debate.

"The single hawser," he thought, "looks very much as though the merchantmen rather distrusted the good faith of the people with whom they have to trade, for one blow of a hatchet, and the sails are hanging quite ready for instant use, and the ship would be clear of the harbour."

The ship's bell struck, and the man called out:

"All's well."

Sheet-Anchor nearly tumbled into the sea as he leant forward to take a closer look at the brig.

"Well," he said, half aloud, "I could have sworn I have heard that call before, but it must be fancy, for I have never been on board the craft."

He looked keenly at the unwieldy run, the thick bows, and the stumpy masts, and came to the conclusion that the similarity of sounds was but fancy.

"Now," Jack thought, "the question is whether I had not better hail the brig, and ask to be taken aboard, but upon second thoughts I think not, for these fellows are but little better than the Moors, or they would not trade with them. No, I will get aboard by that hawser, and when we are out at sea they must take me to the port they are bound for."

He put the project into execution at once, and reached the porthole unperceived by the men on board.

The interior of the vessel seemed familiar, for he had no difficulty in reaching the hold.

"I have been on board this craft before," Jack thought, "or else I have dreamt it, but I'll soon find out."

There was plenty of rope under his feet, and as he had his tinder-box and knife in his pocket, he soon cut a piece of the tarred hemp, and easily as possible struck a light.

The first smoky gleam of the torch revealed to Jack's astonishment, the well-remembered hold of the Wasp.

"This is no place for me," he thought, "Well, I must say the captain is a bold and a skilful hand, to come here and so well disguise his vessel."

The flaming torch shone full upon a barrel of gunpowder, and for a moment Sheet-Anchor stood near it, and thought how easily he could send the privateer and his crew into eternity, but as he would have to make one of the party, he trampled the light carefully out, and ascending the steps crept back to the open port."

"I must try my luck elsewhere," he thought, "this is no use—eh?"

He heard Parker Neville and Tom Grant in conversation just above where he sat, and the privateersman's words caused him to wish himself safe ashore, and in his rustic habitation in the Dey's gardens

CHAPTER XXXI.

THE SCHOONER GOOD HOPE.

When Parker Neville escaped from the Arab flotilla the look-out in the foretop of the saucy little Wasp gave notice of an approaching sail.

The stranger soon rose above the distant line, where the sky and the water seem to blend, and the glasses on board the Wasp made out a clipper-built schooner.

"European," said Parker Neville, "and steering direct for the vagabond's fleet we have just wished a fond farewell."

"Heavily freighted," said Tom Grant, "to judge by the water she draws. "What a pity these infidels should have the plunder of this sweet craft!"

"It is," said the captain of the Wasp. "Suppose we save them the trouble; our voyage, so far, has been confoundedly unprofitable."

"The very thing I was about to suggest," said Grant; "but I feared you might have few scruples about doing the amiable to an English ship, for English she is without a doubt."

"I have many scruples, Tom," said the skipper, "quite as many as a fat parson has when he pockets the tithes procured by the sale of an unfortunate parishioner's goods and chattels."

"If that's how the case stands, we had better have the men at quarters."

The desperadoes were soon at their stations, and when the schooner bore up within range of the Wasp's guns, a shot was sent over the stranger's bows as a gentle hint for the schooner to heave to.

To the surprise of the privateersmen a column of smoke puffed out above the stranger's deck, and a huge ball whistled through the Wasp's rigging, carrying away the foreyard, and cutting a number of loose ropes to mark its passage.

"What do you think of that, Tom?" said Parker Neville, raising his hands to check his men as they were about to send a shot in reply; "that's an unpleasant answer to our invitation, eh?"

"I think we had better belong to the peace party," answered the first officer; "for half an hour's work with that big, ugly gentleman, will put an end to the Wasp's flight."

"I think so. Run up the English rag or German, I should say, for the tight little island has been taken possession of by a colony of the Teutonic race since the first German came over to rob and govern us."

The flag was answered by the schooner displaying the Union Jack, and soon afterwards the swift schooner ran so close alongside, that the faces of the men on each ship were plainly distinguishable.

Parker Neville uttered an exclamation of surprise, so did his officer, as they saw a tall, handsome man leaning over the schooner's low bulwarks.

"The gentleman," said Parker, "that visited us when we lay in the river."

"Sir Basil Jarvis," said Tom Grant, "by all that's good. He seems in a hurry for you to execute his commission."

"I wish I could," said the privateersman, "for it is not often such a profitable job falls to my share."

"What were you to have if you found the boy?"

"One thousand pounds sterling. Five hundred if I brought reliable information of his death."

"Here comes the gentleman. Go below, half of you vagabonds; we do not want the Wasp's beauty to be spoilt by your cut-throat looking faces."

Half the crew went below, as Parker Neville went to the gangway to meet the man Henry Jarvis fully believed was buried, and received him as he came on board.

"You're welcome," said the baronet, as he shook the privateersman's hand, which was rather rough. "Didn't expect to see me here?"

"I did not," Neville said, "but your reply was a little rougher. How do you manage to keep a gun of that calibre in such a small craft?"

"It is the only one we have," said the baronet, "and very useful we have found it in these waters. Did the shot do you much mischief? The blundering fellow fired too high."

"No; a light spar and a few ropes, that is all; the bullet marks were made by the Algerines."

"You have been——"

"Will you step below, we can speak with less reserve there."

The baronet followed the captain of the Wasp to the luxurious state room, and when an attendant had placed wine on the table the privateersman said:

"I have been driven off the coast by a fleet of corsairs, but to-night I will make the first move towards gaining the information you require."

"It will not be found there," the baronet said; "that is partly the reason I came out in this vessel. Are you prepared to hear a very strange story, Captain Neville?"

"Quite," said the privateersman; "and very strange it must be to surprise me."

"We shall see; what think you of being in the company of a man who has been dead and buried for many weeks?"

The privateersman looked at the baronet; the words were somewhat vague, but ere he could make any remark Basil said:

"I am the man!—you start. Now you shall hear the story. I believe you are acquainted with a certain Saul Mason, are you not?"

"Slightly."

"I am beginning at the wrong end of my story. I have a brother—a reckless, dissolute spendthrift. Some time since I determined to track him to the people who supplied him with money, for I feared he was using my name, for his acceptances were valueless. The result of this resolution brought me to a dingy house at Blackwall, and when my brother left I discovered that one Saul Mason resided there."

"I know the place well."

"Do you? Well, the old rascal walked to the end of the street with my amiable brother, and while I stood near the door a letter fell at my feet, and to my surprise it was addressed to Harry; here it is, read, and judge for yourself."

Parker Neville read the letter; but before he finished it he sprang from his seat and exclaimed:

"Fool, fool, to lose him after all!"

"Lose——"

"It is nothing," the privateersman said; "so the writer of this letter accuses your brother of placing a boy in Saul's hands because he stood in his way; of course the only inference I can draw from it is, the boy Saul sent on board the Gloriana was your son."

The baronet inclined his head.

"This Blendell must have been fond of the lad, for he conjures Captain Jarvis to seek for him, adding that even during the fiercest gale some of the crew at times escape."

"Heaven, I hope, has willed it so in this case.

"Amen," said Parker; "so when you obtained this information you at once left England to search for your boy?"

"No, I stayed some days, and the very hour I came on board this ship my funeral was taking place."

"I scarcely understand the meaning of this."

"I will explain: a dead body was procured from the resurrection men, and buried as Sir Basil Jarvis, my wife went into mourning, and left our town residence to Captain Jarvis.

"But why this——"

"To punish the merciless rascal who has robbed me of my son."

"A light punishment I should say, to give him uncontrolled power over your revenue."

"The fall will be felt with more severity when I return, and he is, after the enjoyment of my title and wealth, compelled to relinquish both."

"I understand your motive now respecting your son, whose childhood has been spent in such an uncongenial atmosphere as old Saul's house. I can only say be of good heart, and perhaps before many days he will be restored to you."

"Your confident manner of speaking tells me you know more than you care to reveal."

"It is so; have patience, Sir Basil."

SHEET-ANCHOR JACK IN THE GARDEN OF THE SERAI.

"Tell me," said the anxious father, "have you heard or seen anything to——"

"If it is your son old Saul sent on board the Gloriana, he stood on this deck a few hours since."

Sir Basil Jarvis gave a glad cry, then fell to the cabin floor in a swoon.

* * *

"I don't think the infidels will recognise this craft again, eh, Tom?"

"Scarcely possible," returned the lieutenant. "Well, now that we have put our heads in this hornet's nest, what is the next move?"

"Hans Kleb," said the privateer captain, "is now staining his hands and face to go ashore; the fellow understands Arabic, therefore, I do not expect we shall be long before hearing of this Sheet-Anchor Jack's whereabouts."

"How unfortunate to lose him such a short time before the arrival of the schooner Good Hope."

"Very; but he must be found, and if any one can ferret out the place where the Moors have taken the lad, Hans Kleb is the man."

Sheet Anchor, sitting in the port just below where the speakers stood, heard these words and not knowing the good fortune that was in store for him, made his way back to the shore as quickly as he could.

He went back the way he came, and just as his feet touched the bank, the sound of drums and cymbals was heard, then came the glare of torches, and winding from one of the narrow streets a crowd of spearmen and attendants approached following the Dey.

Jack ran off as fast as possible, but as the procession came in the same direction, he took refuge in a doorway, and hoped by flattening himself against the door to escape detection.

CHAPTER XXXII.

JACK BEGINS TO LEARN ARABIC AND ELOPES WITH AILEY, THE APPLE OF LOVE.

THE cause of all this uproar in the streets of Algiers was to do honour to his mightiness the Dey, who chose that unseasonable hour to attend the mosque.

His escort was followed by a noisy rabble, and in fact the Moslem population behaved much the same as the more enlightened people of the Christian metropolis behave when any of the royal family leave that dreary block of buildings known as Buckingham Palace.

Sheet Anchor wished their loud raised loyalty and themselves anywhere but in the narrow street where he had taken refuge, for as they came near he found it would be impossible to escape unnoticed.

They were not more than a hundred yards from him when he resolved to demand admission to the house in the portal of which he stood.

The doorway was like the doorways of all Eastern towns, let in a wall which surrounded the dwelling-house, for the Asiatics make no display of wealth externally.

The practice of building mean-looking walls around even the most splendid dwellings, originated in the hope of escaping from the tax-gathers, for these rapacious gentlemen tax according to the appearance of wealth. Hence a traveller in the East sees little else but mud-plastered walls and knows not that inside there may be a mansion. The decorations upon the walls and ceilings of a single room may have cost £700 or £800.

It would repay one of the Oriental assessors to come to a certain tight little island, for he would there learn, not how to tax according to the ability to pay, but to levy a ruinous duty upon the necessaries of life, the payment of which is wrung from the poorest man in the same proportion as from his brethren, in purple and linen.

Before Sheet Anchor could put his design into execution, the door in the wall was opened by some one inside, and as Jack had squeezed himself very close to the wood-work, when it gave way he tumbled backwards, and in his fall overset the person who was about to emerge.

"What the devil do you want here? Hech! As I live, it's the lad."

These words spoken in English by the tall Moslem-garbed individual, as he struggled to his feet, caused Jock to feel a little astonished, but this soon passed away when he recognised the speaker as the august Baba-da-Chuk.

"Really, I'm very sorry," Jack began, and to his relief, Baba closed the door while the noisy procession passed. "I hope I have not hurt you?"

"What are you doing here?" Baba asked, not noticing the young prisoner's apology, "I left you in the gardens of the Serai."

"You did," said Jack, "but unfortunately I fell over the wall, and when this door was opened, I was trying to find my way back."

Baba-da-Chuk screwed up one eye, placed his finger against his nose, and looked as wise as an old owl peeping through an ivy bush, as he said:

"Tumbled over a wall thirty feet high? Weel, weel, it may be so, but your legs don't seem long enough for that—trying to find your way back. Weel, it's lucky you met with Baba, for he is going that way, and will show you."

"Much obliged," Jack thought, "but it strikes me, I shall make a bolt before we get as far."

He was mistaken, for Baba clapped his hands and a dozen Moors ran towards him, and when he went towards the Dey's palace the slaves drew their scimitars and surrounded Baba and Sheet Anchor Jack.

"So," mused Jack, when he found himself again in his rustic dwelling, "this Scotch Moslem seems determined to make my fortune as he terms it."

He rolled himself in his carpet, and soon fell asleep; he was too well used to changes of fortune to allow the small matter of his recapture to trouble him long.

He was early astir next morning, and at work in the garden—a watchful Arab, warned by Jack's previous escape, and the chance the guard had of losing his head, in consequence of the captive's loss, did not lose sight of him for a moment.

Jack fell to work with spade and rake to trim the ill-kept garden, and about noon, when he was about to retire to escape the burning rays of the sun, the gate that led to the harem garden was opened, and one of the guards came to relieve the fellow who had been paying such particular attention to Jack.

The Arabs left the gate open for a moment, and to the profound astonishment of Sheet Anchor, the figure of the half-witted lad who he believed had gone down in the Gloriana walked in.

Jack's heart gave a thump when he saw the apparition, and the half-wit seemed petrified at the sight of Sheet Anchor, for he wrung his hands and moaned—

"A ghost! a ghost! I killed him—shot him with a big pistol."

Then as Jack went towards the weak-brained fellow, he held out his hands to prevent the ghost from coming nearer, and cried out—

"It was Saul—old Saul Mason—told me to do it; go and haunt him! he told me—he——"

Sheet Anchor got within a dozen paces of the half-wit when the latter turned and fled, and before Jack could pass through the doorway the Arab sentry warned him back.

"So Mr. Saul Mason told the poor fellow to shoot me," thought Jack as he went back to his arbour, "and he nearly carried out the old rascal's wish. Poor Ted, he would do anything old Saul desired, for the villain had a strange power over him."

When the heat of the sun had a little abated, Jack returned to his work, but the guard, in place of watching him as the one who was on duty during the morning did, took up an easy posture under the shadow of a wall, and with his scimitar across his knees, indulged in a quiet nap.

Jack went on digging, and thinking over the half-wit's words; and the more he thought, the more he felt at a loss to understand Saul Mason's wish to be rid of him.

"I never did the old man any harm," Jack thought, "yet he seems to have pursued me with relentless ferocity, and—"

A footstep upon the gravel walk behind where he stood caused Jack to turn, and to his surprise, he beheld the beautiful Arab girl Kora Ailey.

She held a flower in her hand, and when she saw Jack turn, she advanced and threw the flower at his feet.

The words of Baba-da-Chuk came to his memory, and as he stooped and raised the flower, a vision of the lawless yet romantic life pictured by Baba floated before his mind.

The situation was embarassing, but, thanks to the vocabulary Baba had given him, Jack and the Dey's lovely odalisque were soon able to exchange sufficient language to declare love to each other.

She left him when the voice of the Muezzin called out for the faithful to assemble for prayers.

Jack's captivity began to wear a different aspect; the girl, though dark of skin, was very beautiful.

Jack was very young, and his heart was easily captivated, especially when he knew the Arab beauty would aid his escape from the Dey's power.

Jack began to imagine himself upon the island Baba had painted; in fancy he saw his fleet of Corsair vessels lying in the creek ready to pounce upon their prey.

He looked at his dirty seaman's dress, and thought how much better he would look in Moorish garb, and a gorgeous sash stuck full of jewelled weapons.

He gave his mind full swing over this pleasant subject, then drew his carpet to the door of the summer-house and went in for a hard study of Arabic, and by the time the moon rose he could put the following questions to an old cypress tree that stood near.

"Do you love me?"

"Shall we escape from here?"

"Will you find a horse and arms?"

"Can you get a ship to meet us somewhere on the coast?"

"When shall we go away?"

"That will do for the present," said Jack; "to-morrow morning I will have a go in for a few more phrases. What a pretty girl she is! Well, I don't wonder at her not liking the Dey. Why he is old enough to be her grandfather."

Jack slept soundly, despite his attempts to feel like a love-sick swain; but he was up at daybreak, and, book in hand, questioning the old cypress tree again.

Kora Ailey visited the gardens after the blaze of the noon-day sun had subsided, and Jack was surprised to see the sentry, as on the day previous, sitting cross-legged fast asleep against the wall.

* * * * *

The Dey was seated in his audience chamber, his august back supported by soft cushions, and between his lips the jewelled mouthpiece of his "nergilhe."

His mightiness was in one of his pleasant moods, for he had only kicked his grand vizier once that morning, and endeavoured to break his pipebearer's head also only once since that useful servant entered the room.

The household were at peace under such a blissful state of things, and the body-guard were even seen to relax their grim features into a melancholy smile, when their royal master perpetrated a little joke.

The butt of forbidden liquor he had received from the Jew of Oran, in exchange for the English maiden, perhaps had something to do with this suavity of mind, for the Dey, instructed by his faithful friend Benardin, knew how to do away with the feeling of sickness that usually followed a too close application to the seductive drink.

It was like the excessive calm that precedes a violent tempest, for there was one brewing that the Dey or his followers could not have imagined.

The chief of the harem guard suddenly entered the chamber, and presenting himself before the Dey, said:

"Most high and mighty prince, this day thy servant beseeches thee to call in Mirza, that this head, no longer fit to be upon my shoulders, my be struck off."

"Rise, good and faithful Aljai, keeper of the serai; rise, thy face is white in our presence."

"Master," said the Nubian, "let me die by the bowstring before my tongue shall blister with the news I bring."

"What ails my faithful Aljai, that he shakes thus?"

"Master, I bring great and sad news. May I speak?"

"Thy zeal for us Aljai magnifies the merest trifle into great and sad news; but thy master listens, full well knowing that no words of thine can disturb the peace of mind he now enjoys."

"Oh, that another tongue could have told thee of thy loss," said Aljai, wringing his hands; "oh that other eyes than mine should behold thy face pallid with the grief——"

"Speak, good Aljai, we listen."

"Master," said the chief eunuch, cowering as he spoke, "thy favourite slave, the young, the beautiful, the moon-faced sweet apple of love, has——"

"Has what, good Aljai?" keep us not in suspense."

"Fled, noble and high prin——"

"What!" yelled the Dey; "speak, but my ears drink in none of this."

"Gone," said Aljai: "left the harem, and gone with the accursed Giaour."

The Dey jumped from his seat, then plumped down again, and said with unwonted calmness:

"Let my faithful Aljai tell me more of this."

"Gracious lord," said the trembling slave, "I went to the chambers of the harem to tell thy slaves it was the hour for them to walk in the gardens. Kora Ailey was not in her chamber. I sought for her in the gardens, and found the guard slain by the knife of the Giaour, and the gate open, and outside the hoof-prints of a horse, and fluttering from the nail in the door-frame a piece of the skirt of silver tissue worn by the moon-faced Kora Ailey——"

"O-o-o!" howled the Dey; "but go on."

"I went back to the chamber and found she has taken the armlets of gold, the tiaras of dia——"

"Dog, you lie!"

"My head answer for it, O Dey, if it is not the truth."

"Go on."

"All things that were of value she has taken."

The master of the horse rushed into the chamber, and, presenting himself, said:

"Sun of the Universe. Lord ——"

"May a jackass sit on thy mother's grave," roared the Dey; "speak, and to the point, or by Allah I will make you shorter by a head."

"Thy steed, gracious lord, thy barb beyond price, thy milk-white Arab, has been taken from the stable by thy favourite slave, and she——"

The Dey's scimitar leapt from its sheath, and the master of the horse gave a prudent roll sideways, then jumped to his feet, and bolted from the room.

Scimitar in hand stood the Dey, his fierce little eyes glaring from one to the other of his attendants, hoping to detect a smile upon their visages.

But one and all pulled such doleful faces, that, had an enterprising undertaker been present, he would have engaged them for mutes.

He was about to annihilate the boy whose duty it was to keep the imperial pipe alight, when the curtains were dashed aside, and the great Baba-da-Chuk rushed in.

"Another," howled the Dey. "Speak, dog! what is the matter, thou long-legged, pitiful cur?"

"Master," said Baba, coming to the point at once, "thy favoured slave, Kora Ailey, has by some means seduced six of thy captains from their allegiance to thee, and they have left with their war galleys to meet the false Kora Ailey and the Giaour."

"Thy master, Benardin Allah?"

"He has gone in pursuit, but with little hope of finding them, for he knows not what part of the coast they are steering for."

The Dey stood for a few moments boiling with passion, then he roared out—

"Accursed be the whole infidel race; to

horse! to horse! by Allah's aid, we may yet overtake them."

The Arab horsemen sped upon the trail of the white horse, and came in sight of the fugitives after a hard ride of twenty miles of rough ground.

The Dey spurred his steed and yelled out the direst curses upon the head of the ungrateful young seaman and his companion, Kora Ailey.

But the curses and commands to halt were alike unheeded, and the white horse, put upon his mettle by hearing hoof-strokes behind, flew onward like the wind.

Five miles further and their course lay along the verge of the cliffs. Below, on the quiet water, the Dey beheld the six war galleys that had been bribed to follow the fortunes of Kora Ailey.

He also beheld, a mile or so out at sea, the noble proportions of Benardin's vessel, the stately Fezi Baria, and between the Fezi Baria and the war galleys he saw two vessels of European build and rig, one a schooner, the other a brigantine.

He felt a little more at ease now, for he knew Bernardin's vessel was a match for a dozen war galleys, and as for the two European ships, he imagined they were prizes.

His joy reached its culminating point when he saw the white horse that carried the double burden, suddenly began to limp and slacken his pace.

"Bismillah!" muttered the Dey. "Glory to the Prophet, for in a few minutes I shall have the pair of lovers tied neck and heels together and thrown into the sea."

The white horse became lamer at every stride, and as Sheet Anchor guided the fiery Arab down the declivity that led to the sea, the Dey drew a pistol from his belt and shot the horse that had carried the lovers from the serai.

CHAPTER XXXIII.

THE TABLES ARE TURNED.

Entangled for a moment in the trappings of the fallen horse, Sheet-Anchor and his companion could not extricate themselves until the Dey and his followers had pulled up and surrounded the prostrate grey steed.

Sheet-Anchor knew but little of swordmanship beyond the handling of a common ship's cutlass. Although he placed his left arm around the Arab beauty's waist and menaced the Dey's followers with the broad-bladed scimitar he held, he was soon disarmed by the skilful Arab swordsman, and beautiful Kora Ailey torn from his grasp by the exasperated Dey.

It would soon have been all over with Sheet-Anchor, the humiliation of whose defeat was not lessened by the disappointed Arab girl calling him all the cowardly sons of Christian dogs, and other epithets peculiar to her race and language, had not Parker Neville, followed by a dozen of his men, run up the slope.

Parker and the Dey at once fell to with their blades, but the old Arab's arm was like a child's when opposed to such a master of fence as the privateer captain.

He was soon disarmed, and the Arab girl, whom he had clutched by her long hair, torn from his grasp.

The Dey saw the hour was against him; for simultaneously with his defeat his followers were put to the rout by the privateersmen.

"The curse of Allah upon the dogs!" said the Dey; "may they be shut out of Paradise and roasted by the dark Angel of Death!"

He jumped to his saddle, and leaving the Arab girl to Parker Neville, he rode after his followers; when he reached a portion of the cliff overlooking the sea he drew rein and watched the Fezi Baria approach the war-galleys that had deserted his standard.

"Allah be good!" he muttered, stroking his beard; "for now will my faithful Benardin destroy not only these dogs who have left me, but he will sink or burn the ships of the Christian dogs and their unfortunate crews!"

What the Dey saw from the cliff, so far from carrying out this idea, caused him to tear out his beard in tufts, then, howling with rage, he turned his horse's head and fled to his palace, and soon after the alarm bell pealed out, and the whole of the population capable of bearing arms were soon hastening to the market-place.

Sheet-Anchor, although grateful to his rescuers, was not over well-pleased to find himself again in the power of Parker Neville.

"Fortune has favoured you again," he said to Neville; "while I——"

"The favours of the fickle lady are yours young man," said Parker; "so come, jump into the boat, there is one on board anxiously awaiting your arrival."

Sheet-Anchor looked at the Arab girl and asked:

"What is to be done with this poor girl? She must not be left here, yet she cannot go on board your vessel."

"She shall determine for herself. Hans Kleb."

"Here, cap'en."

"This way, my man."

Hans Kleb spoke Arabic fluently; he had learnt it when a prisoner among the Moors.

"Ask this girl whether we shall leave her here," Parker said, "or whether she will go on board with this youth."

Hans Kleb interpreted this, and to the surprise of Parker and Sheet-Anchor, the girl's answer, as interpreted by Hans, was this:

"The young Giaour is not old enough to protect the maiden who loved him. Kora will go with the handsome unbeliever who has saved her from the Dey; I will be his slave if he will take me."

"Mermaids and griffins!" exclaimed the privateersman, "will I take her? I must be a block of wood to resist such a request. Tell her I will make her queen of my island, for we intend to settle down now, Hans, and do business upon a quieter and more comfortable scale than roaming about the dull ocean."

Hans told Kora this, with a few additions of his own; and the beautiful girl, crossing her hands over her breast, stood meekly before her future lord and master, who gallantly took one of her brown, jewelled hands and raised it to his lips.

"So much for my fleet of corsairs and island home," thought Sheet Anchor as he stepped into the boat. "Now I wonder if I was to appeal to the captains of these galleys who have come to serve me whether it would be any use. They might snuff this gentleman out. Ah! here's a frigate bearing down upon us—the Fezia Baria too. Well, go it, my natives. I am glad there is a prospect of a fight after all."

It was evident the Algerine frigate had no hostile intentions, for, after exchanging a private signal with the war galleys, who were preparing for action, she dropped anchor quietly in their midst, then a boat put off from her side, and went towards the small vessel that lay clear of the Wasp.

Parker Neville sat in the stern of the boat, apparently on the best of terms with his Arab companion; and Jack, who looked upon Kora's sudden transfer as anything but flattering to his dignity or manhood, sat in the bows, and wished the light craft and its crew at the bottom of the sea.

"Pull to the Good Hope," Parker Neville said, as the boat bore up for the Wasp, "with a will, my lads, or the boat from the Feri Baria will outstrip you."

The seamen thus put upon their mettle, endeavoured to reach the schooner before the boat from Benardiu's ship; but the infidel rowers shot alongside, and, to Sheet Anchor's astonishment, he saw a female form garbed in European fashion, ascend the accommodation ladder.

Jack's astonishment was not lessened when Parker Neville told him to go on board the schooner, and when the privateersman reached the deck, he desired the young sailor to follow him to the cabin.

"Here is your son, Sir Basil," said the privateersman, leading Jack forward to the baronet, who came with outstretched hands, and grasping the young sailor by the shoulders, looked eagerly into his face, and exclaimed:

"Thank God, thank God! Found at last!"

The young mariner, who had been buffeted about like a football by the wayward dame, was dazed by this unexpected turn, and could not speak for some minutes.

When he found his speech, he could only stammer but a few incoherent words; and the baronet, deferring an explanation until his son was a little more composed, led him to a seat. Then another surprise greeted Jack, as Milly Mason stepped forward and bade him welcome.

"I had never hoped to have seen you again in life, Milly," he said, "until that old Arab there told——"

"Hush!" the young girl said; "that Arab is my father."

"Your father! You have found one, Milly. I am not alone in my good fortune. These things seem very strange. Father! How strange the word seems to me! Yet, father, will you kindly explain all this to me?"

"I will, my boy," said the baronet. "You were stolen from me when scarcely two years old, and placed with Saul Mason. I heard nothing of you until a short time since; then I was told you had been sent to sea and wrecked on this coast, and sufficient was said to lead me to the belief that you were a prisoner among the Arabs. When Captain Neville's vessel was in the Thames I had an interview with him, and the result was, he promised to seek for you and obtain your release. While he was thus occupied I made the discovery that the story I had been told was false; therefore I chartered this ship and came to join Captain Neville in the search for you, but in another part of the ocean; but Providence has willed it that we should meet here."

"But this Captain Neville," Jack began, "was the cause of my being ship——"

"Your father knows all," said Parker, "therefore as we have but a few moments to spare, to arrange a multiplicity of business, spare the recital until you are on your voyage home."

"I have to thank Captain Neville," said the baronet, "for rescuing you at the last moment from the Arabs; for had he not come to your assistance they would have slain you."

"That's true," Jack said, "therefore we'll drop the matter; but Miss Mason here—what extraordinary chance has——"

"You shall hear, young gentleman," "Benardin said; I have had the good fortune to find this young lady on board a vessel I captured, and to my joy also discovered her to be my daughter."

"You are Saul's brother?"

"I am, and the rascal, believing me dead, has sent my child away where he hoped she would be wrecked, in order to possess the little fortune, which, in the event of her death, reverts to him."

"The old villain!" Jack said. "Here's another portion of the mystery. How is it I find you here among the vessels that were destined for my piratical crew? Not you alone, but my father's vessel and the Wasp."

Benardin and Parker Neville laughed, and the former said:—

"Well, that is soon explained. I was walking on the quay a night or two since, and saw the Wasp moored to the side, but disguised so as to deceived the faithful, but not disguised so as to deceive me. I went abroad, for there was no danger, for the quay side was lined with my galleys, and to my surprise I came across Parker Neville, whose throat I had attempted to cut at a time you may remember, young gentleman, when I had the pleasure of your company on board the Fezi Baria.

"I remember, nay do not forget that to obtain that pleasure you kindly dragged me part of the way to your ship, after first hauling me overboard."

"It has all happened for the best," laughed Benardin. "Well, in my late enemy I recognised a lad who had served under me as a midshipman when I held a commission in the English navy. Old associations caused me to make myself known, and in place of meeting as foes we discussed matters over a bottle of wine; and then I learnt that Neville, like myself, being disgusted with the English service, had set up on his own account, and that his mission to Algiers was to find you, and as I hoped to manage matters for him as far as you were concerned, I told Baba—you know Baba?"

"I do."

"To further the plan he had spoken to you about, and so arrange that you should be restored to your father at this place."

"But," said Sheet Anchor, "what has that to do with these galleys here? They were for the lady who has, without any compunction, transferred her affections to Parker Neville."

"Has she?" said the Bey; "well, that is fortunate, for we were rather puzzled to know what to do with her."

"She has saved you every trouble."

"Now, I intend to leave Algiers at the first opportunity, and as my old friend Parker seemed to fancy the life Baba had marked out for you, I made an agreement with him by which he is to hand over the Wasp to me, and in return I, in place of bringing the traitorous galleys to a just punishment for their treachery, give him the Fezi Baria, and have no doubt the galleys will serve under him when they find he can blow them out of the water."

"No doubt they will," Jack said; "especially now he has the Arab beauty for whose service they had deserted the Dey."

"No doubt," said Benardin. "Now, young gentleman, are you satisfied?"

"Quite," Jack said. "I ought to be, considering I have been the pivot, around which has been worked as nice a piece of rascality as—— but there, it serves the old Dey right. What will he think of it?"

"You can judge for yourself," Parker Neville said. "Here's the glass. Look at that group on the edge of the cliff."

"He certainly does not seem pleased," Jack said, when he had the glass. "Surely, he will take measures to recover these vessels."

"He will," said Benardin; "therefore, the sooner we are off the better, then our friend Parker can steer to the inlet I have marked on the chart, and if he mounts a few guns on the rocks, and anchors the Fezi Baria across the mouth of the inlet, he can give the Dey's galleys and xebecs as much as they want."

The arrangements were soon made; those of the privateer's crew who wished to return to England, remained on board the Wasp to navigate her home, but by far the greater portion went on board the Fezi Baria, the delights of the luxurious life before them being better than a return to the dull routine of a seaman's duty.

The men that stayed with Parker knew, as the privateer captain's crew increased, he would officer the vessel with his old crew, and many a tarry Jack looked forward to command a galley, and wear the picturesque Moorish costume.

The Bey, or Philip Mason, and his daughter would have gone to England in the Good Hope, but Philip did not consider the schooner able to fight her way single-handed through a host of galleys, for there were other States of Barbary besides Algiers, that existed by piracy.

Philip gave Parker Neville a plentiful supply of rich Eastern dresses, and by the time the many changes had been made between the vessels, Parker appeared on the Fezi Baria's deck a full-blown Bey.

Bernardin recommended his late crew of cut-throats to serve their new master well. Pointed out how much better they would be as far as far as worldly wealth was concerned (and that was a great object with the infidels, who take very much after Christians in that respect), and as a climax he led forward Kora Ailey, and told them the beautiful Arab would be their queen.

The infidels fired their pistols and matchlocks in token of their joy, and the chief officers came forward and kissed the hem of Parker's robes in token of their fealty.

This over, the late Bey, now garbed in European costume, returned to the Wasp, and as the swift vessel and the schooner Good Hope were shaking out their sails that were to waft them to England, Parker Neville passed slowly down the fleet of war galleys, and was received in the joyful manner peculiar to his future followers.

A gun was about to be fired from the Wasp as a farewell signal to the Fezi Baria, when Jack, who stood with his father on the raised deck, suddenly exclaimed :

"Look this way, Mr. Mason, here's a xebec flying down towards us."

Philip perceived the light craft, and said :

"It is Baba. I had almost forgotten him."

It was Baba : he had been left behind to tell the Dey Benardin had gone in chase of the disloyal galleys. This had been done in the hope of keeping the Dey harmlessly chafing in his palace until all danger of instant pursuit was over ; but circumstances had willed it otherwise.

Baba had brought with him his twelve wives, and when he scrambled to the Wasp's deck he made known the unpleasant intelligence that the whole of the Arab fleet were getting ready for sea.

"Your just in time then," Philip said; "where's your spoil ? "

"On board the xebec with the women."

"The what?" Philip looked over the side. "You must be mad, Sandy, to think of taking these women to England."

"To England !" Baba repeated. "I'm not going to that foggy land."

"Where the ——. Where are you going ?"

"I don't know, if the young chap won't take me. I'll ask him. Of course he will. He can't get on without some one who knows a little about these fellows. Good bye, Bey. Silly man to go back to that miserable country. Good bye. Maybe I shall be grand vizier yet ; that is if that young chap has any spirit in him."

"Good bye, Sandy. May your shadow never grow less, and your frame widen."

The Scotch Moslem waved a parting salute, and his men set the xebec's sail, and those on board the Wasp saw Parker Neville welcome his new ally and his twelve wives, and twice that number of children.

"Now for England," said Philip. "I hope I may be in a merciful mood when I meet my brother Saul."

"The punishment Henry will receive at being deprived of his wealth and position will be sufficient for me, said the baronet. I forgive him all he has done, now my boy has been restored to me."

The winds bore the light vessel gallantly on to the white cliffs of their native land, and Sheet-Anchor began to like the ocean better now that he had no rough ropes to handle or dirty decks to clean.

CHAPTER XXXIV.

THE LAST OF SAUL MASON.

The freshwater nautical population of Blackwall were highly incensed when they heard the story Bill Webb told upon his release from the watch-house.

The first manifestation of public feeling was given by the juvenile members of the riverside community, for Saul could never leave his house without a crowd of these troublesome attendants following close upon his heels, and shouting the least polite expressions they had gathered from the bouquet of elegant language used by the watermen and "bargees " of those days.

Saul did not care much about this sort of thing, but when they added stones, mud, cabbage stalks, and other garbage that found a resting-place in the gutters of that certainly not sanitary period, he began to think their attentions were far from agreeable.

Having come to this conclusion, he resolved to keep within his doorway, and the juvenile mob, baffled, tried to break his windows ; but as old Saul had every window guarded with a network of iron, the juveniles failed in their laudable object.

The watermen, bargees, riverside porters, and others of this refined class, finding their hopeful sons could effect nothing in the way of annoying old Saul, took it in their heads to pay the old gentleman a visit.

Bill Webb was in front, and only forced to attend the demonstration by the threats of his compatriots, for Bill Webb was a peaceful, and withal a somewhat timid man.

The possession of these peculiarities did not fit him for a public man, especially a man to head the swarm of rough gentlemen who would, whether he liked it or not, see he had his rights.

Unconscious of the coming crowd, old Saul sat in his office rubbing his hands and chuckling audibly at the success he had lately achieved.

"Fifty pounds from Bill Webb, hum—hum—hum," he hummed; "to-morrow Henry—Sir Henry—ho, ho—Jarvis's first year's money will be due; next day I am to receive the snug little fortune left by Philip for me should his girl die—ho, ho—hum, hum—now I will collect all these sums, and with the nice little bags I have leave this musty corner and set up a mansion

SAVED FROM THE BURNING SHIP.

Perhaps the mob had a distinct notion that Bill Webb would stand an unlimited supply of beer if he obtained his rights, perhaps they thought a raid upon old Saul's house would well repay the trouble.

Whatever resolution they had agreed upon, one thing was most unpleasant to William Webb's timid nature—this was having to march at the head of an army that Falstaff would have been ashamed to own.

at the West End; and who knows but that I may become a member of Parliament, perhaps get knighted by the King, and in fact become a minister of state—ho, ho—Sir Saul Mason—that would sound very well—Sir Saul Mason, K.C.B.—eh!—Ned Blendell, what is that noise?—go and see, Ned."

Ned went to see, and when he returned he told Saul that a mob was outside who threatened to fire the house if Bill Webb was not instantly repaid the money Saul had taken from him.

The old rascal reflected for a few moments, but as the hammering at the door continued, and as the unsavoury oaths of the unwashed crowd became louder, he went to his desk and opening it with the requisite number of turns said to Blendell:

"Open the door and let Bill Webb in; he shall have the money he wants."

Blendell departed, and old Saul continued:

"He shall, he shall—ho, ho, ho—I have two or three bags of counterfeit coins, Bill Webb shall have one, and hum—hum—hum—before he finds out the difference, I shall be far away from Blackwall—eh!"

"I told them," said Ned Blendell, "and they said if you did not at the same time give them money for the trouble they have had in coming here, they will have the house down."

Saul shut down the desk savagely.

"Tell them," he said, "that Bill Webb shall not have a farthing; as for the dirty crowd of vagabonds, I will go to one of the upper windows and fire upon every man that comes near the door."

Ned Blendell left the room, and before he could reach the small wicket to parley with the mob, a huge stone was hurled against the panels.

Saul heard the crash of the splintered wood, and running to his desk he thrust the key nervously in the keyhole.

"They mean it," he muttered, and his teeth chattered with fear; "they mean it." Ho! ho! they shall open the desk, yes, they shall, and two or three of them will go to kingdom come, or——ha! the door is broken in. Here they come. Curse the hole, how many times have I to turn the key to the right, once, of course, it must, and another turn——"

Bang! bang!! bang!!!

There was a loud shriek, mingled with the triple discharges, and Saul Mason fell to the floor, the contents of the three pistol barrels in his breast.

He was dead by the time Ned Blendell and Bill Webb entered the room.

"He's gone," Blendell said, stooping over the corpse. "Died by the infernal contrivance he had intended to kill others. Ah! the rabble are making their way in here. Quick, Bill Webb, take as many of these bags as you can carry, I will do the same, then follow me, and we will leave the remainder for the mob."

Ned Blendell's faith was not very strong, respecting the honesty of the gentlemen who were crowding in the passage, afraid to advance in consequence of the triple report; for they fully imagined the old man was firing at Bill Webb, and much preferring Bill Webb's body being a target than any of theirs, they hesitated until all was quiet before they broke loose all over the house.

"Quick," said Ned to the trembling waterman. "Remember if we are caught by these fellows we shall not reap a penny profit from this misfortune. Come man, this way, there is plenty left for them if they divide fairly, a thing impossible, among such a crowd.

The mob took courage after the silence in the old house had continued for some time, and when the leaders saw the open desk and the bags of gold, they thought not of the strange absence of Bill Webb.

They saw not the blood-bedabbled body on the floor. Their eyes were only for the open desk, and soon the bags were torn out, and as the rooms filled those who were not in time to secure a goodly share of the booty caught and dragged at the money bags their companions had secured.

The golden coins were soon strewed upon the floor. Then there arose a cry of fire, and the old house blazed and crackled as the dry wood caught.

But the men still tore at each other, as they grappled, cursed, and fought upon the floor in their eagerness to pick up the scattered money.

They heeded not the body of old Saul, for in their thirst for the ill-gotten money the corpse was trampled upon, rolled over, and buffeted about; and to augment the horror of this dismal scene the flames rose higher and higher, and those who had fired the building shouted and yelled to their companions to come out.

Battling their way through fire and smoke the men who had been engaged in that brutish struggle to obtain a few pieces of Saul's accursed money, reached the street just as the roof fell in.

A blackened heap of ruins was all that was left of Saul Mason's house, and when the authorities sought for the ship-chandler they found a blackened heap of flesh and bone fused into one, and in the midst of these charred remains of what had once been a human being were a pair of diamond shoe buckles and a brooch set with similar precious stones, both of which were the only tokens by which the blackened remains were recognisable from the surrounding heaps of burned wood.

Bill Webb and Blendell kept their own counsel, and the former, although he became rich in comparison to his former state, never passed the spot where the house had stood without a shiver running over his well-clad form.

Ned Blendell, in the peaceful retreat of a rural village soon forgot his sufferings, and the last dread scene that brought Saul Mason's life to a close.

CHAPTER XXXV.

THE RESURRECTIONISTS.

"Fool—fool," exclaimed Sir Henry Jarvis, Captain in the 1st Regiment of Guards, when he heard of Saul Mason's death; "had I but waited I should have had no occasion for the services of this Peter Quills; old Saul burnt to a cinder, his house razed to the ground, and all the papers destroyed—had I but waited—had I but waited. Well," he added, "I have not yet signed the cheque Quills filled in, there may be yet a chance of saving the thousand pounds, for Basil has so tied up the property, that I can scarcely touch a penny more than I have spent for the next year. Come in."

The door opened and the captain's valet entered the chamber.

"Well, Edwards," said the Guardsman, "what news of the Lady Constance? she is still very much depressed in mind, I suppose?"

"No, Sir Henry, she has left off her mourning, and told her maid only yesterday she was going to meet her husband."

"Madam's grief is not long-lived; who is the happy gentleman?—did you find that out, Edwards?"

"Well, Sir Henry, the maid says it is Sir Basil she is going to meet."

"The girl must be mad, Edwards, to talk in that manner."

"Just what I thought, Sir Henry, but of course I didn't say so. But, Sir Henry——"

"Well?"

"There's two men down below wants to see you very particularly."

"Did they not send a message explaining the nature of their errand?"

"No, Sir Henry, they wouldn't do that; they both said it was very particular, and something only for your ear."

"Very well, I will see them when I have finished dressing."

Edwards dressed his master, who went down to the dining room, and to his surprise was confronted by two ill-looking men.

They rose at his entrance, and one of them said,

"Your servant, sir."

The Guardsman replied with a stiff bow:

"I beg your pardon, sir," said the man who acted for the pair, "but we nas something to tell you, if so be as you likes to hear it."

"Much obliged, I'm sure," Sir Henry said. "May I inquire the nature of the communication?"

"Something," said the suspicious-looking gentleman, "as will be for your good; won't it, Bill?"

"No mistake about it, Tony; so go on, tell the gentleman all about it. I hates any roundabout dealings, so up and square it off. If the gentleman likes to drop us a quid or two for what we tells him, so much the better; if not, why there's no harm done."

Tony evidently thought his companion's advice was worthy to be followed, for he drew the cuff of his shabby claret-coloured coat across his mouth, and said:

"Well, you see, sir, a short time ago a party from this house gave Bill and I an order to get a stiff——"

"A what?"

"A stiff, sir—a corpus."

"I really do not understand you."

Tony scratched his head, then looked reflectively at the rusty steel buttons on his coat, and finally looked at his companion, and said:

"Bill, the gentleman don't understand what I means."

"Tell him, then, Tony. Tell him it was a dead 'un. A dead body, you know, sir."

CHAPTER XXXVI.

CONCLUSION.

Did a person from this house," the Guardsman said, "order you to procure a dead body. Is that what you mean?"

"Yes, yes," Tony eagerly said, "that's it. He wanted a stiff, and he was mighty particular about the colour of the stiff'un, and his weight, and all that sort of thing, but, as he paid well, we got him what he wanted."

"You did," Sir Henry said, feeling a little uneasy. "Well, what then?"

"Well, sir, we leaves the stiff here, thinking all along it was a doctor as wanted it," continued the resurrectionist; "but my pal here, Bill, happens to pass this here house a day or two arterwards, and I'm blessed if he didn't see a grand funeral."

"Ha!" exclaimed the Guardsman, "go on, pray."

"Well, we elt a bit curious like, for we finds out the gentleman wasn't a doctor, but a real gentleman; so Bill and I follows the funeral, and saw where the coffin was put, and at night we opens it, and I'm blowed if it wasn't the same stiff as we got for the gentleman as wasn't a doctor, and when Bill and I reads the name on the plate, we says, here's a rummy go, which it was, sir."

The Guardsman was deadly pale, for he began to remember that the grief exhibited by the lady was not so violent as he thought consistent with the sudden loss she had sustained.

He remembered, too, that the room was darkened when he came to view his brother, and these things added to his man's words about the Lady Constance being on the point of meeting her husband, revealed the whole truth to him.

He gave no outward sign of agitation, but placed a couple of guineas in Tony's hand, and said:

"The gentleman was rather eccentric to give out that he was dead; but as he will soon be back, I daresay he will reward you both for keeping your tongues quiet about the affair."

"Mum's the word," said Tony, pocketing the money; "mum, sir, with Bill and I; we shouldn't have told you only we thought you'd like to know."

"Quite right," the Guardsman said; "good evening."

The resurrectionists left the house, and Sir Henry drove to the War-office, and being a member of the King's regiment and a baronet, he was soon admitted to the great man's presence.

After the usual greetings the Guardsman said:

"The seventh regiment sails to-morrow for the Low Countries, I have come to ask you to transfer me at once to it, as I have a desire to go on active service."

"With pleasure, Sir Henry, you shall have your papers before you have obtained your uniform or packed your luggage."

The Minister kept his word, and next morning at daybreak the Guardsman sailed from England.

* * * * *

"We are both too late," said Sir Basil to Philip, "perhaps it is as well so, for we can afford to forget the past now we are blessed with those we have so long lost.

During the voyage home, Sheet-Anchor or Basil Jarvis, heard from a passenger they saved from a burning ship that his elopement with the Arab girl had so offended Milly, that she refused to listen to his professions of love, and as he had contracted a better liking for the sea than heretofore, his father at once set about obtaining him a post in the royal navy.

He was successful, and young Basil had the happiness to be appointed to La Minerva frigate, commanded by Commodore Nelson.

The rising officer welcomed Basil on board, and in the glorious career which he followed he soon forgot all about Milly Mason.

The rich Philip Mason soon became a member of Parliament. The friendship he had contracted with Sir Basil still continued, and it was owing to Philip's persuasion that Sir Basil and Lady Constance forgave Henry Jarvis; and when he returned from the war, wounded, and his breast covered with decorations for bravery in the field. Milly Mason, like Desdemona, loved him for the dangers he had passed through.

They were married, and young Basil, now a captain in the navy, was present, and at the banquet he amused his father and Philip by saying:

"Yes, I touched at Algiers to visit the Dey, concerning certain ships his galleys had captured, and to my surprise his mightiness turned out to be our old acquaintance Parker Neville."

"Was Sandy there?" Philip asked.

"Yes, he was prime minister, and a jolly evening we had. I'm afraid the followers of the Dey must have suspected we were anything but decorous, for Parker, I beg his pardon, his mightiness the Dey had some capital wine, which we drank in spite of all the edicts of the Koran."

"And Sandy helped him I'll be sworn?"

"That he did," Captain Jarvis said, "quite as willingly as he had helped to place him on the throne."

"I suppose you saw the lovely Kora Ailey," Philip's said, exchanging a glance with Sir Basil, "unless Parker was too good a Moslem to allow you to see his favourite wife."

"Yes, I saw her," the young captain said "and Parker, strange to say, cares so much for his handsome Arab wife, that he will not have any but her in the barem. In fact, whatever the Dey may be to his subjects, he still adheres to his European habits in private, and well and happy they all seemed."

Captain Jarvis outlived his friend Nelson and when the time came for him to inherit his father's title, he was Rear-Admiral of the Blue

www.ingramcontent.com/pod-product-compliance
Lightning Source LLC
Chambersburg PA
CBHW081157170626
46813CB00009B/3218
9781535810876